Rebelonging
Unbelonging
Book Two

SABRINA STARK

ISBN-13:
978-0615997506 (Mellow Moon)

ISBN-10:
0615997503

PROLOGUE
LAWTON

I glanced down at my left wrist. The pain was nothing. I wound the rope tighter and gave it another sharp, seesaw tug. The coarse fibers chewed at my skin.

Not enough.

I gave the rope another tug, and then another. I didn't stop until it came away slick and dark.

With a clinical detachment, Bishop looked down at my wrist. "So that's what the rope was for?" He shook his head. "You poor fucked-up bastard."

"Like you're one to talk," I said.

I'd grabbed the rope on my way out here. What I should've grabbed was barbed wire. Except I didn't exactly have any lying around.

Bishop looked unimpressed. "It's not gonna win her back, you know."

"This?" I shrugged. "It's not about winning her back. It's about penance."

He glanced toward the house, dark and quiet. "If it's not

about her, then why are we here?"

We stood side-by-side on the darkened sidewalk, hidden in the shadows of a tall oak tree. I stared past the long driveway to zoom in on the big two-story brick house. Something in my gut twisted.

That was where she lived. The girl I loved. The girl I lost.

Chloe.

There it was again, that gnawing ache where my heart used to be. I glanced again at the driveway. Her car was gone. Where was she?

A friend's house? A hotel? I swallowed. The hospital? I gave the rope a vicious yank, and then another.

Bishop's voice cut through the mist. "That's enough."

He might've been my brother, but he wasn't my boss. I twisted the rope three times over and yanked twice as hard.

"For fuck's sake," he muttered. "At least switch wrists, will ya?"

Silently, I unwound the rope from my left wrist and wrapped it around my right. I gave it the same seesaw tug. And then another.

Bishop shook his head. "My brother, the psycho."

"Half brother," I said.

"Yeah. And all psycho."

"No," I said. "Not psycho. Fair." I glanced over at him. "It's what we do, right?"

"No. I'm pretty sure this is a first."

"Get real," I said. "If I were some other guy, this is exactly what we'd be doing to him. I know it. You know it." I tugged again, savoring the burn as it tore into my flesh. "Why should I be different? Like I'm so fucking special."

His voice was quiet. "You didn't know."

"That the cuffs were tearing up her wrists?" I heard myself

2

swallow. "Yeah? Well, I should've known." I looked down. "And what kind of monster does that shit? You know how long I left her there, in those fucking handcuffs?" My voice broke. "Hours." I gave the rope a vicious tug. A strand of rope splintered from the rest, drooping slick and loose at my side.

With a sound of disgust, Bishop snatched the rope and moved it out of my reach. "That's it. You're done." He coiled the rope loosely around his wrist, but he didn't tug.

He didn't need to. He wasn't a monster.

I was.

I didn't deserve her. I never had. And she sure as hell didn't deserve what I'd put her through.

Chloe had it all. Looks, money, and the kind of class I'd never have, no matter what my bank account said. I'd known her, really known her, just a few weeks. But I'd loved her for years. Not that she ever knew.

These past weeks, I kept waiting for her to put two and two together, to come up with my face, to remember. But she never did. And I never told her.

"My guess?" Bishop said, "She's at work."

I gave him a look. Why the hell would she be there? To forget what happened? To forget about me? She sure as hell didn't need the money. That much was obvious.

"No." I shook my head. "She's not there. Not after what happened."

At the memory, I felt a dull, deep pain that had nothing to do with my bloodied wrists or bruised knuckles. God, I'd been such an asshole. Why?

But I knew why. I'd been so damned determined to not be played that I'd fucked up the only thing that had ever given me peace.

Peace, now that was a foreign concept. I used to watch her when she slept, curled on her side, or curled in my arms. The memory made me want to scream.

I blew out a breath. Sleep. That had been scarce too. Until Chloe.

For her sake, I should walk away for good. She'd be better off. She already had it all – looks, personality, probably a nice family too. Not that she'd ever brought me around to meet them. I knew why. She was ashamed. And who could blame her? Shit, at this point, I was ashamed of myself.

And now she was gone. But for how long?

Best-case scenario, she was at some friend's house, telling her what an asshole I was. Worst case – My stomach twisted. I didn't want to think about it.

"Just in case," Bishop said, "we'd better find a new drop point."

But what if she was at work? Would I be able to see her? Make sure she was okay?

"No," I said. "The drop point stays."

"So you want her to see this thing? Is that it?"

I shrugged.

"You know what you're acting like? You're like some cat who just tore up the couch," he said. "So what you do is drag home a couple of dead mice and fling 'em at the owner's feet. Look, a present. But I'm telling you, it's a mistake."

"Fuck you," I said. "Our mice aren't dead."

"Yeah. And you sound real happy about that." He gave me a serious look. "But about that cat, you know what happens, right?" He paused. "The owner freaks. Especially if it's a girl."

"Yeah? So what's your point?"

"If Chloe's there," he said, "she's gonna freak."

"No, she won't. Besides, she deserves to see this." A cold

rage washed over me. "After what those guys did to her."

"Almost did to her," Bishop said. "And even that —" He shrugged. "—wasn't as bad as we first thought."

I looked over at him. "You can't be fuckin' serious. Wasn't bad? They tried to drag her into their car, for fuck's sake. You think that's alright?"

"I never said that. I'm just saying, it's too personal. You're all twisted up."

I glared over at him. "Wouldn't you be?"

He turned to study the house. "No."

"Bull."

"I don't get twisted up," he said.

I made a scoffing sound. "Yeah. You're a cold motherfucker. I get it. But you're a fuckin' liar too. If it were your girl this happened to, those guys would already be dead."

"No." A slow smile spread across his face. "They'd just wish they were."

In front of us, the house hadn't changed. It was still dark. Still quiet. There was nothing to see and no reason to linger.

"Think the car's done yet?" I asked.

"Probably."

"Alright," I said. "Let's do this."

☐

CHAPTER 1

I always knew Keith would show his ass someday. I just didn't expect it to happen so literally. Standing in the frigid parking lot, I stared at the foggy mess that was his car window. Pressed up against the glass were two skinny cheeks and a giant black squid.

The cheeks were real. The squid was inked. Either that, or Keith had a serious problem on his hands. No, make that another part of his unremarkable anatomy. I couldn't see his hands through the foggy glass, but I'd seen them often enough to know they were squid-free.

About the rest of him, let's just say I was getting a lot better view than I'd ever wanted.

Keith was the night manager at the Two-Bit Diner where I worked as a waitress. That pompous dipshit had been making my life hell for weeks. Just an hour ago, he'd called my cell phone with an ultimatum. Come in to see him within the hour, or lose my job for good.

Standing outside his car window, I pulled out my cell phone and checked the time. I'd met his stupid deadline, but just barely. Again, I glanced at the cheeks. The squid was moving again.

Apparently, Keith wouldn't be returning to his office any time soon.

I'd busted my butt to get here. I'd cleaned up my tear-stained face, squeezed into my trampy uniform, and plastered on the required makeup even thicker than usual, complete with the bimbo-blue eye shadow and enough foundation to hide the fact I was pale as death, with dark circles under my eyes.

My bare legs trembled in the freezing night air. It was the cold, I told myself. Just the cold. Not nerves, not exhaustion, and certainly not the remnants of the worst crying jag I'd ever indulged in.

I'd had a hellish night. Yet somehow, I'd managed to not only get ready, but make the twenty-minute drive in just under fifteen. And now that I was here, I wasn't about to lose my job because Keith wasn't actually in his office.

Screw it.

I knocked on the glass.

Instantly, the squid flew away from the window. A moment later, Keith's surprised face appeared in its place. From what I could see, he was utterly naked, except for his standard striped necktie, hanging loosely around his thin neck.

Somewhere on the other side of the backseat, a woman was squealing at top volume. I chalked it up to embarrassment. Somehow I couldn't envision Keith causing the other kind of squealing, even in the fanciest of hotels, much less a Lincoln Town Car with a pine tree air freshener hanging from the rearview mirror.

Keith's eyes were wide, and his thinning brown hair was a disheveled mess. "Damn it, Chloe!" he hollered through the glass. "What the hell's wrong with you?"

Me? I wasn't the one banging some strange chick in the back parking lot.

Then again, that angle wasn't exactly banging-friendly.

Maybe their interlude involved more mouth and tongue than —

I shuddered. This was Keith, after all.

Stop thinking about it.

I knew why Keith had demanded to see me. Officially my shift began hours ago. Unofficially, I'd been too indisposed to come in.

Tied up.

Okay, handcuffed.

And not in the fun way either.

True, I'd been nearly naked. And true, the guy with the handcuffs was hot as sin, with perfect pecs, glorious abs, and a face to launch a thousand fantasies. But all that aside, the experience wasn't half as much fun as it sounds, even if a million other girls would've gladly taken my place.

I'd been handcuffed because my jerk of a boyfriend — correction, ex-boyfriend, if he'd ever truly been my boyfriend at all — had mistaken me for some kind of greedy, lying scumbag looking to exploit his fame for my own financial gain.

But I couldn't think about that now. I'd rather kiss that squid a hundred times than cry in front of my idiot boss and some random car hoochie.

I swallowed the pain and focused on Keith. He covered his privates with both hands while the girl in the backseat continued to screech. Keith leaned toward her and muttered something I couldn't hear. A moment later, the screeching stopped, and a second face appeared in the window. My jaw hit the pavement.

It was Brittney.

The girl who tried to have me kidnapped.

The girl who almost got me fired.

And apparently, the girl who was screwing my boss.

CHAPTER 2

Standing in the cold parking lot, I looked from Keith to Brittney and back again.

I totally didn't see that coming.

"You are so fired!" Brittney hollered through the glass. Her long blonde hair hung in surprisingly perfect waves, but her dress was definitely off-kilter, like she'd been wrestling a monkey in the back seat. Whatever she and Keith were doing, she apparently hadn't bothered to undress.

I couldn't really blame her. If I were doing Keith, I'd keep most of my clothes on too.

"You can't fire me," I hollered back through the car window. "You don't even work here."

Smiling, she reached a hand toward the door. The car window slid halfway down, revealing both of them in all their sweaty glory. No wonder the car had been running. Clothed or not, the night was way too frigid for a backseat bang-a-thon.

Brittney turned to Keith. "Go on, baby," she said. "Tell her."

I looked at Keith. "Baby?"

Keith cleared his throat. "Well, uh, you never showed up for your shift, and um –"

"And," Britney said with a flip of her hair, "you're totally fired."

Again, I looked to Keith. He was still covering his privates, but his jaw was set in that stubborn line I knew all too well.

"Is that so?" I said with a lot more surprise than I felt.

In truth, I had expected to be fired. I had a pretty good idea why Keith had called me here. He wanted the pleasure of firing me in person. If I had any dignity whatsoever, I'd have told him to take his ultimatum and shove it. But dignity was a luxury I couldn't afford.

So here I was, waiting for the hammer, but hoping for a miracle.

Keith squared his shoulders. "You know the rules," he said. "Section three, item two, under employee conduct." He spoke like he knew the employee manual by heart, which he probably did. Oddly enough, quoting the thing word-for-word was the one thing he was actually good at.

His voice picked up steam. "Employees who miss their shifts will be subject to disciplinary action, up to and including termination."

I nodded. "Uh-huh. And what does the manual say about, oh, I dunno, screwing skanks in the parking lot?"

"Hey!" Brittney said. "I'm no skank."

This wasn't true. If you searched on the word skank, you'd find a picture of Brittney, along with her friend, Amber. They were the worst kind of groupies. Except they didn't specialize in rock stars, or even restaurant managers, regardless of what it might look like now.

They specialized in billionaire bad boys from Detroit. Okay, one in particular. Their latest conquest had been Lawton Rastor – former underground fighter, famous reality star, fitness mogul, and yes, the guy with the handcuffs.

I rubbed my wrists. The skin was still raw, but not half as

raw as my aching heart. Walking away from Lawton tonight had been one of the hardest things I'd ever done, especially after he'd begged me to stay.

But I wasn't that girl, the one who'd excuse the inexcusable just because the skeletons in some guy's past were rattling too hard for him to handle.

"We weren't screwing," Keith said. "And besides, I'm on break." He stuck out his chin. "What I do on my own time is my own business."

Keith was almost always on break. Restaurant management was an incredibly hard job, but somehow Keith managed to log a lot of hours without actually working. We all figured he had naked goat pictures of the owner or something.

"Really?" I crossed my arms. "You do realize you'll be on a permanent break if this gets out?" Was it true? Hard to say. But I was desperate. It was worth a shot, right?

Keith narrowed his eyes. "Are you threatening me?"

"I dunno," I said. "Are you threatening me?"

His gaze slid to Brittney, and then back to me. "You know the rules," he said. "No exceptions."

I gave him a hard look. "Is that so?"

"It wouldn't be fair to the other girls," he said.

I let my gaze drift downward. When it reached the land of Squidville, I gave him a long, slow nod. "Uh-huh."

With one hand, he reached up to straighten his tie. He stopped in mid-gesture when he discovered no shirt-collar to secure it to. A trickle of sweat inched down his brow. "Go ahead," he said. "Tell someone. You can't prove anything." He gave me a nasty smile. "It's your word against mine."

"Yeah," Brittney said. "Who's gonna believe a ditz like you, anyway?"

I stared at her. A ditz? Sure, I played one at work, but in

real life, I was anything but ditzy. If nothing else, I was smart enough to know I couldn't afford to lose my job.

I had too many bills and an accounting degree that was getting me nowhere. Waitressing was the closest thing to a career I had.

Pathetic, I know.

Thinking about everything – the stalled career, the bills I couldn't pay, and the obligations that were piling up – I felt my hands tighten into fists. That's when I realized something. My hands weren't exactly empty. In one hand, I had my purse. In the other, I still held my phone. That phone had a camera.

I looked at Keith, naked except for the necktie. I looked at Brittney, not naked, but decidedly disheveled. I looked down to my phone.

I shouldn't.

But I did. ☐

☐

CHAPTER 3

Josie lowered her voice. "Watch out for Keith tonight. There's something funny going on."

Absently, I nodded. If she only knew the half of it.

We were standing at the waitress station. She was throwing together a couple of salads while I topped a tray of sundaes with whipped cream and cherries.

I gave Josie a sideways glance. Her auburn hair was way too big, her tight white blouse showed too much cleavage, and her flared pink skirt was a couple inches too short to be considered decent. Or maybe it just seemed that way because of those little bobby socks that, if anything, made the rest of her getup seem that much more obscene.

But who was I to judge? I was dressed exactly the same way. Except tonight, I wore clunky red bracelets on each wrist. The bracelets clashed with the rest of the outfit, but I couldn't afford to care. It was either that, or explain away the red, raw skin where the handcuffs had been not so long ago.

Maybe I shouldn't have tugged so hard against them. It's not like it had done any good. If Lawton hadn't finally unlocked them after realizing his epic screw-up, I'd probably still be trapped in his basement, watching him watch me.

In my mind's eye, I could still see him standing there, his eyes flat and his jaw set. The way he looked at me, I'd never forget. It was burned into my brain like the time my Mom called me a slut in fifth grade for holding hands with Shawn Proctor.

Like she was in any position to judge.

"We were taking bets," Josie was saying. "Odds of you getting fired were running five to one."

I tried to smile. "Which way did you bet?"

If I were Josie, I'd totally bet against me. I'd already been on probation. I'd been hours late for my shift. I wasn't exactly the manager's pet. No doubt, I was supposed to be fired.

Saved by a backseat blowjob and an itchy camera finger. Well, that was one for the record books.

But who was I kidding? Eventually, Keith would find some way to get rid of me. If he couldn't do it directly, he'd have to get creative. It was only a matter of time.

"It was because of the flu," Josie was saying.

I squinted over at her. "Huh?"

"The flu," she said. "It's still making the rounds, so I figured you'd be safe another week at least." She grinned. "I made fifty bucks. Sonya was so pissed."

"Nice to know she's rooting for me," I said.

"Eh, don't take it personal. She's having a rough day. She's only been here since lunch."

"Twelve hours?" I said. In the world of waitressing, that was a lifetime. "Why so long?"

"She's covering for some girl on the day shift. Even me, I should've been gone hours ago." She winced. "My feet are totally killing me."

"Who are you covering for?" I asked.

"Well, you, actually. When you didn't show up, Keith told me I had to stay. He didn't even ask. He just barked out an order, like a drill sergeant or something."

"Oh. Sorry." I felt the color rise to my cheeks. "But I'm here now. Can't you go home?"

She shook her head. "We're still short. Listen to this. Before you got here, Jasmine threw up in the parking lot."

"Our parking lot?" I could totally sympathize. I felt like throwing up too. But in my case, it had nothing to do with the flu. Still, poor Jasmine.

"Oh yeah," Josie said. "Right outside the front door. It was pretty disgusting, actually. So get this. Keith hears about it, and he totally flips out."

I rolled my eyes. "Like that's a surprise."

"No kidding," Josie said. "So he goes outside, and he practically drags her back to his office. And guess what he does next?"

"What?"

Josie was grinning. "The moron threatens to fire her."

I stared at Josie. As someone who'd been on the firing line myself, I saw no reason to smile.

"Oh, don't give me that look," she said. "You haven't heard the funny part. So Jasmine starts crying. And she gets so worked up, get this. She throws up again. But this time –" Josie's smile widened "– it's on Keith."

I felt the first tug of a real smile. "Seriously?"

"Seriously. He had to change his pants and everything. You should've seen him. He was madder than hell until –" Josie's smile faded "– some blonde in this super-tight dress shows up asking for him."

My smile faded too. Brittney the Skank. It had to be. I was almost afraid to ask. "So what happened then?"

"So Keith and Blondie, they're in his office maybe five, ten minutes. And when they come out, Keith's looking all happy. It was kind of creepy, actually."

Creepy? She should've seen the squid. I stifled a shudder and nodded for Josie to continue.

"So Keith walks her out, and he's gone forever." She snorted. "It's like they went to some cheap hotel or something."

Yeah, I thought. A pine-scented hotel on wheels.

Working on autopilot, I added the last cherry to the sundaes. I glanced down for a final check. "Oh crap," I said. "Look at these things." They were half melted already. I picked up the tray. "Save that thought. I'll be right back."

Josie grabbed my arm. "Wait," she said. "There's a reason I'm telling you all this."

Something in her voice sent alarm bells ringing. Slowly I returned the tray to the counter. I turned to face her. "What is it?"

Josie glanced around. "The blonde? The way I hear it, she's gonna be your replacement."

▢ ▢

CHAPTER 4

My mouth fell open. "Brittney's taking my job? Here?"

"Yeah, sorry." Josie gave me a sympathetic look. "Freddie the cook heard them talking out back. Apparently, she starts next week. As soon as she's trained, you're outta here."

"That jerk!" I glanced across the dining room. I spotted Keith lounging against the hostess stand. When he saw me looking, he gave me a slow, toothy smile.

A sick feeling settled into my stomach.

But this didn't make any sense. I had that photo of him, with Brittney too. He couldn't fire me. Not anymore. Josie's information had to be outdated. Right?

"So anyway," Josie said, "it's gonna take a lot more than the flu to save you this time."

Shit. She was right. Even if by some miracle, I was able to keep my job, I'd be working alongside the bimbo from hell. And that bimbo happened to be sleeping – or whatever – with my boss.

I felt like screaming. That was the best-case scenario. Worst case, I'd be gone. And she'd be taking my place. It wasn't like this was my dream job or anything, but until I found something better, this was the closest thing I had.

I was having a hard time catching my breath. Would Brittney be taking my place elsewhere too? In Lawton's bed?

They'd been intimate before. With me out of the picture, would Brittney slide back in? I made a sound of disgust. More accurately, he'd be sliding back into her.

I squared my shoulders. Fine. Brittney could have him. In fact, they deserved each other. Totally.

So why did I feel like throwing up? An ugly image slithered into my brain. Lawton and Brittney, naked, together. I choked back a wave of nausea.

If I was lucky, it was just the volcanic flu.

"I'm really sorry," Josie was saying.

I gripped the counter. "Yeah, well, I'm not gone yet," I said, trying to sound more confident than I felt. "And besides, if I had a dollar for every time I was supposed to be fired, I'd probably own this place."

"Well, you have been on a roll lately," she said.

I blinked hard as I stared down at the pathetic sundaes. Some might call it a roll. I'd call it a giant suck-fest of bad luck and worse choices. When I reached for the spoons, my hand was shaking. Was Keith going back on our deal? So soon?

"That asshole," I muttered.

"Yeah," Josie said, glancing toward Keith. "He really does hate you, doesn't he?"

Well, if he didn't hate me before, he definitely did now.

I'd learned a few things tonight. One, it's hard for a guy to chase you when he's not wearing pants. Two, it's not any easier for a groupie in stiletto shoes. And three, I wasn't above blackmail when push came to shove.

In the end, Brittney broke a heel, Keith broke down and said I could keep my job, and as for me, I broke a nail hanging onto that cell phone like my life depended on it.

In a way, it did. One lost paycheck, and I'd be back on my Dad's basement couch, sucking up the smell of sour milk while the rest of the household slept on therapeutic mattresses with Egyptian sheets.

While dodging Brittney in the parking lot, I'd miraculously managed to text that picture to my best friend, Erika for safe-keeping. Two copies were better than one, right?

I should be ashamed of myself.

Except I wasn't.

Still, something was definitely off. In the parking lot, Keith had been panicked, scared even. I snuck a quick glance across the dining room. Now, he looked ready to strike. Something was very wrong. I turned back to Josie.

At the look on her face, I stopped short. She was studying my sundaes with an odd, vacant expression. I followed her gaze, and stifled a gasp. One of my bracelets had shifted forward, exposing the raw, angry skin for the whole world to see.

I looked up. Slowly, her eyes met mine.

Her voice was quiet. "What's that?"

I shoved the bracelet back in place. "Nothing." I felt my eyes water, just a little. Damn it. I gave a quick shake of my head. I wasn't going to do this. Not now.

I summoned up what I hoped was a smile. "Weird cooking accident." I gave a quick wave of my hand. "Long story, you don't want to know."

"Oh." She frowned. "Okay. Well, if you ever want to talk--"

"I don't. But thanks."

I picked up the tray too fast. The sundaes wobbled dangerously, clinking and slopping globs of fudge over the sides. This was just great. They now looked nothing like their menu picture. Talk about a mess. Me and the sundaes.

Before Josie could say anything else, I turned and plunged

into the dining area.

On autopilot, I made my way through the maze of tables and booths. Cooking accident? Seriously? Was that really the best I could do? Maybe I was a ditz.

Silently I delivered the sundaes. No sass. No attitude. Probably no tip either. Leaving the table, my breath was coming too short and too fast. I tossed the empty tray on a dirty table and ducked into the crowded ladies room.

I dove for the farthest stall and locked the door behind me. I leaned against the cool tile wall and closed my eyes. I had three hours left. Damn it. I so needed the money. If I were smart, I'd make every hour count.

I wouldn't think about Keith. And I definitely wouldn't think about Lawton.

It was Lawton's fault I'd been late for work. And it was his fault that Brittney was out to get me. Finally, it was his fault that I was having a hard time holding it together.

He'd stolen my heart, and then smashed it to pieces.

That fucker.

I wrapped my arms tight around myself and made a solemn vow. For the rest of my shift, I wouldn't think about anything except my job, and making up for lost time.

I could do this. I had to do this. I took several deep breaths and thought happy thoughts – the feel of sunshine on a warm, spring day, the smell of an open campfire, the sound of Lawton screaming as I whacked him with a baseball bat.

In real life, I'm not prone to violence. And the odds of Lawton actually screaming were slim at best. But hey, they're called fantasies for a reason. When I ditched the bat for a tire iron, the screaming seemed a lot more genuine.

Ten minutes later, I left the stall just as shaky, but a lot more determined. Miraculously, the restroom had emptied, giving me more privacy than I had any right to expect.

I stood alone in front of the long mirror and made myself smile. It felt fake and foreign, and no matter how hard I tried, it never did quite reach my eyes.

But a stranger wouldn't know the difference, right? Besides, I didn't have to be cheerful, not exactly. I only had to be entertaining.

For once, I thanked Heaven and Earth that this wasn't your average waitressing job. If I had to be perky right about now, I'm pretty sure I'd end up killing someone.

With that stiff smile plastered in place, I left the restroom, grabbed a fresh tray from the waitress stand, and hustled to my next table. With an overblown sigh, I plopped down into an empty chair.

"So, how's the food here?" I asked. "Anyone got a menu?" I looked around. "I'm totally starving." I glanced at the woman's purse. "Hey, got anything to eat in there? Gum? Chocolate?" I leaned closer. "A pizza?"

This time, my intro was technically true. I really was starving. How many hours had it been since I'd eaten, anyway?

But the couple laughed, and eventually I took their order. Soon I was delivering their drinks. After that, it got a little easier. It got easier still when Keith disappeared into his office in the back. If I were lucky, I wouldn't see that weasel – or his squid – for the rest of the night.

An hour later, I was finally getting into a groove. The place was swamped with the after-bar crowd, which was probably all for the best. Running from table to table and juggling too many things to count, I could almost forget my life was a walking disaster zone.

But then, Keith made his first move.▢

CHAPTER 5

I was at the waitress station, processing a credit card payment when Keith emerged from the back office. "Alright," he announced, "time to send one of you girls home."

Next to me, Josie's jaw dropped. Mine too. Outside, the line was scary long. Inside, every table was taken, either with actual customers or stacks of dirty dishes as the lone busboy struggled to keep up.

"What?" I stared at him. "Why?"

"Because we're overstaffed, that's why."

"You've got to be kidding," I said.

His gaze narrowed. "You think I'm out here for the fun of it, is that it?"

I snorted. "I'm surprised you're out here at all."

"Hey!" he said. "You wanna compare jobs?" He looked down at my skimpy uniform. "Well mine's a little harder than dropping off food and shaking my ass."

As someone who'd actually seen his ass, I sincerely hoped he wouldn't be shaking that thing at anyone.

Next to me, Josie pointed toward the dining area. "But we're totally slammed," she said. "Look at this place."

He gave the dining room a cursory glance. "Not according to sales figures," he said. "Do I need to remind you girls? It's calculated by receipts, not customers."

I glared at him. "So?"

"So," he said, "if you wanna justify the manpower –" he smirked "– or should I say girl power, then maybe you should work a little harder at suggestive selling, huh? "

"Hey!" Josie said. "I suggest the shit out of stuff."

His jaw clenched. "What'd you just say to me?"

Josie rolled her eyes. "Fine. Crap. I suggest the crap out of stuff. It's not my fault if people don't go for it."

"Yeah," I said. "And besides, we can barely keep up as it is."

He turned to smile at me. "Then you'll be happy to know that you're the girl who's going home."

My mouth fell open. "What? Me? But I just got here."

Was this his way of firing me without firing me? I'd dealt with him before. Agreement or not, he always found a loophole.

I felt my jaw clench. I still had that photo of him with Brittney. Maybe I needed to find a loophole, too, like a billboard off I-75.

Next to me, Josie spoke up. "Alright. Fine. Whatever. But if someone needs to go home—"

"It'll be Chloe," Keith snapped. "Not you."

Josie was glaring at him now too. "I was going to say Sonya."

"Oh, so you're making these decisions now?" Keith said. "Last time I checked, I was the manager, not you."

"But have you seen Sonya?" Josie said. "She's not looking too good."

"Nice try," Keith said, "but I think your little friend can speak for herself."

"What little friend?" I asked. "Me? Or Sonya?"

"Doesn't matter," he said. "You're the one leaving. First in,

26

first out. Just like the manual says."

"But I was here last," I said.

"Only because you were late."

"But Sonya's been here since noon."

"That's the day shift," he said. "Not my problem."

"But—"

"No buts. You," he said, pointing at me. "I'm clocking you out as of now." He pointed at Josie. "You. Cover her tables."

Josie gave him a desperate look. "But I can't even cover my own."

"Again, not my problem," he said.

"Hey," I said, "You can clock me out all you want, but I'm staying 'til my tables are finished."

"Why? So you can turn around and sue the restaurant later?" he said. "Tell them how I forced you to work for free?" He puffed out his chest. "Not gonna happen. Not on my watch."

And with that, he turned and stalked back toward his office.

I stared after him. "So he's gonna clock me out?" I said. "Is that even legal?"

Josie rolled her eyes. "I dunno. Check the fucking employee manual. God, what a turd." She picked up her tray and turned toward the dining area. I watched her go. And that's when I saw them.

The flashing red and blue of police lights. □

    □

    □

CHAPTER 6

I looked over the crowd, wondering how I hadn't noticed all the commotion before.

Against the long bank of front windows, customers were pressing their faces to the glass, cupping their hands around their eyes to shut out the glare. Behind them, others stood to peer over their shoulders, or craned their necks to see around them.

Whatever was going on, it was happening in the front parking lot. And apparently it wasn't your average traffic stop.

Suddenly, a stocky guy with shaggy hair stood and bolted. He strode toward the front exit, leaving his dinner partner, a petite redhead, scowling after him. Fork in hand, she glared daggers at his back as he pushed through the people waiting to be seated and disappeared out the front door.

Sitting by herself, the redhead looked madder than hell, and I couldn't say I blamed her. I'd just delivered their food a few minutes earlier. Now she'd be eating it alone.

And she wasn't the only one.

As if Shaggy's departure had somehow granted everyone else permission, a slew of other diners followed after the guy – a couple near the far wall, a trio of college guys near the waitress station, a lone older man who'd been standing at the bar. Within a few minutes, at least thirty people, maybe more, had wandered outside.

I made my way to the front windows and peered out. Across the parking lot, the lights were still flashing, reflecting red and blue off of two large, silver tour buses that I'd noticed on my way in.

Josie dashed over breathlessly, tray in hand. "Hey, you wanna do me a favor?" she said. "Find out what's going on, will ya? The customers are asking."

She glanced around, taking in the empty seats. "Well, the ones who are still inside anyway." Then she was gone, heading toward one of the many tables that I'd been forced to abandon, thanks to Keith and his employee manual.

If I couldn't help her with those tables, at least I tell her what was going on. I owed her that much. I dashed to the back room and grabbed my coat off the rack.

A minute later, I was shivering outside with the rest of them. I stood on my tiptoes, trying to catch some sort of clue. It was no use. Between the shifting crowd and massive tour buses, a good vantage point was proving impossible to find.

Near the back of the crowd, the shaggy-haired guy was awkwardly taking pictures, or maybe video, with his cell phone. As I watched, he held the phone above the crowd, pressed a button, and then pulled down the phone to take a look. He frowned as he studied the tiny screen.

I hustled to his side and tapped him on the shoulder. "What's going on?" I asked.

"Got me," he said, lifting his phone again. This time, when he studied the screen, he gave a low chuckle. "But I think it's gonna be good."

"Why?" I said. "What is it?"

"Hang on," he said, lifting the phone yet again. This time, when he studied the screen, he gave a sigh of irritation.

"Damn it."

"Why don't you just get closer?" I asked.

He gave me a look. "Why don't you?"

I glanced at the crowd, crammed shoulder-to-shoulder in front of me. The parking lot was huge, but the commotion seemed centered between the two buses, leaving only a narrow alley between them.

Unless I was willing to shove someone aside, this was as close as I'd be getting.

"See?" Shaggy said. "You don't wanna get your ass beat neither, huh?" He cleared his throat. "Besides, I already tried. People take this shit seriously."

"But you were the first one out here," I said. "How come you're not up front?"

"Because," he said, "I had to grab my phone out of the car." He glanced toward the restaurant. "You can thank my girlfriend for that."

He mimicked a high-pitched female voice. "You love that stupid cell phone more than me. Can't you leave it outside just once so we can have a nice dinner?" His voice returned to normal. "So I leave it outside, and what happens?" He flicked his head toward the crowd. "This."

I looked toward the commotion. I still didn't know what this was.

"She'd better be grateful," the guy said.

I'd seen the look on the redhead's face. When he returned, he was more likely to get a fork in the eyeball than anything resembling gratitude.

"Um, yeah," I said, as I craned my neck in a desperate bid for a better vantage point.

"Hey, I've got it," he said. His eyes were bright with excitement. "You wanna see, right? I know. Lemme give you a boost."

"A boost?"

"Yeah. Get you higher for a better look." He grinned. "For a price."

I narrowed my gaze. "What kind of price?" My skirt was almost obscene as it was. One lift above eye level, and I might as well be charging him.

"Video." He thrust his phone into my hand. "Zoom in on the car, will ya?"

"What car?"

"You'll see." He licked his lips. "Oh man, this'll be great on my site. Total viral. You just watch."

I glanced toward the commotion. The lights were still flashing. A few paces ahead of me, someone laughed long and hard.

It had been a hellish night. If there was one thing I could use, it was a good laugh. Probably, so could Josie.

Still, this was beyond strange. I bit my lip. "I dunno."

"Aw c'mon, please?" He looked at me with puppy dog eyes. "I'm desperate. Help a guy out, will ya?"

He looked so ridiculous that I had to smile. The sensation felt utterly foreign after faking it far too long. Something inside me uncoiled, and I felt an odd surge of gratitude for the unexpected release.

"I can't believe I'm actually considering this," I said.

He grinned. "Just be careful of the phone, alright? I just replaced it last week." He smile faded, and he looked around. "Some psycho smashed the piss out of my last one. Can you believe it?"

Oddly enough, I could.

A second later, he leapt behind me and called out, "Ready?"

I didn't move. Sure, I owed Josie and all, but how would this work? I looked down at my skirt. It was way too short for what the guy was suggesting.

But then, almost before I knew what was happening, I felt Shaggy's head plow between my knees and his hands on my waist. "Hey!" I yelled, clutching his head for balance as he lifted me skyward. "What are you doing?"

"The favor. Just like we talked about."

"Yeah, but—"

"Now c'mon. Get me some good stuff, will ya? Remember," he said, "the car. Anyone pops out of it, get a shot of 'em, alright?"

Already, this had been one of the strangest nights of my life. I glanced down, relieved to see my skirt – and not my panties – pressed tight against the back of his neck.

If nothing else, at least I wasn't giving the guy's neck a hoo-ha massage.

I shifted my gaze to the commotion, eager for a laugh, or at least a distraction. There was only one problem. What I saw there wasn't exactly the chucklefest I'd been hoping for.

CHAPTER 7

Wobbling on Shaggy's shoulders, I caught my breath. Memories flashed in my brain. Two guys in ski masks. A dark sedan. A knife at my throat. Concrete at my back. A gloved hand mashed across my mouth.

Had it really been only just a few hours ago? Unsteadily, I reached a hand to my throat. That knife, it hadn't even been real. But it sure had felt real. My fear, that was more real than anything – until a rescuer had shot out of the darkness to change everything.

Lawton.

If I closed my eyes, I could still see his face, a shadowed profile of unrestrained fury as he beat the living crap out of the guy who'd been on top of me. If Lawton's brother hadn't pulled him off, well, let's just say the guy's odds of survival weren't looking too good.

Now, staring at that all-too-familiar vehicle, my legs felt rubbery. It couldn't be the same car. It just couldn't. And yet, something in my gut told me it was, in spite of the car's new and oddly profane paint job.

Below me, Shaggy called out. "The hood – what does it say?"

I looked around. It wasn't exactly a crowd-friendly phrase. I glanced at the guy closest to us. It was that older guy who'd been standing at the bar. My mouth opened, but no words came out.

"Oh for Pete's sake," the older guy said, "just spit it out, will ya?"

"Fine." I shot him a look. "Asshole patrol."

His bushy eyebrows lowered. "Well, you don't have to get all personal about it."

I rolled my eyes. "Not you. The car."

Below me, Shaggy called out, "Oh man, sweet! That's what I thought. You got the video, right?"

Dutifully, I turned back to the car. I held up the phone and pressed play.

"Make sure you catch everything!" Shaggy called out. "The hood, the doors, whatever you can get!"

But I couldn't. Because I wasn't even looking at the car. Not anymore. I was looking at a face in the crowd. I knew that face. I knew it so well that my heart ached.

My mouth went dry, and I forgot to breathe. The face looked haunted, with hollow eyes and a grim mouth.

Like some kind of pathetic sponge, I soaked up the sight of him. He wore a dark hoodie with the hood thrown back, revealing that tousled hair, those chiseled features, and the barest hint of the tattoos that decorated his amazing body.

It was Lawton, the guy I loved. And the guy I hated.

He wasn't looking at the car either.

He was looking at me.

☐ ☐

CHAPTER 8

A metallic, clattering sound jolted me back to reality.

"Hey!" Shaggy hollered. "My phone! What'd you do that for?"

I looked down, and there it was, the phone, lying on the pavement a couple paces in front of Shaggy's feet.

Suddenly, I was practically body surfing as Shaggy dove toward his phone. When he bent nearly double, I flew off his shoulders, and my feet hit the pavement too hard to keep my balance. I stumbled into the people ahead of me, who turned to give me dirty looks.

Shaggy swooped up his phone and gave it a good, long look.

"Damn it," he said. "This thing's brand new."

My eyes were on the phone, but my thoughts were on Lawton. What was he doing here? Had he come to see me?

"If it's broke," Shaggy said, "you'll get me a new one, right?"

My jaw dropped. "You've got to be kidding me."

"Sorry, but it's only fair," he said. "You were the one who dropped it, not me."

"Hey," I said, "you're the one who told me to get up there. Remember?"

"Yeah. And I also told you to be careful." His tone grew

snotty. "Remember?"

"Oh shut up," I said. "It's fine." I looked down. At least, it looked fine.

"Yeah?" he said. "Well, I'll need your name in case it's not."

He wanted a name? Fine. I'd give him a name. "Betty," I said.

It was the same name I'd given him earlier, when I'd introduced myself as his waitress. Of course, back then I'd been joking. Now, this was no joke.

Sure, he could get my real name if he really wanted it. But until then, I was Betty. And I was gonna stay Betty.

His gaze narrowed. "You don't look like a Betty."

"Neither do you," I said.

His forehead wrinkled. "What the hell's that supposed to mean?"

Honestly, I had no idea. I didn't care what the guy's name was. I could barely remember my own. Lawton was here. I wanted to run. To him? Or from him? My head felt on the verge of exploding.

Across from me, Shaggy was typing something into his cell phone, probably on some digital notepad. "And your last name?" he said.

I crossed my arms. "Boop."

"No shit?" He shook his head. "Man, it must've been hell for you growing up, huh?"

If he only knew the half of it. Of course, my rocky childhood had nothing to do with what my parents had named me, which definitely wasn't Betty. And besides, my last name was Malinski.

Sure, the name wasn't the most glamorous in the world, but it was better than being named after a cartoon character.

"Poor kid," Shaggy said, looking down at his phone. The digital notepad was gone, and I saw stills of the video footage. His fingers flew across the tiny screen. Suddenly, he did a double-take. "Holy shit," he said. "Is that who I think it is?"

Oh crap. This wasn't good. I clamped my lips together to keep from groaning.

"Check it out." Shaggy thrust the phone in my face. "Lawton Rastor. Am I right?"

Reluctantly, I studied the video still. And there he was, the man of my nightmares, the man of my dreams. He stood a few paces behind the car, his hands thrust into the front pockets of his dark hoodie. His gaze bored straight into the camera.

At me.

How on Earth had I missed that? But I knew exactly how. When I'd hit the play button, I'd been focused on that car.

Oh shit. The car.

That thing was definitely the same car my attackers had been driving. It had to be.

Had Lawton dropped it off? And if so, why here? Why now?

In front of me, Shaggy was licking his lips. "Oh yeah. It's totally him."

I shook my head. "I don't think so."

"Goes to show what you know." He straightened. "I'm a professional. And I'm tellin' ya, it's him." He grinned. "And you know what I say to that?"

Hell, I didn't even know what I'd say to that. I shook my head.

"Cha-ching!" Shaggy slapped me on the back, buddy style. "You know what, Betty? Tonight's your lucky night. Because this little video's gonna make my rent."

My stomach was churning. "Yeah. That's me. Lucky."

He grinned. "So, are you ready to take some more?"

"Hell no," I said. "I'm not gonna make that mistake twice."

"Oh c'mon, Betty," he said. "Don't be that way." He pulled out his puppy dog face and turned it on full-force.

Some puppy. I felt like swatting him with a rolled up newspaper. "No way," I said.

Not eager to be hoisted again, I turned and plunged into the crowd, no longer caring whether there was room or not.

Whatever was going on, it involved Lawton, and it involved me. And, if my hunch was correct, it involved two guys in ski masks who'd attacked me not that awful long ago.

Squeezing between the closely packed bodies, I jostled my way forward, ignoring muttered curses and grunts of disapproval. At least no one threatened to kick my ass. Well, not that I noticed anyway.

Finally, I stood near the front of the crowd. I looked to the spot where Lawton had been standing.

He was gone.

☐ ☐

CHAPTER 9

I scanned the scene in front of me, trying to make sense of it. The police cruiser was parked on the opposite side of the dark sedan. The lights were still flashing, giving the faces in the crowd an odd, disjointed appearance as people craned their necks for a closer look.

Two uniformed police officers stood behind the defaced car. They studied the trunk with expressions that I could only describe as perplexed.

I turned to the guy next to me, a lanky guy in a black wool coat. "What's going on?" I asked.

"Not sure," he said. "Every time I try to get close, the cops tell me to back off."

I glanced at the car. Something near the rear was thumping. The thumping sounded familiar.

"Sweet!" said a voice behind me. "Something's in the trunk. I'm betting it's mobsters. It's always mobsters."

Damn it. I recognized that voice. I turned around, and there he was. Shaggy. He was holding out his phone again, capturing whatever was in front of him.

"What the hell are you doing here?" I said.

"Hey, you paved the way," he said. "I just followed in your wake." He grinned. "Nice job with the elbows, by the way. I could learn a thing or two from you."

Suddenly, my fondest wish was for the guy to be gone. "What about your girlfriend?" I said, thinking of the redhead. "Are you ever going back inside? That's a hint, by the way."

"Yeah? Well what about my waitress?" he said. "Is she ever going back inside?"

"Oh shut up," I said. "I'm not your waitress anymore. They sent me home."

He shrugged. "That's the breaks, Betty."

With a sigh of irritation, I turned around to face the commotion. The trunk was still thumping. Mobsters, my ass.

A second later, Shaggy jostled his way between me and Wool Coat. "I'm telling ya," he said, "ten bucks says it's mobsters."

"You're on," I said. My gaze narrowed. "But I wanna see the cash up front."

Shaggy made a show of patting his pockets. "I'm a little short," he said. "Take an I.O.U.?"

"Hell no," I said.

Wool Coat spoke up. "No sense in betting," he said. "It's not mobsters. It's just a couple of frat boys."

"Really?" I leaned around Shaggy. "How do you know?"

"The police have been talking to 'em ."

"How?" I said.

"Through the trunk."

"If it's a frat thing," Shaggy said, "it's gotta be Sig-Eps. Those dudes are totally whacked." He elbowed me in the side. "Heh, whacked. Get it?" He chuckled at his own joke. "See, maybe they are mobsters."

"If anyone's whacked," I said, "it's you."

He beamed. "Thanks, Betty."

"It wasn't a compliment." I leaned toward Wool Coat. "Why don't they just open the trunk and get it over with?" I asked. "What are they waiting for?"

Just then, a big tow-truck rumbled up behind the police car, moving slowly to allow the crowd time to shift out of the way.

Wool Coat pointed to the truck. "They're waiting for that, I guess."

"Alright, people!" the shorter of the two police officers yelled. "Everybody back!"

Soon, a burly guy with a beard emerged from the tow truck. He grabbed a tool box from the back and approached the officers. And then, flanked by them, he approached the back of the car and went to work.

A few minutes later, the sedan's trunk flew open. The crowd grew absolutely silent, waiting and watching. The officers leaned in for a closer look.

Between them, the tow truck driver scratched his chin. His eyebrows furrowed. "Now, that's a first," he said.

Slowly, a couple of figures emerged from the trunk – two half-naked men in ski masks.

At first, no one made a sound. And then, a woman behind me snickered. That's all it took. A second later, the crowd burst into laughter as the two guys stumbled out onto the pavement.

Next to me, Shaggy was practically salivating onto his phone. "Oh man," he said. "This is gonna be the best payday ever."

Aside from the masks, the guys wore only two things – bling and their underwear.

"Huh," Shaggy said. "You know what? I've got underwear exactly like that."

I glanced at the guys. One wore striped boxer shorts. The other wore tiny black briefs that left very little to the imagination. I gave Shaggy a sideways glance. "Uh, the boxers?"

Please be the boxers. Please be the boxers.

"Wouldn't you like to know?" he said.

I shook my head. "No. I'm pretty sure I know way too much already."

Unsteadily, the two guys crawled out of the trunk. They looked beyond ridiculous, especially with all the jewelry – thick gold necklaces, expensive looking wristwatches, and giant rings that glittered on almost every finger.

They'd worn the same kind of the night I'd first met them. I'd been their waitress, unfortunately. They'd been the customers from hell – drunk, rowdy, and obscene, just like their dates, Brittney and Amber, the skanky duo.

"Look at those rings," Shaggy said. "See, they are mobsters." He turned to smirk at me. "Goes to show what you know." He held out his hand, palm up. "I'll take my ten bucks now."

I glanced down at the hand. "Dream on," I said.

Besides, those guys weren't mobsters. They were two player wannabees who had tried to kidnap the wrong girl.

Me.

On instinct I backed up, trying to melt into the crowd. As far as I could tell, neither guy had noticed me. And for some reason, I definitely wanted to keep it that way.

When the guy in the black briefs finished climbing out of the trunk, he turned to face the crowd and yelled, "What the hell are you looking at?"

On the side opposite us, a heavyset woman spoke up. "You tell us, Loverboy!"

The crowd burst into fresh laughter.

"Hey, Loverboy!" Shaggy hollered over the distance. "Take

off the mask, will ya! Show us your face!"

The guy lifted both hands, extending both middle fingers. "Fuck off, asshole!" he yelled. "I'm not showing you dick!"

The nearest cop grabbed him by the shoulder and hustled him toward the police car. A moment later, he and his friend were shoved unceremoniously into the backseat. The car door slammed behind both of them with a decisive thud.

"Why would I want to see his dick?" Shaggy said. "God, what a dumb-ass." He held out his cell phone and started circling the vandalized sedan, stopping every few seconds to zoom in on something or other.

Nearby, the rest of us watched as the police cruiser pulled slowly out of the lot, leaving the tow truck driver to deal with the defaced sedan.

I never did see the guys' faces. But unlike Shaggy, I didn't want to.

But there was someone I wanted to see. And probably not in the way he wanted.

As I stood shivering in the cold parking lot, an even colder rage settled over me. I hated drama. For years, I'd been trying to escape it – the drunk-ass mom, the psycho stepmother, a dad who was indifferent at best.

Even tonight, I'd forced myself to walk away, not just from Lawton, but from the chance to give him hell for what he'd done. And he had done plenty.

So what does he do? He brings drama literally to the doorstep of where I worked. What the hell was he thinking? Did the guy think at all?

I looked around. He had to be here somewhere. I just knew it.

Maybe I hadn't given him what he deserved earlier, but I sure as hell wasn't going to miss the opportunity now.

That fucker had earned a piece of my mind. And drama or not, it was time to give it to him.

CHAPTER 10

Away from the heat of the closely packed bodies, the temperature dropped hard. But I barely noticed as I stalked through the parking lot. Methodically, I went from row to row in search of Lawton's vehicle, whichever one he might be driving tonight.

Near the restaurant, the crowd was already breaking up, with most of the gawkers straggling back into the diner, chattering to each other as they went. The few exceptions fanned out into the parking lot, where they got into their vehicles and drove off one by one.

As for me, I wasn't going anywhere. If Lawton was here, I'd sure as hell find him.

Finally, I spotted what I was looking for. In the very back row, there it was, Lawton's vintage muscle car. I was no car expert, but I'd recognize that thing anywhere.

Its bold, masculine lines screamed pure power -- just like its super-charged engine, and just like its owner.

The car was one-of-a-kind. From what Lawton told me, he had restored it himself, taking months to get every detail just perfect.

I still didn't get it. Why would he do such a thing? If I had that kind of money, I'd just buy something fantastic and be done with it.

But then again, I wasn't a car buff. And besides, I could barely check my oil.

I would've spotted the car sooner, except for a tight grouping of tall vehicles in the previous row. Was Lawton hoping to hide? If so, he was going about it all wrong. If he didn't want to be noticed, he should've driven a different car.

I stalked up to the car and rapped against the driver's side window. When it slid down, I felt my lips purse in annoyance.

It wasn't even Lawton. It was his dick of a brother.

He studied me with a marked lack of enthusiasm. "Can I help you?" he said.

I glared down at him. "Where's your brother?"

"Which one?"

"Oh, cut the crap," I said. "You know which one."

"My guess? He's out looking for you."

"Nice story," I said. "But I saw him earlier. And then he disappeared. So he sure as hell isn't looking for me."

"Yeah? You check your car lately?"

My car was in the back parking lot. Actually, I hadn't checked. But that was beside the point. I knew the brush-off when I saw it.

"You know what?" I said. "You two are assholes. You know that, right?"

He shrugged. "Pretty much."

"Those guys in the trunk? You brought them here, didn't you?"

"Well, they sure as hell didn't drive themselves, if that was your other theory."

"Why here?" I demanded.

"Hey, it wasn't my idea."

"You dick," I said. "I'm gonna lose my job over this."

He glanced briefly toward the restaurant. "Doubtful."

"Listen." My voice rose. "I don't give a shit what you idiots think! I'll get fired just as soon as those guys tell the cops I was involved somehow. Word'll get back to the restaurant, and I'll be out on my ass before morning."

Bishop looked unimpressed. "Look," he said, "I admitted to being an asshole. And possibly a dick –"

"Which you are," I said.

"Yeah. But idiot? Now you're just reaching. Here." He motioned me closer. "Lemme give you a hint."

I didn't budge.

He continued anyway. "If you wanna insult someone," he said, "you've gotta have an element of truth. Otherwise, it's just a waste. You end up looking stupid." He grinned. "So who's the idiot now?"

"Oh for God's sake!" I yelled. "Will you just stop already!"

"Hey!" An all-too-familiar voice sounded just behind me. "What the hell are you doing to her?"

I whirled around. And there he was, close enough to touch, close enough to kick.

Lawton.

Breathless, I stared up at him, trying to recall all the insults I'd been practicing in my head. But my brain was worse than empty. Instead of coherent thoughts, it contained a jumbled pile of nonsense, like someone had shredded a crossword puzzle and scattered it at my feet.

As my brain churned, I tried not to notice Lawton's absolute perfection, those stormy eyes, his chiseled jaw, a body to die for. But one thing about Lawton, he was impossible to ignore. ☐

☐

CHAPTER 11

He was giving Bishop a murderous glare. "Answer me!" he said.

Behind me, I heard the car door open. I turned around to see Bishop slowly getting out of the car. Automatically, I moved to the side. Bishop shut the door behind him and tossed Lawton the keys.

As if by reflex, Lawton snagged them in mid-air.

Bishop turned toward the restaurant. He started walking.

"Hey!" Lawton called after him. "Where do you think you're going?"

Bishop didn't turn around, but his voice carried across the cool night air. "To get a burger, beer – hell, a cab, I dunno. You guys work it out. I'll catch you later."

"Hey!" I cupped my hands around my mouth and hollered "There's nothing to work out, dipshit!"

No reaction. No twitch. No hesitation. No nothing. I glared at his receding back. That jerk. He must've heard me. He was just like his brother, maddening beyond description. I wanted to scream.

Next to me, I heard Lawton's amused voice. "Did you just call him a dipshit?"

I whirled to face him. "You think it's funny?"

He raised his hands in mock surrender. "Nope. Not me."

"Then why are you smiling?" I said. "God, you are such a—" I shook my head. "I don't even know what to call you."

His smile faded. Slowly, his gaze traveled the length of me as if cataloguing my body parts, as a doctor, not a lover.

"You're okay?" His voice caught. "You look okay." He reached for my hand. "But what are you doing here? Shouldn't you be home?" He visibly swallowed. "In bed or something?"

I yanked my hand away. "Oh, because some psycho locked me in his basement?" I laughed, a foreign, hysterical sound. "No big deal. Happens to me all the time. Life goes on, right?"

His face crumpled. "Baby–"

"I already told you, don't call me that." I pointed toward the restaurant. "So why'd you do this here? You want me to lose my job? Is that it?"

"No. I get it. You love this job. I know that."

"Oh yeah. That's why I'm working here. Because I love it soooo much."

His eyebrows furrowed. "You don't?"

"Hell no," I said. "But I still don't want to get fired." I reached up to rub my temples. "I can only imagine what those two guys from the trunk are saying right about now." I closed my eyes. "God, what a nightmare."

"They're not saying anything," Lawton said.

I opened my eyes to look at him. "What are you? Some kind of mind-reader? Admit it, you don't know squat."

"I know one thing," he said. "They won't talk."

"Why?" I said. "Because they're too afraid that I'll talk too? Yeah, like that's gonna happen."

"What do you mean?"

"I mean," I said, "that I don't want to get dragged into some police station." My voice rose. "I don't want to be sitting there all night, telling my pathetic story of how they tried to drag me into a car and –" I let the sentence trail off. What had they been planning to do, anyway?

"Hey, don't worry," Lawton said. "Nobody's dragging you anywhere. They won't talk. And you won't have to either."

"How can you be sure?"

Lawton's voice was quiet. "Because they know better. They're not gonna say one word about you."

I glared up at him. "Yeah? How do you know?"

"Because if they do," he said, "they'll find themselves dropped off someplace worse next time."

My gaze narrowed. "What next time?"

Lawton shrugged. "Depends on them."

Tonight, they'd been dropped off in a crowded public place. There'd been people and police and even some paparazzi club wannabe. I looked around. "What could possibly be worse than this?"

His face hardened. "My old neighborhood."

From the look on his face, I didn't have to guess what kind of place it was. I didn't want to think about it. I didn't want to talk about it either.

"So answer me this," I said. "Why, of all places, did you bring them here, where I work?"

"You wanna know why?" he said. "Because this is exactly where they were gonna drop you."

I felt my forehead crease. "What?"

"Yeah," Lawton said, an edge creeping into his voice. "They were gonna strip you down to your bra and panties and dump you right here. In this parking lot." His jaw tensed. "Want to know what they called it? A prank. Just a fucking prank."

"Seriously?" I said. "That's all they were gonna do?"

Compared to what I'd feared, yeah, it sucked. But it wasn't half as bad as the other scenarios that had run through my mind.

"All?" he said. "Isn't that enough?" He made a strangled sound deep in his throat. "God, Chloe. They hurt you. They scared you."

"Yeah." I gave him a hard look. "And they weren't the only ones, now were they?"

"No." His voice was quiet. "They weren't."

"So what was all this?" I said. "Your idea of justice?"

"Something like that." His gaze bored into mine. "We did exactly to them what they were gonna do to you. Seemed fair enough."

"Fair?" I made a scoffing sound. "Yeah, but you didn't stop there, did you?"

"What do you mean?"

"I mean," I said, "that you also beat the crap out of them. And, you ruined their car. So it wasn't exactly an eye for an eye, was it? "

He gave me an incredulous look. "You're sticking up for them?"

Was I? In truth, those guys got exactly what they deserved. And I sure as hell didn't feel sorry for them. But if Lawton was expecting me to run into his arms just because he delivered some well-deserved payback, he had another thing coming.

Tonight, a handful of people had suffered. Me. Those guys. But as far as I could tell, one person who hadn't suffered one single bit was Lawton. After what he did, not to those guys, but to me, he didn't deserve my understanding. And he sure as hell didn't deserve some kind of hero's welcome.

So, was I sticking up for those guys? Did it matter? I

shrugged.

"You are serious. Aren't you?" he said. "After what they did to you? You think that's alright?" He turned to glare across the parking lot. "Because I'm not gonna lie to you, Chloe. I'd do it again in a heartbeat. And if they ever pull that crap again, especially with you, they're not gonna get off so light."

I gave him a smirk. "So they got off light, huh? Well, what about you?"

"What about me?"

"You got off lightest of all, didn't you? Look." I pointed directly at his chest. "You're fine. Not a scratch on you, is there?" I turned toward his car and pointed again. "And look. Your car's fine too." I turned to face him. "Seriously, what has any of this cost you?"

"Chloe." His voice was very quiet. "It's cost me everything."

"Yeah." I rolled my eyes. "Right."

"Everything that matters."

"You know what?" I said. "That's real easy for you to say." My voice rose. "Me? I'm an inch away from losing my job. Those guys, they got their car trashed. But you? This has cost you nothing." I took a step closer. "Nothing!"

With an anguished expression, he reached out for me. I slapped his arms aside. "So who's gonna kick your ass? Who's gonna get you fired? Who's gonna trash your car?"

"You want someone to kick my ass?" He threw up his hands. "Go ahead. I'd welcome it."

"Sure you would."

"Think I'm lying? You think I don't know that I deserve it?"

"Yeah? Well, words are cheap." I turned to go.

"Wait," he said.

I stopped. "For what?"

"Proof."

☐

CHAPTER 12

As I watched, he strode toward the back of his car. He popped the trunk and rummaged inside. A moment later, he slammed it with a thud.

He emerged with an old-fashioned tire iron. He held it out in his open palms. "Here," he said.

I glanced down. "What would I want with that?"

"Take it." His eyes met mine. "And hit me."

"Oh shut up," I said. "I don't want to hit you."

"Alright," he said. "Get someone else. Have them do it."

Not too long ago, I'd fantasized about such a thing. And here it was, the chance to make it a reality. This was just my luck. A fantasy comes true, and it's not even a good one.

I shook my head. I should've fantasized about winning the lottery.

He glanced toward the restaurant. "Go ahead, find someone. I'll wait."

"Oh c'mon, you can't be serious."

"Why not?" His voice was raw. "I deserve it. Just like you said."

"You are seriously messed up. You know that, right?"

"Hell yes, I know it! You think I'm liking myself right now? You think I don't know that I deserve an ass-beating?

You think I don't wish it was me 'suffering,', as you say?"

From the look on his face, he was suffering plenty. Fearless, that's what he was. But looking at him now, he looked almost terrified, like the ship was sinking, and the last lifeboat was filling up fast. I wanted to rescue him. And I wanted to throw him overboard.

Damn it, Chloe. Just stop. I wrapped my arms tight around my body, both for warmth and to keep myself from melting into him. Or slapping him silly. Or both.

There was a word for how he made me feel.

Psychotic.

Just like him.

"Alright, here's the deal," I said. "You –" I lifted a hand to point at his chest "– need to stay the hell away from me. Stay away from where I work. Stay away from where I'm living. And stay away from anywhere else you think I might be."

"Chloe–"

"You already said that."

"Please." His voice was ragged, and he moved toward me, slowly, like he knew he shouldn't but couldn't seem to make himself stop.

I raised my voice. "I mean it."

He stopped, his expression anguished, but his body rigid. The muscles in his forearms were coiled masses of restrained force matched only by the look of absolute control that slowly settled over his face.

"Chloe, please. Hit me. Yell at me. Do something." His voice choked. "Anything but this."

My heart twisted at the sight of him. But I couldn't afford to let him know that. Not after what he'd done. And I couldn't afford to encourage him either. This had to be over, once and for all.

"You heard me," I said, turning to go.

"Chloe." It was an odd, strangled sound. "Wait. Please."

Slowly, I turned back to face him. "For what?"

"I know what you're thinking," he said.

I crossed my arms. "I seriously doubt that."

"I can see it all over your face. You're thinking talk is cheap."

"So?"

"So you don't want someone to beat my ass? I get that. But you want me to pay, am I right?"

I shrugged.

"Believe me, Chloe. I want to pay."

Oh God, he wasn't going to offer me money, was he? Lord knows I could use it. But the whole idea made me just a little bit sick.

I recalled him peeling off those hundreds for Brittney. It had happened that first time I'd been inside his house. Officially, the money was payment for a destroyed purse. Unofficially, it felt like something a whole lot different. I'd seen the look in his eye when she'd taken the cash.

It wasn't so much a judgment as a dismissal, like she'd lived down to his expectations, and he didn't give a crap one way or another.

But my integrity, it wasn't for sale. "I don't want your money," I said.

"I know."

"You don't know anything," I said.

"I know you want something else."

"Oh yeah?" I said. "What's that?"

"This." He shifted his grip on the tire iron. He took one long stride toward his car. Before I could digest what was happening, he bashed it against the windshield, leaving a

59

cracked, spider-web pattern on the formerly smooth glass.

"What the hell are you doing?" I yelled.

As an answer, he raised the iron again and smashed it against the side view mirror. Another hard blow, and the mirror hit the pavement, breaking on impact.

I dove toward him and grabbed his elbow. "Don't!"

Slowly, he turned to face me. "Why?"

"Because it's stupid!" I was shaking as I looked at the destruction. Oh my God. His car. His beautiful car. I didn't know how much it was worth, money-wise, but I knew exactly what it meant to him personally.

"Isn't this the kind of justice you wanted?" he said. "My car trashed? That's what you said, wasn't it?"

"No!" I gripped his elbow tighter. "This isn't what I wanted."

"Well, I do." Gently, he removed my hand from his elbow. "Because, Chloe, let me tell you something. Compared to you, this car means nothing to me."

He strode to the passenger's side. He raised the iron again. "Compared to you, it means less than nothing."

I watched helplessly, frozen by disbelief, as he bashed off the other mirror, and then destroyed both headlights, leaving scattered bits of glass on the dark pavement.

"Stop it!" I yelled.

He gave a sad shake of his head and raised the iron high above his head. He slammed it down on the hood, leaving an ugly dent in the beautiful finish. He raised the iron and struck again. And again. Soon, the hood was mangled almost beyond recognition.

I was having a hard time catching my breath. He loved that car. He'd spent countless hours restoring it with his own hands. Now he was destroying it right before my eyes.

I couldn't act. I couldn't think. I staggered backward and hit something unexpected.

And then, I heard that dreaded voice. "Sweeeeet."

I whirled around, and there he was. Shaggy. With that damn cell phone.

CHAPTER 13

Shaggy was holding the phone out in front of him, directly toward Lawton and his mangled car.

I glared at him. "What the hell are you doing here?"

"Taking video," Shaggy said. "What else?"

Helplessly, I looked toward Lawton. He stood near the passenger's side door, watching us with a blank expression. The iron dangled loosely in his right hand. And then, it clattered to the pavement. An instant later, he was at my side.

"You." He glared at Shaggy. "Get away from her. Now."

With a shrug, Shaggy took a couple steps away from me. He turned back toward the mangled car. "Oh man," he said. "That is so messed up." He held out his cell phone. "Total viral." He stepped closer, zooming in on the hood.

"Stop that!" I said.

He shook his head. "No way."

I gave Lawton a pleading look. "Are you just gonna stand there and let him take video of – " I waved my hands on a useless gesture "—this?"

Shaggy chuckled. "It's called freedom of the press, baby." He turned to call over his shoulder. "Am I right, or what?"

"Got that right," said a distant, unfamiliar voice.

Wildly, I glanced around and came to a horrible realization. Shaggy wasn't the only one invading our privacy. Around us, maybe a dozen people stood clustered within spitting distance.

I saw wide eyes, eager expressions, and more than a couple of cell phones, held out camera-style, just like Shaggy's.

"Oh my God," I groaned. I leaned my head down and covered my face with both hands. "This isn't happening."

I felt a hand on my elbow. "Chloe," Lawton said. "You okay?"

I heard myself laugh. A foreign sound with jagged edges, like it came from someone else. I heard it grow louder, drowning out everything – the murmur of voices, Shaggy's stupid commentary, and the beating of my own heart.

Too soon, laughter turned to sobs, quieter than the laugher, but infinitely more unsettling. Lawton's arms closed around me. He gathered me to his chest, shielding me from everything – the crowd, the sight of his car, and Shaggy with his stupid phone.

"God, this is all my fault," he murmured into my hair. "I'm so, so sorry. Baby, c'mon, don't cry."

Suddenly, his body tensed. When he spoke, his voice was hard, with an undertone of menace so sharp that I fought the urge to step away.

"You take one more shot of her," he said, "and you're gonna be out more than just another phone."

Another phone?

Oh God, was Lawton the psycho who smashed Shaggy's last one? He had to be. Shit. How well did I know this guy, anyway?

I couldn't think. I couldn't breathe. This was a living nightmare. Except I couldn't wake up.

Lawton's arms tightened. He shifted his position as if hiding me from someone's view. "Get the fuck away from her!" he yelled.

And then I heard a new voice, ferocious and female. ☐

☐

CHAPTER 14

"Chester!" she yelled. "You son of a bitch!"

Startled, I pulled my head away from Lawton and looked toward the sound of the voice. And there she was, the petite red-head. She stood on the opposite side of Lawton's car, near the passenger's side door.

Her face was flushed, and her hair was wild. She was glaring at Shaggy. "I knew it!" she yelled.

I glanced toward Shaggy. His eyes were huge, and his mouth was half open. He glanced frantically around as if seeking the fastest avenue of escape.

"You bolt now," the redhead warned, "and you're walking home." Her voice rose. "And when you get there, guess what? You're gonna find the locks changed, because I've just about had it with this crap!"

Shaggy offered up a shaky smile. "Heeeey Jen. So what are you doing out here?"

"Me?" she shrieked. "What am I doing out here? You're kidding, right?"

"Yeah. I mean no," he stammered. "I thought you were gonna wait for me."

She glared across the car at him. "You mean in the fucking restaurant? Where do you think I've been the last hour?"

"An hour?" Shaggy glanced toward the restaurant. "Oh

c'mon, it hasn't been that long."

She reached into her big red purse and pulled out a foil-wrapped container. "Still want that romantic dinner?"

Shaggy took a step backward. "No, I'm good, but uh, thanks."

Jen laughed. "Oh, you haven't been good for a long time. And you wanna know why? Because of you and your stupid Web site!"

She dug through the foil container. "You know how many times you've left me sitting alone while you chased some stupid story?" Her hand emerged from the container with – was that a shrimp?

Shaggy took another step backward.

"And you know how many places?" She raised her arm. A jumbo shrimp went flying toward Shaggy's head.

He ducked to the side. "Aw c'mon Jen! Not again!"

She reached into the container again. "At my sister's wedding!" She hurled another shrimp. This one hit Shaggy's chest and bounced onto the pavement.

From about a car-length away, something flashed. A camera? Shaggy's head whipped toward the flash. "Hey!" he yelled. "No pictures! C'mon, dude!"

"At my class reunion!" Jen yelled. "At my uncle's funeral!" She reached into the shrimp container and pulled out a whole fistful. She flung the whole mess in Shaggy's direction. It scattered across the pavement near his feet.

She stalked around Lawton's car. Her fists were clenched as she headed straight for Shaggy. He looked wildly around, like escape still might be possible. But in the end, whether frozen by terror or her threat of changing the locks, he held his ground.

Before I could blink, she was on him. She ripped the

phone from his hand and hurled it to the pavement. It crashed down, shattering into broken bits.

Shaggy looked down, his eyes half-crazed. "My phone!"

Jen gave a bark of laughter. "Your phone? Your phone?"

"Hey, you gave it to me," he said.

"No. I let you use it," she said, "It's my phone! And what did you promise?"

"Uh—"

"You promised to leave it home tonight. But did you?" She turned toward the crowd. "Did he?"

Around us, gawkers nervously shook their heads. Someone near the back was still taking pictures, illuminating the area with random flashes that made the whole sordid scene that much more unsettling.

Shaggy turned toward the source of the flashing. "Dude, c'mon!" he yelled. "Cut that out! Give us some privacy, will ya?"

Suddenly, I heard a burst of laughter. It sounded half-crazed.

Oh my God. It was coming from me. Through this entire spectacle, I'd been too transfixed to move. But now, I couldn't help it. I pushed away from Lawton and stumbled toward the shattered phone. I looked down.

"It doesn't look okay anymore," I said, with another snort of laughter.

"What's so damn funny?" Shaggy said.

"Do you really have to ask?" I turned to the redhead. "Sorry, I know it's not funny. I just –" I looked to the phone. "Oh my God. I so wanted to do that."

Her eyebrows furrowed. "Weren't you our waitress?"

"She's not gonna be anyone's waitress," said a male voice somewhere behind me, "if she doesn't get her butt back to work pronto."

CHAPTER 15

I stifled a groan. I knew that voice. I turned around, and sure enough, there he was, the worst boss ever.

Keith elbowed his way to the front of the small crowd. He stopped and put both hands on his hips. "Break time's over," he said.

"What break?" I said. "You sent me home. Remember?"

"No," he said in a tone of forced patience. "I sent you on break."

"Get real," I said. "You did not."

"Oh yeah? Check the schedule," he said. "You've got three hours left. Or did you forget that too?"

"I didn't forget anything," I said. "You were the one who clocked me out."

Shaking his head, Keith took a long, lingering look at the scene surrounding us, taking in the battered muscle car, the destroyed cell phone, the crowd of gawkers. And then his gaze stopped. His eyes widened. I turned to see what he was staring at.

It was Lawton, standing directly to my right. He was studying Keith with flat, hooded eyes. Lawton's hands, loose at his sides, twitched like he wanted to throttle someone. Who that someone was, I had no idea, given the wide range of possibilities. Shaggy? Keith? I swallowed. Me?

"Hey," Keith said to Lawton, "aren't you –"

"Yeah," Lawton said, flicking his head in my direction. "Chloe's boyfriend."

I whirled to face him. "You are not."

Lawton stared down at me, his eyes pleading. He reached for my hand. Our fingers brushed, and I fought the urge to fall into his arms, safe from everything.

There was only one problem. I wouldn't be safe from the most dangerous person of all. Him.

Blinking hard, I pulled my hand away.

Somewhere near Lawton's car, I heard Shaggy's voice, low and earnest. "Hey Dude, can I borrow your phone?"

"Screw you," a male voice said.

"Aw c'mon," Shaggy said. "Be a sport, will ya?"

"You touch that phone," a female voice said, "and you're a dead man."

Shaggy groaned theatrically. "Aw c'mon, Jen!"

Nearby, Keith cleared his throat, far too noisily for it to be genuine. I glanced in his direction.

"Chloe," he said through clenched teeth. "Might I speak with you a moment?" He gave the crowd a calculating look. "In private."

I returned my gaze to Lawton. "You should go," I told him.

He shook his head. "Not before we talk."

What the hell? Was he trying to get me fired? "I can't," I said. "I've gotta go."

"Then come by later," he said. "Promise me."

Slowly, I shook my head.

"Alright," he said, flicking his gaze to his car. "I'll wait here."

For all I knew, he'd be waiting three hours. Maybe more.

"You can't wait here," I said. "It might be all night."

He looked unimpressed. "I don't care."

Shit. I should make him wait. It would serve him right. But damn it, I'd never be able to focus on my job, knowing that Lawton was out here in the parking lot. I was barely holding it together as it was.

"Alright, fine," I said. "I'll stop by. But it might be morning before I get off work."

Something in his shoulders eased. He gave a slow nod. "I'll be waiting."

Nearby, Keith cleared his throat again. "Yeah," he muttered. "Waiting. I know how that feels."

"Alright, I'm coming!" I turned back to Lawton. "Go, alright? Please?"

When he gave a small nod, I turned toward Keith, who motioned me to follow him. With a sigh, I kept pace with him as he strode several car lengths away. When we were out of earshot, he said, "Look, I don't know what kind of game you're playing here, but we simply can't have this."

I studied him with raised eyebrows. "This? Which 'this' are you referring to?"

He crossed his arms. "Do I need to spell it out for you?"

I crossed my arms too. "Apparently."

He glanced at my arms. "Are you mocking me?"

"Look," I said, "whatever you've got to say, just say it, alright?"

"Oh, I'll say it, alright," he said. "And you'd better listen good, because this is a professional establishment. We can't have —" he gave a little wave of his hands as if searching for the words "—domestic disturbances here on the premises."

"Domestic disturbances?" I said. "Seriously?"

His expression hardened. "In case you forgot, this is your

place of employment, not a pickup joint."

I couldn't help it. I laughed in his face. "Says the guy who screws customers in the parking lot."

Keith looked around and lowered his voice. "She's not a customer." He lifted his chin. "She's my girlfriend."

I rolled my eyes. "Oh yeah? Since when?"

"That's none of your concern."

"I heard she's gonna be working here," I said. "Is it true?"

"So what if she is?" he said. "She applied, and we're short-staffed. She's not getting any preferential treatment, if that's what you're implying."

I squinted at him. "Doesn't the employee manual expressly forbid dating between managers and their employees?"

He gave me a nasty smile. "Not when no one knows about it."

I gave him a nasty smile right back. "Well, that's the thing, Keith. I do know about it. And I can prove it too."

His smile widened. "Really? How?"

I felt my own smile falter. He knew exactly how. Unless – did he know something I didn't?

My phone was still inside the restaurant. But it wasn't like I should need to worry about it. It was locked in one of the back lockers, along with my purse and a few other personal items.

"I'm glad we had this little chat," Keith continued. "Now get back to work before I have to write you up."

"For the last time," I said, "you sent me home."

"And for the last time," he said in a mocking tone, "I sent you on break."

"Oh c'mon, you clocked me out yourself. Remember?"

"What I remember," he said, "is that according to the manual, no one except the employee can clock his or herself in or out. So, to answer your question, no, I don't remember because that would be a clear violation of company policy."

I rolled my eyes. "Whatever."

"I'll ignore your attitude, and tell you what I do know," he said. "Your break ended thirty minutes ago, and rather than return to your station, you're out here, living it up with your boyfriend."

My jaw dropped. Living it up?

"If you still want a job," he said, "I suggest you get back to work." He gave me a thin smile. "Before I send you home, permanently."

I stared at him, thinking of all the times he'd threatened my job within the last few weeks. The first time, it had rubbed me raw. Now, I felt like one giant callous. Or maybe that was only the fatigue talking.

But all that aside, if I had the chance to work a few more hours, I'd be stupid to not take it. It was nearly three in the morning, prime time for the after-bar rush. The tips alone would go a long way toward Grandma's rent money.

I turned toward the restaurant and started walking.

"About time you listened," Keith said, falling in beside me.

As I made the long trek across the parking lot, I took one final look over my shoulder. Lawton stood, leaning against the hood of his car, his arms crossed and his gaze on me. Nearby, Shaggy was scooping up remnants of his – correction, his girlfriend's – cell phone. Other than Shaggy's girlfriend, most of the gawkers were gone.

"When you get back," Keith said, "the next table's yours. Got it?"

"Oh, I've got it alright," I said. "But first, I'm checking my timecard."

"Why would you wanna do that?"

"Because," I said," "if I'm clocked out, you'd better believe I'm clocking back in."

He cleared his throat. "Well, if you are clocked out, just remember, it wasn't me who did it."

I gave him a sideways glance. "Uh-huh."

Besides, there was something else I needed to check.

My phone. Because I had a bad feeling it wasn't exactly the way I'd left it.

CHAPTER 16

I stood in the back room, staring down at my phone. For the third time, I frantically scrolled through its photos.

It was stupid, really. The phone was relatively new. I'd taken only a handful of shots, including several by accident.

The worst, or the best, depending on how you looked at it, had been an image of Lawton stark naked. That picture I'd finally deleted, but not before it caused me all kinds of grief by giving Lawton the worst impression of me and my intentions.

But right now, there was only one photo I was looking for – the one of Keith and Brittney in all their backseat glory. It was the very last photo I'd taken. It should've shown up first. Instead, it wasn't showing up at all.

I glanced again at my locker. I'd locked it myself, using my own combination lock. The lock was intact when I'd returned. Had I deleted the photo myself? Maybe by accident? It seemed unlikely.

Thank God I'd texted a copy to Erika. I scrolled through my outgoing texts, and there it was, along with her response, a simple "LOL."

Laugh out loud. Yeah, it was pretty funny. But right now, I wasn't laughing. Someone had tampered with my phone. I just knew it. And if the missing photo wasn't confirmation enough, Keith's attitude told me all I needed to know.

He wasn't scared. He was an obnoxious asshat. Like he always was.

"Hey Chloe!" he called from somewhere out front. "You coming out here, or what?"

Speaking of asshats.

I tucked my phone back into my purse just in time to see Keith round the corner, carrying a yellow timecard. I slammed the locker shut and gave the lock a few spins – not that it would do any good, assuming my suspicions were correct.

Still, I felt myself smile as I considered the thing Keith didn't know, that I had another copy.

"What are you so happy about?" he said.

"Nothing." I looked to his hand. "Is that my timecard?"

"Yeah," he said, thrusting the thing in my face. "Initial here. It does seem that someone clocked you out." He puffed out his chest. "But you'll be happy to know I did the adjustment personally."

I rolled my eyes and pulled a pen from my apron. Wordlessly, I added my initials to the adjusted entry and turned to leave the locker area.

"You're welcome!" he called to my receding back.

A minute later, I was out in the dining area, running my butt off with the other girls. I still owed Josie an explanation of what I'd seen outside. But between the packed dining room and Keith's new habit of popping in and out of the waitress station, talking to her was nearly impossible.

In a way, I was glad. I wasn't sure what to say.

Just before my shift ended, I was going from table to table, refilling the salt shakers when Josie sidled up next to me.

"Alright," she said in a hushed tone. "I got the scoop."

It was almost dawn, and most of the tables were vacant.

"Scoop?" I said, glancing around the nearly empty

restaurant.

"Scoop. News. Whatever," she said, waving away my confusion. "About the guys in the trunk." She put her hands on her hips. "By the way, you were supposed to be giving me these juicy details."

I grimaced. "Sorry about that, but Keith's been dogging me all night."

"No kidding," she said. "He's like your own personal shadow. What's up with that?"

I shrugged.

"Forget Keith." She grinned. "You're gonna love this."

I paused in mid-reach, the salt shakers forgotten. "Yeah?"

"Totally." Josie looked around. "Well, remember the guy at the bar?"

"Which one?"

"Older guy. Name's Bruce. But that's not important. Anyway, he got the whole story from one of the cops."

"Really? How?"

She shrugged. "They're buddies or something. But check this out. According to Bruce, those two guys ended up locked in their own trunk because of this stupid fraternity prank that got totally messed up."

I stared at her. "Messed up? How?"

"Apparently," she said, "they were supposed to end up at some sorority bash, and got dropped here instead. Can you believe it?"

No. I couldn't believe it. I knew better. Less than twelve hours earlier, those same two guys had tried to drag me into that same dark sedan. But instead, they'd been handed their asses by Lawton and his brother, and then locked in their own trunk.

No way I'd be sharing that little nugget though. "What

about the ski masks?" I said.

This ought to be good.

"Oh that's the best part," she said. "So apparently, they were supposed do some panty-raid, burglar skit when they got there –"

"Where?" I asked.

"The sorority house. But they ended up here." She grinned. "In their underwear. God, what a couple of dumb-asses."

I stared at her. That had to be the dumbest story I'd ever heard. "And the cops actually bought that story?" I said.

She squinted at me. "Why wouldn't they? You can't make that shit up, right?"

Time to change the subject.

I stopped to give her a serious look. "Can I ask you something? You did hear Keith say he was clocking me out, right?"

"Yeah. Why?"

"Because according to him, he was just sending me on break. Wanna hear what he did? He tracked me down in the parking lot and practically dragged me back inside."

Josie grinned. "Ohhh, that. I know why."

"Why?'

"Because remember Sonya, how she wasn't looking so good?"

I nodded.

"Well, maybe ten minutes after you left, she threw up in Keith's office."

I leaned forward. "On Keith?"

"No." Josie frowned. "In his wastebasket. Unfortunately. Still, she had to be sent home. We won't be seeing her for a week or two."

"So that explains it," I said.

"Yeah, good news for you, huh?"

"How so?"

"Two words," she said. "Job security."

I felt my shoulders slump. It was a sad day when you had to wish the flu on your co-workers just to make ends meet.

"What's wrong?" she asked.

I summoned up a smile. "Nothing. Just a long night, that's all."

"Alright, here's something that'll crack you up. Want to know what else happened in the parking lot?"

I felt my body tense. "What?"

"You know who Lawton Rastor is, right? Remember, you let me wait on him a few weeks ago?"

Mutely, I nodded.

"Well, some guy I waited on claims he spotted him in our parking lot, beating the crap out of his own car." She laughed. "Crazy, huh?"

"Well, he does have that reputation," I mumbled.

"Know what?" Josie said. "I don't even care. I'd totally do him, anyway." She leaned her head back and closed her eyes. "Oh my God, those abs. Want to know what I want? To cover him with chocolate sauce and lick it off." Her voice got husky. "Drop by drop."

I tried to laugh, but it came out wrong. More like a whimper.

Josie opened her eyes to study my face. "You feeling okay? You're not coming down with the flu, are you?"

I shook my head. "Not me. I can't afford to."

I also couldn't afford to think about any other girl, including Josie, licking Lawton anywhere. He and I were done. But if I were honest, the idea of him with anyone else was making me more than a little sick.

Or maybe, if I was lucky, it was just the flu. ☐

☐

CHAPTER 17

The tall, iron fence was as daunting as ever, but the gate was open. Cast in the shadows of thick overhanging branches, I stood on the darkened sidewalk, gripping a cold fence spire in each hand.

My stomach churning, I stared at the massive brick and stone mansion that I'd come to know all too well. The house was utterly dark, except for the barest glimmer of light coming from a single room on the lower level.

I knew that room. Lawton's study.

I glanced at the circular drive. No cars. Not even the one he'd practically destroyed. But that didn't mean he wasn't home. He did have a huge garage after all.

He was definitely inside. He had to be. It was nearly dawn, and the grounds were wide open. Was he asleep? My gaze narrowed. Did I care?

No. In fact, if I dragged him out of a sound sleep, all the better. This meeting was his idea. Besides, I didn't walk here in the darkest part of the night just to turn around and scuttle back to safety without finishing this once and for all.

I pushed away from the fence and made my way along the sidewalk and through the open gate. Too soon, I stood at his front door. But before I could even ring the doorbell, the massive front door swung wide open, revealing Lawton in all his tattooed glory.

He was a dark silhouette against the dim interior. He wore black jeans, a dark gray T-shirt, and an expression filled with such longing that I felt myself swallow.

I took an involuntary step back and looked up at him. He stood absolutely still, framed in the doorway, with his hands loose at his sides and his eyes on me. Slowly, his lips parted. "Chloe."

There was a reason I'd come here, and it wasn't only because he'd cornered me into it. If I played my cards right, I'd be putting all this behind me. No more drama. No more temptation. No more Lawton.

I summoned up the meanest smile I could muster. "Lawton."

When he spoke, his voice was so low, it was barely audible. "You came."

I made a sound of disgust. Like I'd had a choice. "You wanted to talk? " I said. "Well, here I am."

Something in his face eased. His muscles uncoiled, and he took a step toward me.

I held up a hand, palm out. "Not that kind of talk."

He stopped. Behind him, the door remained open, apparently forgotten as he stood between me and the breathtaking place he called home.

His voice was thick when he asked, "Wanna come inside?"

"Uh, no." I gave him a look. "That didn't work out so well for me last time, now did it?"

Funny how getting handcuffed in a guy's basement made you rethink his notion of hospitality.

If I were smart, I probably wouldn't be here in the first place, especially at this hour. But foolish or not, I still believed he'd never hurt me, at least not physically. Mentally, well, that was another story.

If I gave him half the chance, the damage could be infinite. It was my job to make sure that didn't happen, not tonight, and not ever.

He glanced down at the thin hoodie I'd thrown on over an even thinner long-sleeved T-shirt. "But it's freezing out." He flicked his head toward the inside of his house. "C'mon. Please?"

I raised my eyebrows. "Afraid of a little cold, are you?"

Slowly, he shook his head. "It wasn't me I'm thinking about. Cold, hot —" He shrugged. "I don't care." His voice softened. "I'm just glad you're here."

I rolled my eyes. "Oh please. Save it for someone who believes that sort of thing, okay?"

"Baby —"

"Stop." I gave him a hard look. "Listen, whatever reason you seem to think I'm here, that's not it." I steeled my resolve. "I'm here because you didn't give me any other choice, remember?"

He glanced toward the driveway. His eyebrows furrowed. "Where's your car?"

"At work."

"Why?"

"Because," I said, "the stupid thing wouldn't start. And I had to beg the busboy for a ride home." Technically, it wasn't my home, but that was beside the point.

The whole thing had totally sucked. Josie had been long-gone, and no else lived remotely near this neighborhood. I knew exactly why. They couldn't afford it.

Then again, neither could I.

I wasn't a surgeon, a CEO, or even a billionaire bad-ass like the guy standing in front of me. I was just the house-sitter. Not that Lawton knew that.

Maybe he'd never know that. And that was fine with me. Because if I were truly honest with myself, I didn't want him to be missing some temporary house-sitter with barely a penny to her name. I wanted him to miss the girl he thought I was.

I didn't want his pity, and I sure as hell didn't want his charity. I wanted him to eat his heart out.

It was totally messed up. I knew that. With our relationship ending, it shouldn't matter, but somehow, it did. It mattered a lot. □

□

CHAPTER 18

Standing at his front entryway, the silence stretched out. He glanced again at the empty driveway. His mouth tightened. "You should've called me."

"Yeah?" I said. "Well, maybe I didn't want to owe you a favor."

"You wouldn't have owed me anything."

"Yeah, right."

I knew exactly how these things went. He'd rescue me with a ride, and I'd feel obligated to be nice to him. I didn't want to be nice to him.

He looked toward the street. "So you walked here? Alone?"

"Why not?" I said. "I've done it before. Besides, I'm just on the other side of your fence."

He gave me a dubious look. "So you climbed it. That's what you're saying?" From the tone of his voice, it was pretty obvious he knew the answer to that.

"No. Of course not."

His so-called fence was twice my height and made of iron. It practically had spikes all along the top. I'd be stupid to go that way. Besides, I'd already tried that once. It didn't work out so well.

In front of me, he was still giving me that look. "So you

took the long way. By sidewalk."

"Well, I didn't fly here," I said, "if that's what you're wondering."

"It's a fifteen-minute walk," he said.

"So?"

"So it's the middle of the night."

"No. It's early morning."

His jaw tightened. "So you want something bad to happen to you? Is that it?"

I forced out a laugh. "What do you consider bad? Because it seems to me that something bad can happen just about anywhere, anytime." I shrugged. "Driveways, parking lots—" I gave him a look. "Basements."

He briefly closed his eyes, and when he opened them again, there was a glassy quality that hadn't been there before. "You should've called me," he said. "Chloe, I'm serious. Don't do that again, alright?"

"Look," I said. "You were the one who forced me to come here."

"Forced you?"

"Cornered me. Whatever." I crossed my arms. "So here I am. How I got here isn't all that important."

"It is to me."

"Yeah? Well, from now on that's your problem, not mine."

My words hung in the air. His lips parted, but he said nothing. The look in his eyes made me feel about two inches tall.

I was hateful. I knew that. But I had to be hateful. It's what he deserved, and not only as retribution for what he'd done. He deserved to know where we stood. And honestly, I was too mad, too tired, and too torn up to tell him nicely.

I stiffened my spine and broke the silence. "Listen," I said,

"I've had a long night, so can we skip the part where we debate why I wouldn't be calling you for favors?"

His expression froze somewhere between wariness and fatigue. "Alright," he said. "But there's something you deserve to hear. At least come inside, alright?"

"No. I don't think so." I glanced at his front door, still open. Apparently, billionaires didn't worry about little things like bloated utility bills or the furnace giving out. I couldn't even imagine.

I tried not to think about it. If he was too stupid to close the thing, who was I to care? Besides, he had to be colder than I was. His T-shirt looked even thinner than mine, and he wasn't even wearing a hoodie.

I glanced at his arms, bare except for thick athletic tape, wrapped around his wrists. I'd seen the tape before, wrapped around his hands the few times I'd seen him beating the crap out of his punching bag. Had he been lifting weights? In the middle of the night?

I glanced again at his arms. Even relaxed, the powerful lines of his biceps and forearms were a stark reminder that he wasn't just some harmless neighbor guy. He was a brute, even if he'd always been beyond gentle with me.

Well, except for that one time. And even then, he hadn't hurt me. Not exactly.

Somewhere deep in the house, I heard the low hum of the furnace.

"Aren't you gonna close the door?" I blurted out.

Shit.

Pathetic. That's what I was. If I couldn't resist warning the guy about inefficient heat usage, how the hell would I resist the haunted look in his eyes? And how would I resist telling him that the past few weeks had been the happiest of my whole life? Or confessing that when he held me long into the night, I'd felt safe and warm for the first time in forever?

Lawton's attention never wavered. "Screw the door," he said. He leaned a fraction closer. Something about the way he moved reminded me of our first almost-kiss. My heart ached at the memory.

And then, I heard a sleepy female voice call out, "Lawton, who's at the door?"

I froze, too stunned to move, and not just for the obvious reasons.

I recognized that voice.

CHAPTER 19

In front of me, Lawton froze, and any remaining color drained from his face. He glanced behind him and quickly back at me. "Chloe," he said, "it's not what you think. I swear."

But then, just behind him, I saw the girl who went with the voice.

Brittney. She was nearly naked, clad in see-through panties and a matching bra.

Suddenly, it was hard to breathe. It was even harder to think. I stood, rooted in shock, as my gaze darted from Brittney to Lawton and back again.

She gave me a sly smile. "Oh. It's you."

Lawton looked ready to kill. "You were supposed to wait upstairs," he told her.

She blinked at him. "Oh. Was I?"

"And where the hell are your clothes?"

She raised her arms in a slow, leisurely stretch. "Mmm...I dunno. Upstairs?"

I wanted to slap him – her too while I was at it. Or at the very least, I wanted to say something clever and cutting. But when I opened my mouth, all that came out was an odd, strangled sound. I clamped my mouth shut and whirled to go.

Lawton grabbed my elbow. "Chloe, wait! Please?"

I whirled back to face him. "So this is why you invited me here? To throw this in my face?"

"There's no this." His expression was anguished. He turned to Brittney. "Go on, tell her." He gritted his teeth. "Right now."

Brittney smiled. "Tell her what?"

Lawton bared his teeth. "You tell her right now why you're here, or the deal's off. Got it?"

She lifted a bare shoulder. "Whatever you say."

"And for God's sake," Lawton said, "put on some fucking clothes, will ya?"

Her lips formed a pout. "But they're dirty," she said. "And besides, it took her forever to get here."

I was shaking. This was a bad dream. It had to be. Except, in my nightmares, it was usually me in my underwear – standing at some bus stop, or maybe in the mall. That was nothing compared to this.

Lawton gave Brittney a warning look. "You've got five seconds," he told her.

"Oh alright. Fine." She looked to the ceiling and mumbled, "I'm here to apologize."

"In your underwear?" I said. "Yeah. Nice story."

"Brittney," Lawton said in a low warning tone, "you can do better than that."

Already I had heard enough. I'd seen enough too. More than enough actually. Brittney went for the clean-shaven look. All over.

"Don't bother." I gave Brittney the most dismissive look I could muster before turning away. "I don't want your apology."

"Wait," Brittney said.

Against my better judgment, I turned around.

She turned to Lawton. "If she doesn't want me to apologize, our deal still counts, right? I mean, because I tried. And she said 'no.' You saw that, right?"

Oh, that was rich. Suddenly I didn't care if she was nearly naked or wearing a clown suit. I wanted an apology, and I wanted it now.

☐

CHAPTER 20

I pushed past Lawton and stormed into the house. I stopped in front of Brittney. "On second thought," I said, "I'd just love an apology." I crossed my arms. "And I sure hope it's a good one. Because unlike some people, I've got standards."

Her lips pursed. "Hey, I've got standards too."

"Yeah, except yours are too low to measure." I turned to Lawton. "A few hours ago, wanna know what I caught her doing?" My voice rose. "Boning my boss in the back seat of his car."

"Hey!" Brittney said. "We weren't boning. We were doing other stuff."

"Whatever." I turned back to Lawton. "So for your sake, I hope you wore a damn condom." I made a hard, scoffing sound. "You know what? On second thought, I hope you didn't. Because you deserve whatever this skank gives you."

Lawton's face crumpled. "Baby." With two long strides, he closed the distance between us. He reached for my hand. "I didn't wear anything."

I snatched my hand away. "How nice for you."

"Because," he said, "I didn't have to. She's only here for one thing."

Yeah, and it was pretty obvious what that was. "Exactly," I

95

said.

"Not that." He turned toward Brittney. "She's here," he said, speaking very slowly and clearly, "to tell you how very, very sorry she is."

I snatched my hand away. "In her underpants? Do I look stupid to you?"

With a muttered curse, Lawton strode over to the front closet. He reached to the top shelf and pulled out a navy stadium blanket. He hurled it at Brittney. She didn't move to catch it. The blanket hit her torso and slid to the floor.

"Cover up," he said. "Or get out. Your choice."

With a scowl, Brittney leaned over to pick up the blanket, taking her sweet time. With the same languid motion, she stood and draped the blanket loosely around her shoulders, covering next to nothing.

I pointed to her pelvis. "I think you missed a spot."

With a huff, she tightened the blanket around herself, leaving only her bare legs exposed. She gave me a smirk. "Prude."

I gave her a smirk right back. "Squid-fucker."

Brittney turned to Lawton. "Did you hear what she called me?"

Lawton gave her a cold look. "Like I care," he said. "Now, go on. Apologize. Chloe's waiting."

"Oh alright." Brittney blew out a breath and looked vaguely in my direction. Her voice was a bored monotone as she said, "I'm sorry about that little joke."

I stared at her. "A joke?"

She rolled her eyes. "You know. The prank. With Joey and Paul."

Joey and Paul? The guys in the ski masks? So that was their names?

Lawton's voice was tight. "That was no prank."

"Aw c'mon," Brittney said. "Yes, it was. Just a little joke. No big deal." She turned to me. "Go on, tell him. You thought it was funny. Right?"

"Funny?" I said. "So let me get this straight. Two masked men try to throw me in a trunk, and you call that a fucking joke?"

She shrugged. "At least I have a sense of humor. Unlike some people."

"Gee," I said, "maybe some people don't like getting dragged away in the middle of the night. Maybe some people are funny like that. Maybe some people aren't totally fucking nuts!"

"Hey, you're the one who's crazy," she said. "It wasn't the middle of the night. It was like, what, nine?" She turned to Lawton. "See? She's making it sound ten times worse than it was."

Lawton's gaze narrowed. At his side, his hands were fisted so tight that the corded muscles in his forearms looked hard as granite.

Brittney took a small step backward, but then quickly recovered. She tossed her long blonde hair over one shoulder and said, "So like I told you, it's no big deal."

"And like I told you," Lawton said, "it is a big deal. A very big deal. And if you were some guy, you'd be getting a lot worse than the chance to beg Chloe for forgiveness."

"Hey," she said. "No one said anything about begging." She threw back her shoulders. "Brittney Adams doesn't beg for anything."

"Not even car nookie?" I said.

She gave me a look. "It wasn't nookie." She turned to Lawton. "You believe me, right?"

"What I believe," he said, "is that you're supposed to be apologizing."

She pursed her lips and turned back to me. "Alright. I guess I'm sorry. But seriously, it's no big deal. In my sorority, we do that sort of thing all the time."

"Your sorority kidnaps people?" I said. "Seriously?"

With a little huff, Brittney turned to Lawton. "See? She's doing it again. She's making it sound worse on purpose, just to make me look bad."

Lawton gave her a murderous look. "You want to do a shitty job at this, fine." He pointed toward the door. "Get the fuck out. Now."

"But I'm trying to explain," Brittney said. "She won't let me."

He crossed his arms and spoke very slowly. "Try harder."

With an eye roll, she turned to face me. "What we do," she said, "is steal their mascots. Swipe 'em for a day or two." She gave Lawton a pleading look. "But we always return them. It's no big deal. See?"

"No," he said. "I don't see."

"But it was just a joke," she said. "I don't get why everyone's freaking out about it." She adjusted the blanket and gave a dramatic sigh. "But just because you asked, I apologized anyway. So are we good now or what?"

I turned to Lawton. "So this was your idea?"

He pushed a hand through his hair. "Yeah, but—" He gave Brittney a hard look. "It was supposed to go a lot better."

Brittney threw back the blanket, and tapped her bare foot against the floor. She gave me a half-hearted look. "So you do accept my apology or what?"

"Hell no," I said. "That was the worst apology, ever."

"Hey, it was my first one," she said. "I thought I did pretty good." She turned to Lawton. "Didn't I?"

He crossed his arms. "No."

Staring at her, I felt my gaze narrow. "Just how long have you been here, anyway?"

She hesitated a split second before giving Lawton a long smoldering look. "Hard to say. We kind of lost track."

"That's it," he told her. "Get out."

"But I'm not dressed!" Brittney said.

"Whatever. Keep the blanket. Just get out."

"But I don't have my car," she whined.

Lawton reached into his jeans pocket and pulled out a cell phone. He tapped out a quick message, and barely a moment later, there was a knock at the front door. Lawton strode toward it and flung it open. A uniformed driver stood at the ready.

"Take her wherever," Lawton said.

The driver glanced in my direction. "Yes sir."

"Not her," Lawton said. He pointed toward Brittney. "Her."

Oh God, how humiliating was this? He literally had so many girls, the driver was losing track.

"Of course," the driver said with a surprisingly straight face.

With Brittney protesting all the way, the driver hustled her, blanket and all, outside into a dark SUV. Lawton and I watched silently as it pulled down the drive and out the front gate.

From somewhere upstairs, I heard a male voice say, "Well, that went good." □

□

CHAPTER 21

I glanced up and spotted Lawton's brother, lounging against the bannister. He wore dark sweatpants and no shirt, revealing a torso that might've made my mouth water if I were some other girl in some other place. His short, dark hair was mussed, like he'd just crawled out of bed.

I gave him a dirty look. "Eavesdropping again?"

"No. Trying to sleep." Absently, he scratched his lean stomach. "For all the good it did."

I rolled my eyes. "Oh, I'm soooo sorry if we ruined your beauty sleep."

Looking up the stairway, Lawton's eyebrows furrowed. "This is a private conversation," he said.

"Private, your ass," Bishop said. "Bet half the neighborhood heard."

"Fuck off," Lawton said, and then glanced quickly at me. "Sorry."

Bishop looked toward the front door, now closed. "Told you that was a bad idea." He shrugged. "But women, what do you expect?"

"That's it." I threw up my arms. "I'm outta here."

"Hey, don't leave on my account," Bishop said. "I'm heading back to bed."

"Yeah, you do that," Lawton said in a tone of forced

101

patience. He reached up to rub the back of his neck, where the muscles were corded into tight knots.

When I glanced again at the stairway, Bishop was gone.

I cupped my hands around my mouth and yelled, "I hope you sleep like crap!"

No answer.

Muttering, I turned away.

"Chloe," Lawton said. "Don't leave."

Ignoring him, I marched to his front door and flung it open.

"You're not walking," he said.

I turned to glare at him. "We already had this discussion."

"At least let me drive you," he said.

"No."

"Alright, then I'm walking with you."

I knew it was smart. But I didn't feel like being smart. I'd been stupid for weeks. Why stop now? "No, you're not," I said, turning away.

I strode out his front door and didn't look back. But as I reached the front gate, I felt that certain something, eyes on my back. I stopped. Reluctantly, I turned around. And there he was, Lawton, a few paces behind me.

"What are you doing?" I said.

"Making sure you get home okay."

With a huff, I turned back around and started walking again. But after about a block, I couldn't stand it anymore. I stopped again and turned around. He was still a few paces behind me. "You don't need to do this," I told him.

"Yes," he said, giving me a serious look. "I do."

"But it's creeping me out."

"Why?"

"Because I don't like someone walking behind me."

"Then I'll walk with you," he said. "But you're not walking back alone."

I glanced around, taking in our surroundings. Between the street lights, the sidewalk was dark, cast in the shadows of the tall trees that lined the residential street. I crossed my arms. "Fine. Whatever. But it doesn't change anything."

Lawton strode forward, joining me on the quiet sidewalk. For a couple of minutes, we walked in silence. The night air was freezing, and I tried not to shiver. I slid a glance in his direction.

He didn't even have a coat. He was being stupid. But what did I care?

I shouldn't care.

"I want to tell you something," he said.

I kept my voice disinterested. "What?"

"I know you don't want to hear it," he said, "but I do love you, and I'm so fucking sorry."

Something squeezed at my heart. I blinked hard and kept on walking. He was right. I didn't want to hear it. And I wanted to hear it a million times over.

I was a mess. I clamped my lips shut to keep from saying something regrettable either way.

With something like a sigh, Lawton bridged the silence and continued. "Which is why you deserve to know why I flipped out on you."

CHAPTER 22

Silently, I kept walking at a steady pace, ignoring the unsteady beating of my heart.

He had flipped out. Sure, almost anyone would be mad if they thought their girlfriend was planning to trick them into making a sex tape. But he'd taken mad to a whole new level.

He'd gone through my stuff. He'd treated me like trash. He'd tricked me into his basement and locked me down there for hours.

As if taking my silence as an invitation, Lawton continued. "A few years ago, right after that first fight video went vial, I met this girl."

Lawton met a lot of girls. No surprise, considering all his claims to fame. He'd made his money through prizefighting, the kind with bookies, beer, and bimbos. It wasn't hard to imagine what kind of girl he was talking about now.

But I didn't need to imagine. I knew exactly who he was talking about – Brandy Blue, the girl who starred with him in that sex tape.

"It was before that reality series," he said. "But I was starting to make a name for myself. Then there was the money." He paused. "Growing up, I never had any, you know? But it was starting to roll in. Lots of it. At least compared to what I had before."

I knew what he meant. Today, he was a billionaire. Back then, a thousand bucks probably seemed like a fortune. To me, it still was.

"But this girl," he said, "she worked as a cocktail waitress at this club I used to go to. She seemed nice. You know, working her way through college and all that. I don't remember what her major was supposed to be, but she was studying all the time, brought her books to the bar, always talked about what she was gonna do when she graduated."

He blew out a breath. "Wait. I remember. A veterinarian." His voice got an edge to it. "Yeah. An animal doctor. She was gonna take care of puppies and kittens, and nurse them back to health and all that shit."

"Shit?" I said.

"You know what I mean."

"Actually," I said, "I don't." I loved dogs, one in particular. Unfortunately, Chucky wasn't mine, just like a lot of things in my life. I could pretend, but that didn't change anything. Not really.

"Anyway," Lawton said, "I used to hang out at the club sometimes. And we got friendly."

"Yeah, I just bet."

He was quiet for a beat, and then he said. "Not that way. Not at first."

I heard myself ask, "Why not?"

"Because I liked her."

Still walking, I snuck a sideways glance in his direction. Cast in shadows, the angles of his face were sharper than ever, but his voice was very soft, like he was fading off into the past. "In some ways, she was a lot like you. Or at least, I thought she was. Which is why I didn't want us to... you know."

"So let me get this straight," I said. "You didn't want to have sex with her, and somehow she reminds you of me." I made myself smile. "Gee, thanks."

"It's not that I didn't want to. I mean, she was—" He gave a small laugh. "I mean, like I said, she was a lot like you. One minute, she'd be sweet and funny. And then the next minute? She'd be cussing like a truck driver, surprised the crap out of me. And she was–" he cleared his throat "— attractive."

"How nice for you," I said.

He dug his hands into the front pockets of his jeans and kept on walking. "But things were so crazy back then. I had girls throwing themselves at me everywhere I went."

"Like that's changed."

"Maybe. I dunno. But back then, it was all so new, I didn't handle it that good." He pulled a hand out of his pocket and pushed it through his hair. "I dunno. But this girl I liked. We were friends, maybe something more someday. I didn't know. But I wasn't gonna mess it up."

At first, I'd been absolutely certain he'd been talking about Brandy Blue. Now, I wasn't so sure. And the more he talked, the more I didn't even care what her name was. I totally hated her.

"I get it," I said. "You liked her. So?"

"So you know who I'm talking about, right?"

I shrugged.

"Brandy Blue. The girl from, you know, that video."

This didn't make any sense. The girl he had just described sounded nothing like Brandy, other than being attractive, and working as a cocktail waitress. From what I'd read, Brandy had never gone to college. Mostly, she'd been trying to get famous – sometimes as a model, sometimes an actress.

After that video, she'd gone on to do a couple of horror

flicks and a short-lived stint on a doctor drama. I hadn't read much about her lately, but she was still a household name, mostly because of that video with Lawton.

"I didn't know Brandy went to college," I said.

"That's because she didn't."

I stopped walking. Lawton did, too. I turned to face him.

"What do you mean?" I said.

"I mean," he said, "it was all a sham. Everything. The nice girl act, the college thing, the books. It was just one big crock."

"I don't get it," I said. "Why?"

"That's the best part," he said. "This guy – someone I thought was a friend – he gets this idea that I should make a sex tape." Lawton made a sound that was probably supposed to be a laugh. "Everyone was doing 'em. Quick fame, right? That could be me. Famous for being famous. All I needed was a willing partner."

My heart sank. "So you did it?"

Stupidly, I'd come to believe his official story, that the footage had been taken without his knowledge. I should've known better. It's what they all said after the fact, wasn't it?

His gaze met mine. "That's what you think? That I filmed that thing on purpose? That I wanted the world to see me fucking some chick for five minutes of fame?"

The venom in his voice surprised me. I looked down, trying to collect my thoughts.

"You want the truth?" he said.

I looked up and felt myself nod.

"That kind of fame?" he said. "Don't want it, don't need it. But Brandy, she wants it and needs it, because she's gonna be a fuckin' star someday."

"So what happened?" I said.

"So she hooks up with this friend of mine. And this so-called friend tells her everything she needs to know – where I hang out, things I like, things that piss me off. And they agree to this split."

"Of the money?" I said.

"No. He gets the money. She gets the exposure."

"Literally or figuratively?" I said.

"You saw the footage. What do you think?"

I shook my head. "I don't know," I said. "I never watched it."

His mouth tightened. "I saw the disk. Remember?"

I didn't need to ask which disk. Obviously, he meant the one he'd seen lying on the Parkers' kitchen table. The label on the case, handwritten in big, black letters, was a dead giveaway – Rastor Sex Tape.

I was still mad as hell about what he'd done, but the story he'd just relayed was so sickening that my heart went out to him.

My voice was quiet. "Erika brought it over. You know, for my birthday. She didn't know that you and I were together. She thought it would be funny." I shrugged. "You know, because we're neighbors."

I blew out a breath. "But you and I were together. At least I thought we were."

"We were," he said. "I still wanna be."

He was making this so damn hard. His behavior had been inexcusable, or so I thought. But then what does he do? He gives me an excuse that, well, actually made a lot of sense. How would I feel in his shoes?

Oh crap. He'd asked me about the tape, hadn't he?

"Anyway," I said, "it just seemed wrong to watch it. Plus, well, I guess I didn't really want to watch you doing that with anyone else."

At this, he smiled. A real smile. It seemed like forever since I'd seen one.

"Yeah?" he said.

That smile, his voice, the things he said – I was falling. Everything was happening too fast. I needed time to think.

"So with Brandy," I said, "you two ended up having sex anyway, and she taped it?"

His smile faded. "Not exactly. This one night, outside the club, I was supposed to meet her there at closing time. Get a coffee or something. So I pull up to the back entrance, and she's already there." His voice hardened. "And she's crying."

"Why?" I asked.

"Well at first, it was hard to get the story out of her. But from what I did get, a couple of guys jumped her in the parking lot. Tore at her uniform, and tried to–" He paused. "Well, you know."

"Oh my God," I said. "Did they ever find them?"

He gave a bark of laughter. "No. And you wanna know why?"

I nodded. "Why?"

"Because they didn't exist."

CHAPTER 23

I tried to digest what he'd just told me. "What do you mean they didn't exist?" I said.

"It was all a big show," he said. "The torn clothes, the fake tears. By then, she knows me pretty good. Especially with this friend of mine feeding her information. And she knows I can get a little intense when people I love are hurt–"

I swallowed. "So you loved her?"

He shrugged. "I dunno. Not like that. It's not that she was unattractive—"

"You already said that."

"Alright, you want the truth?" he said. "I didn't see her like that."

"Why not?"

"The truth? There was this other girl, someone I'd met maybe a few months earlier, before everything started to hit. And I couldn't get this girl out of my head."

Another one? God, how many girls were there? I felt my jaw clench. "You're changing the subject," I said. "What about Brandy?"

Lawton hesitated a half second and then continued. "So that night, after this so-called attack, she wouldn't let me do a damn thing about it."

"Like what? What'd you want to do?"

"Find those guys, take care of it."

"How?" I asked.

He shrugged. "I had a few ideas."

From the tone of his voice, I could only imagine.

"So what happened?" I said.

"So we go back to her place, and I should've known something was up. The place looked like—" He shook his head. "Well, let's just say it looked like she was expecting company."

"Romantic company?"

"Yeah. And she asks me to hold her, and starts kissing on me, and one thing leads to another."

I snorted. "Yeah. I bet."

His gaze snapped to me. "Go ahead. Joke about it. You and everyone else. I should be used to it, right?"

I felt the color rise to my cheeks. "I'm sorry," I said. "Really." And I was. He might deserve a lot of things, but he didn't deserve ridicule, not for this.

"It's alright," he said. But from the look on his face, it obviously wasn't.

"No," I said, my voice softer now. "It's not. I don't want to be like everyone else. At least, not about this."

"That's the thing," he said. "You're not like anyone else." He reached for my hand. "Not about anything."

I didn't pull away. His hand felt big and strong around mine. I fought the urge to fall into his arms. It always felt so good there, like the home I never had.

"So what happened then?" I said.

"So we had sex. Obviously."

Lots of sex. Although I'd never seen the tape, I'd read plenty about it.

"So a few days later, the footage of it hits all these Web

sites, and Brandy's gone." He made a scoffing sound. "To Hollywood, L.A., whatever. Big surprise, huh?"

"What about your friend?" I asked.

"The next time I see him, he's driving a Jag."

"Did you confront him about it?" I asked.

His voice got an edge. "You might say that."

From the look on his face, I probably didn't want to know how the confrontation ended. "So what about Brandy?" I said.

"What about her?"

"You ever see her again? I mean, I read about that thing in Beverly Hills."

He'd left her half-naked in the bathroom of some posh restaurant, then beat the crap out of the bouncers who tried to stop him from leaving.

"Yeah. About that," he said. "Her acting career? It wasn't exactly taking off."

"It seemed like it was going alright," I said.

"Yeah. She had a few parts. Mostly TV. But she wanted something bigger. So I'm at this dinner—some promo thing for a celebrity endorsement. And she corners me in the men's room."

"Seriously?"

"Yeah," he said. "And the way it looks, she's ready for a sequel."

"You're kidding."

"Only half," he said. "Because Brandy's not stupid. She knows damn well I'm not gonna fall for some secret camera thing again. But she still could use the publicity, right? So she gets half-naked and corners me."

"You did say this was in the men's room, right?"

"Yeah. And as soon as I see her, I take off. But she follows after me, making this big scene. And from what she's yelling, it sounds like we just did it right there in the stall."

I'd seen pictures of their confrontation. It didn't just sound like they'd been having sex. It looked like it too. True, Lawton had been fully clothed, but Brandy was wearing next to nothing.

"So I get the hell out of there," Lawton said, "and she's following after me, acting like I'd just done the wham-bam-thank-you-ma'am. And I see all these photographers."

"She set you up?" I said.

"Yeah. Did a good job of it too. Even hired these bouncers to keep me from leaving. She wanted a full spectacle."

"Boy, she sure got it," I said. The whole thing was still legendary. "How come you never told anyone?" I said.

"I did. I said flat-out that none of it happened. You think that got any coverage? Besides, you think anyone gives a crap?"

"They might've," I said, "if you had told the whole story."

"You think anyone wants the whole story?" His voice grew sarcastic. "Besides, she did me a big favor, right? Right after that sex tape hit, I was signed to that reality show."

Oh yeah. Hard World. He'd slept with practically every girl on the set. I felt my forehead wrinkle. Or maybe not. Was that also fake? "About that show," I said. "Was any of that true?"

"Which part?"

"You." I cleared my throat. "And all those girls?"

He'd slept with practically every girl in the household. But it wasn't the off-screen sex that had people watching. It was the fights -- not with him, over him. The show was abruptly cancelled after one girl threw another one through a plate glass window. She'd survived, but the show hadn't.

His gaze drifted from my face and down to his feet.

"Yeah."

"Oh."

"You've gotta understand," he said, "everywhere I looked, someone wanted something from me. I guess I was pissed off, maybe a little tired of fighting it." He squeezed my hand. "Until you."

"Why me?"

"What do you mean?"

"Why not Amber? Or Brittney?"

He looked at me. "Is that a serious question?"

Was it? Yeah, I guess it was. "Well, take Brittney," I said. "You obviously liked her well enough a few weeks ago. And Amber too. Why not them?"

He blew out a breath. "Girls like Brittney are easy."

"That's for sure," I said.

"I don't mean that." He shook his head. "With girls like her, I know what I'm getting. And they know what they're getting too."

"Girls like what?"

"You know the type," he said. "Girls from the wrong side of town who pretend to be something they're not."

I felt my body stiffen. That didn't only describe Brittney. It described me, too. Still, I made myself ask, "What's she pretending to be?"

"I dunno. Some socialite, I guess. Take that sorority thing. Get this. She doesn't even go to college."

"Not now? Or not ever?"

"Not ever. And probably never will."

"You're kidding."

"Nope."

"How do you know?"

"One night at my place, she got totally trashed. It was just the two of us, and she started telling me how much her life sucked, and how lucky Amber is, compared to her. "

"So Amber's the real deal?"

He shrugged. "Far as I know."

"Does Amber know about Brittney, that she's just pretending, I mean?"

"She's got to," Lawton said. "I mean, they claim to be in the same sorority. And they've got this sister act thing they do."

I recalled the first night I'd seen them. I knew exactly how far that act extended. I felt my jaw clench. "That's seriously messed up."

"Yeah. I guess."

"But she told that same lie tonight," I said. "About the sorority, I mean. Why would she do that if you knew the truth?"

He shrugged. "She probably forgot. Like I said, she was pretty trashed."

"But why didn't you call her on it?"

"Because I didn't care. I figured you wouldn't either. I mean, c'mon, it's pathetic, right?"

In spite of the cold, I felt color rise to my cheeks. I slipped my hand out of his and started walking again.

Lawton fell in beside me. "What's wrong?" he asked.

"Nothing."

Somehow, in the last few minutes, I'd almost forgotten my vow to keep him at a distance. A very long distance. Like from Michigan to the Moon, in spite of the fact we shared a fence.

But after the things he told me, I was having a hard time keeping everything straight. Plus, I was seriously sleep-deprived. It was nearly dawn, and I'd been awake for most of the past twenty-four hours.

"Chloe?"

"Yeah?"

His voice was very quiet. "Will you give me another chance?"

CHAPTER 24

We were getting closer to the Parkers'. It wasn't actually my home, even if I was living there. I was just the house-sitter, dog-walker, plant-waterer, mail-getter, whatever.

When I answered the Parkers' ad, I approached it the only way I thought they'd hire me. I acted like I didn't need the money.

There was only one problem. At the time, I hadn't known about Lawton. I didn't know that we'd get together, or realize how the secrets would pile up. By now, Lawton knew it wasn't my house, but that was pretty much all he knew.

I wanted to keep it that way. And I wanted to tell him everything.

So, what did he think now? That I was some rich guy's mistress? The niece of the owners? Some surgeon's love child?

I took my agreements seriously. As part of the deal with the Parkers, I had a strict confidentiality clause. They didn't want a single person to know they were out of town, and I honestly couldn't blame them.

And even if I wanted to tell someone, Lawton would be a terrible choice. He had baggage of his own, starting with his brother, who had a nasty little habit of breaking into people's houses when they weren't there.

But was that my only reason? I recalled what Lawton had

said about Brittney. He'd practically called her a poser. In truth, I was a poser, too. Sure, I was a paid poser, but did that make it better or worse?

My head was swimming, and the silence stretched out.

Lawton's question hung in the air, getting heavier with every step. After a couple of minutes he said, "Is this your way of telling me no, that it's over?"

Up ahead, I spotted the Parkers' house, a two-story brick Tudor nestled behind a long, tree-lined driveway. It wasn't my home, but it almost felt like it. I'd been here weeks already. I was scheduled to be here most of the winter. Chucky felt like my real dog. Lawton felt like my real neighbor.

More than my neighbor, actually.

I felt like I belonged here. There was only one problem.

I didn't.

Eventually, whether I told him directly or not, Lawton would learn that for himself. When that happened, would he call me pathetic too? Would it be any less pathetic if I told him directly?

And if I did, would he tell his brother that the owners were out of town? And would his brother use that information to steal more than a glimpse at my driver's license?

There were too many questions on not enough sleep. At the foot of the Parkers' long driveway, I stopped, turning to face him.

He stopped too, looking down at me with parted lips and wary eyes

As I studied his face, I considered how easy it would be to melt into his arms and tell him everything. We could start over, no more secrets, no more barriers.

Or maybe, he'd decide I was just another Brittney. Maybe I was just another Brittney. Were we really that different?

"Chloe," he said. "I do love you."

I looked down at my feet. "I love you too. But I'm not sure it's enough."

"It's enough for me," he said. "The first time I saw you, I just knew."

I looked to the horizon. The first streaks of pink appeared in the eastern sky. "It's really late," I said.

He turned to follow my gaze. "No. It's early, remember?"

"Lawton," I said. "I'm not sure you really know me. And if I'm being really honest, that's my fault not yours. But it is what it is."

"I do know you," he said. "At least all that matters."

"No. You don't," I said. "And honestly, I probably don't know you very well either."

"You wanna know me?" he said. "Come with me tomorrow."

"Where?"

"You'll see."

I was too exhausted to plan anything for tomorrow. If I didn't get some serious sleep, I'd never make it through my shift. "Tomorrow's not good," I said.

"Then how about the next day?"

"Monday?" I said. "I'm working that day, too."

"But you don't go in 'til late, right?"

"Yeah. But I can't afford to be late anymore."

"I won't make you late," he said. "I promise."

I bit my lip, thinking about it.

"C'mon," he said. "It's my last day in town this week. Say yes."

"You're taking a trip?" I said.

"Not a vacation. Work. This event in Vegas. You wanna come?"

SABRINA STARK

"Very funny," I said.

"You think I'm joking?"

"I don't know what to think, but it doesn't matter. I'm working every day 'til Friday."

"Then c'mon, say yes for Monday." His gaze met mine. "Please?"

I stared into his eyes, and something in my heart gave way. "Maybe," I said.

His eyes softened. "I'm taking that as a yes." He glanced toward the house. "Can I walk you to the door?"

I shook my head. "Nah, that's alright." Awkwardly, I gave him a little wave and headed toward the house. As I walked down the long driveway, I felt his gaze on my back, but I didn't turn around.

When I unlocked the front door and went inside, I peered through the window blinds and saw him still standing there, a dark silhouette on the quiet street. I left the window to flick on the living room lights. When I looked out the window a second time, he was gone.

I found Chucky asleep in his favorite basket.

Five minutes later, I stumbled upstairs and fell into bed, fully clothed, in the Parkers' guestroom. Just before sleep claimed me, I saw Lawton's face, looking at me the way he used to, before all the drama, all the heartache.

It would be nice to see him look at me that way again.

But would he, if he knew who I truly was?

CHAPTER 25

The low sound of harp music felt like a jackhammer to my brain. Groaning, I glanced at the digital clock on the nightstand.

One hour. That's how long I'd been asleep. It wasn't nearly long enough.

With muttered curses, I reached past the clock and fumbled for my cell phone, still making that dreaded sound. With bleary eyes, I studied the display.

Shit. It was Loretta, the stepmother from Hell.

I had a choice to make. Suffer a little now? Or suffer a lot later?

I did the smart thing. I answered. "Hello?"

"Don't tell me you're still asleep," she said.

"Not anymore."

"There's no need to get snippy," she said. "Not all of us can sleep the day away, you know."

I felt my jaw clench. "You do remember I work nights, right?"

"Save me the sob story," she said. "You've had a chip on your shoulder as long as I've known you. And to be perfectly honest, I'm more than a little sick of it."

Damn it. I should've suffered later. If I hung up on her now, would she forget that I'd answered? No. She wouldn't.

Loretta never forgot anything.

I forced myself to think of Josh, my thirteen-year-old brother. Unlike me, he lived in Loretta's house. He ate Loretta's food. And if I didn't pull it together fast, tonight he'd be taking Loretta's shit – insults, nitpicking, verbal abuse. And my Dad wouldn't do a damn thing.

Better me than Josh.

I closed my eyes and choked out an apology. "I'm sorry."

"As far as apologies go," she said, "that was barely adequate."

If she didn't like mine, she should've seen Brittney's.

"I'm sorry for that too," I said.

"Are you being sarcastic?"

Was I? Probably. Should I apologize for my apology? Damn it. I should've let it go to voicemail. My body might've been awake, but my mind was still out cold.

"Are you still there?" she said. "You fell back asleep, didn't you?"

"No, I'm still here."

"If you say so."

What the hell was that supposed to mean? What did she think? That she was talking to a recording?

Still, in a lame attempt to sound friendly, I made myself smile as I said, "Is there a particular reason you called?"

"Are you laughing at me?" she said.

"No. I'm not laughing at anything. I was smiling into the phone, just like you told me the last time we talked."

"Alright, whatever." She gave a loud sigh. "I'm just checking in about Thanksgiving. You are still bringing the dessert right?"

"Wait a minute," I said. "I thought I was bringing a salad?"

"Oh for God's sake," she said. "Not this again."

"Not what again?"

"Don't be dense." With another sigh, she pulled out her overly patient voice and spoke very slowly. "Yes, I did ask you to bring a salad, but you pitched such a fit that I switched the menu around just for you."

"So I'm bringing the dessert?"

"That's what I said, wasn't it?"

I rubbed my eyes. She was doing this on purpose. I just knew it. "Okay," I said. "What kind of dessert? Pie? Cake? Something else?"

"Look, you've got one thing to bring," she said. "Me? I've got a whole meal. Is it really that much trouble to figure out the dessert on your own? Or do you want me to send you a recipe book too?"

"Sorry," I said. "I'll bring a pie."

"Well, I guess I shouldn't be surprised."

"Why?"

"Because Lauren Jane hates pie. You just love to stick it to her, don't you?"

Lauren Jane? She had to mean Lauren, her natural daughter. But I'd never heard the Jane part before. It must be new.

Lauren was about my age, but I had no idea what she liked, or didn't like. In truth, I barely knew the girl. She was the upstairs daughter. As for me, I'd been relegated to the basement from day one.

"I'm sorry. I didn't know," I said. "I'll bring a cake then."

"For Thanksgiving? What do you think this is? A birthday party?"

My brain was foggy, but my head was pounding. For the life of me, I couldn't think of another single dessert. I was gripping the phone so tight, I feared it might shatter.

I tried to keep my voice calm as I said, "Okay, then I'll bring a surprise."

"Oh, I'm sure you will."

And then, before I could respond, she hung up without saying goodbye.

I turned off the ringer and flopped back onto the bed. For at least an hour, I stared at the ceiling, willing myself to fall back asleep. But that woman got under my skin like almost no one else.

It didn't help that I knew she was doing it on purpose. Someday Josh would move out, and I'd be free to tell her exactly what I thought of her and all her games.

Until then, I was screwed.

I should be used to it by now. But somehow, I wasn't.☐ ☐

CHAPTER 26

I'd just drifted back to sleep when the sound of Chucky's barking jolted me awake. Groaning, I flopped onto my side and wrapped the pillow around my head, mashing it tight against my ears.

It was no use. Even muffled, there was no ignoring it. When I heard the ding-dong of the doorbell, I hurled the pillow against the wall and stumbled out of bed.

There was only one person it could be. Lawton.

So much for giving me some space.

I jumped into my rattiest sweatpants and marched downstairs, leaving a trail of profanity in my wake. By now, Chucky was going nuts, barking his furry head off and skidding across the hardwood floors as he ran from window to window.

Grumbling, I snapped on his leash before getting within ten feet of the door. I'd learned all his tricks the hard way, and I wasn't about to fall for them again. With Chucky securely at my side, I stomped to the front door, flung it open, and bellowed, "What!"

Erika stood, blinking in the dappled sunlight. "So, uh, is this a bad time?"

Before I could form an answer, a furry land-rocket shot past my ankles. I looked to my hand. The leash was still there.

Chucky wasn't. Instead, he was tearing full speed ahead toward the front sidewalk.

"Chucky, you come back here!" I hollered.

Giving Erika a frantic look, I plunged barefoot out of the entryway to sprint after him. The ground was frozen, sending shockwaves of icy jolts into the bare soles of my feet. Still, I pursued Chucky across the front yard, twice around a giant pine tree, straight through a dormant flower bed, and back toward the house.

Halfway to the front door, he stopped long enough to let me almost reach him. But just as I leaned down to scoop him up, he gave a yip and raced toward driveway.

I threw up my hands. "Fine! Go! See if I care!"

Ignoring my tirade, he circled my car and skidded to a stop near the driver's side door.

And then it hit me. My car. What was it doing here? Last time I'd seen it, it was stalled at the restaurant. Wasn't it?

I was mentally scratching my head when suddenly Chucky's body tensed. His ears twitched, and his nose turned toward the house.

A moment later, he took off at full speed toward Erika. She was crouching near the front entrance holding something in her outstretched palm. It looked suspiciously like a breakfast biscuit.

When Chucky dove for the biscuit, she scooped him up, biscuit and all, and dashed into the house, slamming the door behind her.

Wordlessly, I stalked up to the door and twisted the doorknob. It didn't budge. What the hell? I tried again. Nothing. I hollered through the door. "Hey! Erika! The door's locked. Let me in, alright? "

A moment later, the door flew open. Erika stood with

insanely messy hair and Chucky held tight at her side. "What!" she screeched, barely keeping a straight face.

I glared at her. "Is that supposed to be funny?"

She grinned. "Yeah. Totally. Wasn't it?"

Probably on any other day, it would've been. Today, not so much. "You know," I said, "I'm really not in the mood for this."

"Oh c'mon," she said. "I rescued your dog, didn't I?"

"He's not my dog." I jostled my way inside and slammed the door behind me. My feet were numb, and the rest of me was only slightly less miserable. I looked down to see clumps of dirt lodged between my bare toes. "Stupid flower beds," I said.

I trudged into the living room, leaving a trail of dirt behind me. Just great. I mentally added floor-cleaning to my to-do list. I sank onto the front sofa and buried my face in my hands.

Erika flopped down on the recliner across from me. "That was your biscuit by the way."

I looked up. "Yeah. I figured."

"Want half of mine?" She held out a white paper bag.

I gave it a dubious look. "Does it have bacon?"

"Sorry."

"That's alright." I waved the bag away. "You go ahead. Eat. Honestly, I'm not hungry, anyway."

She reached into the bag and pulled out the biscuit. "Rough night?" she said, unwrapping it and taking a bite.

"You have no idea." I glanced over at Chucky, settling into his favorite basket. If only I had a basket. I'd probably never come out. I returned my gaze to Erika. "So what are you doing here?" I said. "I thought you were heading back to State."

"Yeah. I'm on the way now, actually. But I couldn't find my dorm key. You haven't seen it here, have you?"

I groaned. "Oh crap. I'm sorry." I vaguely recalled seeing a strange key last night while rushing around getting ready for work. "I meant to call you, but…" I shook my head, not sure where to start.

So I started at the beginning and kept going.

When I was done, Erika sat in stunned silence. I'd just told her everything that had happened since I'd seen her last, starting with the so-called kidnapping attempt and ending with everything Lawton had told me during the walk home.

Her mouth hung open. "And all this happened since I saw you last?"

I nodded.

"But that was only last night."

"Tell me about it," I said. "So now, Lawton wants another chance. But I'm not so sure."

She laughed. "You liar."

"I'm not lying," I said.

"You are, too. You're totally nuts for him."

"Maybe. But he's a total psycho."

"Oh, c'mon. He's not that bad. At least not the way you tell it."

"Oh yeah?" I pulled up my shirt sleeve and thrust out my wrist. "Look." The bruises had darkened overnight, making the raw skin that much more ugly. "You believe me now?"

Her gaze narrowed. "That asshole."

"Exactly."

"So," she said, "you think he'd do it again?"

I didn't even have to think about it. "No. Definitely not."

She leaned back in her chair and said, "Hmm…"

"What's that supposed to mean?" I said.

She shrugged.

"Look," I told her, "you know how this goes. As soon as some girl thinks, 'Oh, he'd never do that again', that's when she's totally screwed."

She raised her eyebrows. "Because?"

"Because they always do."

"Uh-huh," Erika said. "Except you just said he wouldn't."

"Don't listen to me," I said. "I mean, what if I'm one of those girls."

"Which girls?"

I launched into a high-pitched imitation. "Sure, Bobby cheated on me like a dozen times with my sister, but I'm telling you, he's a changed man. He told me so and everything."

Erika gave me a look. "Trust me. You are so not that girl."

"Yeah? How do you know?"

"For starters," she said, "you're not exactly the most trusting person in the world."

"I'm not so bad."

"Yes, you are."

"Okay, fine. But maybe there's a good reason for that."

"Maybe," she said. "But here's a question. When you told Lawton you were just the house-sitter, what did he say?"

"Are you kidding?" I said. "I didn't tell him."

She pretended to scratch her chin. "Hmmm…I wonder why that is."

"You know exactly why," I said. "I promised the Parkers. Remember?"

"But you told me," she said.

"Yeah, but you're different."

"Why?" she asked.

"You just are."

"As flattered as I am," she said, "there's something you need to hear."

"What?"

"Alright." She leaned forward in her chair. "I hate to tell you this, but you brought a lot of this on yourself." □

□

CHAPTER 27

I stared over at her. So here, I'd spilled my guts, expecting a shoulder to cry on. But what I got was a kick to the teeth.

"Gee," I said, "maybe I should've called Loretta. At least when she insults me, it's not exactly a surprise."

"Yeah but Loretta's a bitch. Me? I'm just delightfully honest."

"I wouldn't exactly call it delightful," I said.

"Want to hear my theory?" she said.

"Probably not."

"Too bad," she said. "That agreement with the Parkers? That's just your excuse."

"For what?" I said.

"Do I seriously need to spell this out?"

I crossed my arms. "Apparently."

"Alright, admit it. You liked the fact he thought this was your house."

"Oh shut up."

"So you passed the test. Congratulations, you fit in. You belong. Yippee for you."

"I don't fucking believe this."

"Hey, I'm not judging you." She grinned. "Last weekend? I told this guy I was a stripper. He totally got off on it."

"You know what?" I said. "You're not as smart as you

133

think you are. Did I tell you about Lawton's brother?"

"What about him?"

"Apparently, he has this thing for breaking and entering."

Her eyebrows furrowed. "How do you know?"

"Because," I said, "he broke into here once."

She looked around. "So what'd he do? Make off with the TV? Raid the liquor cabinet?" She waggled her eyebrows. "Panty-raid?"

"Oh stop it. Technically, he didn't steal anything."

"So what'd he do? Break a window, smash a door? What?"

"No, it was nothing like that. But he did look at my license."

"Oh, heaven forbid. I hope you called the FBI."

"C'mon, this is serious," I said. "You know where my license was? In my purse. Right here in this house. And I wasn't even home."

"And Lawton put him up to it?"

"Well, no," I admitted. "But still, the guy's his brother. They're related."

She gave me a look. "Just like you and your Mom are related?"

"Hey, I'm not my Mom."

"Oh. I see."

"No," I said. "I don't think you do."

"So lemme ask you this. Does Lawton even know his brother broke in?"

"Yeah, he knows."

"So Lawton was the one who told you about it?"

"No. I just overheard them talking, that's all."

"Oh," she said. "So you were eavesdropping."

"No. It wasn't like that."

She shrugged. "If you say so."

"Jeez, what's up with you today?"

"Nothing." She crossed her arms. "If you can't handle a little truth, it's not my problem."

"Yeah? Well, maybe instead of judging me, you should look in the mirror."

"What's that supposed to mean?" she said.

"You know what started all this? Our little birthday party, with that stupid movie poster."

In the poster, a gag gift designed by Erika herself, Lawton had been shirtless with beads of sweat glistening on his bare chest and a woman's arms encircling him from behind.

That fictional woman had my face, just like the fictional movie had its own title, Riding the Rastor. The whole thing had been a joke, right until Lawton saw the poster and assumed it was real.

"So now my poster's stupid?" she said.

"No," I said. "Sorry, I didn't mean that. Honest."

"Well, what did you mean?"

"It's just that between the poster and that stupid sex tape you brought over, well, Lawton went a little nuts when he found everything. He thought I was this crazy stalker chick looking to make a porno on the sly."

"Well, excuse me for wanting to celebrate your birthday." She stood. "You know what? I really don't have time for this crap. Where's my keys?"

"Crap?" I said.

"Do you have my keys or what?"

"Oh, so that's your big problem? You can't find your keys? Poor you."

"What's that supposed to mean?"

"I mean," I said, "that you have no idea what it's like to be me. Wanna know what'll happen if you lose your keys? Your

135

parents will buy you new ones. Wanna know what happens to me when I lose my keys? I get locked out." My voice rose. "And I don't have a single fucking person I can call."

"Yeah? That's funny," she said, "because actually, you've called me plenty of times. And my parents. Or do you pretend those are yours too?"

I felt my face grow hot. "That's unfair, and you know it."

"Whatever." She started walking toward the door. "You know what? Fuck the dorm keys. You're right. I'll just have my rich Mommy and Daddy bail me out like they always do."

"Erika, c'mon. I'm sorry, alright?"

"Why should you be sorry? You're exactly right. I wouldn't know a real problem if it bit me on the ass."

"C'mon. I never said that."

"Whatever. I'm just saying, so what if you're just the house-sitter? It's not like you're Hitler, for God's sake."

"I never said I was."

"And if you like this guy enough to let him stick his dick in you, then you sure as shit should like him enough to be honest with him."

With that, she opened the front door and stalked out toward her car.

"Oh yeah?" I yelled out the open doorway. "Tell that to the guy who thinks you're a stripper!"

CHAPTER 28

After Erika peeled out of the driveway, I slammed the door, stumbled back to bed, and cried myself to sleep. By the time I woke, it was late afternoon.

Lawton aside, the argument with Erika haunted my thoughts. We'd argued before, but never like that. It was my fault. I just knew it. I'd been crabby from the moment she showed up. It was no wonder we'd gotten into a huge, screaming fight.

I pulled out my cell phone and gave her a call. It went straight to voicemail, and I didn't leave a message. When I apologized, I wanted to do it directly.

About Lawton, maybe she was right. Maybe she wasn't. But I had no right to snap at her just because she'd given me an honest opinion. And in truth, I loved that poster. She'd made it herself. She'd come all the way down from college just to give it to me.

If anyone was spoiled, it was me.

Heading out the front door to walk Chucky, I stopped short at the sight of my car in the driveway. I vaguely recalled noticing it earlier, but with everything else going on, I hadn't done more than wonder.

After the walk, I got Chucky settled in the house and returned to the driveway alone. Holding my breath, I settled myself into the driver's seat and turned the key in the ignition. It started on the first try.

This had to be Lawton's doing. Other than the busboy who'd given me a ride home, Lawton was the only one who knew about my car troubles.

I turned off the car and dialed Lawton's cell phone.

When he answered, I said, "So, I've got this mysterious car in the driveway."

"Yeah?" he said. "How mysterious?"

"Well, it looks like mine. But apparently, it can drive all by itself."

"Hmm."

"Even when it's broken down."

"Or maybe," he said, "it was just a dead battery."

"Aha!" I said. "You went and got it, didn't you?"

"It depends," he said. "If I did, is that a good thing? Or a bad thing?"

It was definitely a good thing. Without a car, I was hosed. Still, it made me feel a little funny to think of him retrieving my car when we weren't exactly together anymore.

I stalled. "What if it is a good thing?"

"Then it was all me."

"And if it's a bad thing?"

"In that case," he said, "blame Bishop."

"Your brother?" I laughed. "Why him?"

"Because he's already on your list, so I figure, eh, what's the difference?"

"Heeeey," I said, "you're on my list too."

"I know," he said. "And I'm trying like hell to get off it."

"So, that's why you did it?"

"Nope. I'd have done it anyway."

"I've gotta ask," I said, "how'd you do it? It's not like you had my keys."

"Long story," he said.

"Yeah, I just bet," I said. "Still, thanks for the help. Seriously."

"Hey Chloe?"

"Yeah?"

"You might wanna get a new battery."

I winced. "Really?"

"Yeah. The car's starting okay now, but you know how these things go. Vintage cars. They're tricky, right?"

Vintage my ass. Old was more like it. Last winter, my entire exhaust system had gone out piece by expensive piece. But Lawton's car? That truly was vintage, all sleek lines and shiny paint. Well, until last night.

I felt a pang at the image of his once-beautiful car. Here he had gone to a lot of trouble to retrieve my car, a total piece of crap, but he hadn't even mentioned his own. Was it still at the restaurant? Would he be able to fix it?

My voice was quiet as I asked, "How about your car? Is it, uh—"

"It's fine."

"Oh c'mon Lawton," I said, "I know it's not fine. I was there. Remember?"

"Yeah. I remember."

"Why'd you do that?"

"Because," he said, "it needed to be done."

"No, it didn't."

"Yes," he said. "It did."

"Why?"

"Because I meant what I said. For what I did to you, I deserved a good ass-beating. Still do. But somebody wouldn't take me up on it. So that car, it was the closest thing I had."

I thought of all his possessions – the breathtaking mansion he called home, the fleet of late-model vehicles, the clothes, the electronics. The logic made a weird kind of sense. Of everything he owned, the car was probably the only thing that was truly irreplaceable.

Still, it was majorly messed up. Who does that sort of thing?

"You shouldn't have done it," I said.

"You're right," he said. "I shouldn't have done it. But I'm not talking about the car."

I didn't know what to say. My head was swimming. "Speaking of cars," I said, "I've got to leave for work in a little bit, so I'll catch you later, alright?"

"Alright," he said. "We're still on for tomorrow, right?"

"Yup, it's a date."

Oh crap. A date? I didn't know what our plans were, but it seemed far too early, or maybe too late, to be thinking of this as a date.

I heard the smile in his voice. "A date, huh?"

Crap. He'd caught that?

Distracted, I mumbled something about meeting up sometime in the late afternoon, and then disconnected the call.

Lawton did funny things to my brain. And even funnier things to the rest of me. What he did to my heart, well, there was nothing funny about that.

Pushing Lawton out of my thoughts, I picked up my phone again and gave Erika another try. Again, she didn't answer. This time, I couldn't help myself. I left a message, mostly an apology.

But all of that was forgotten, at least temporarily, a couple hours later when I walked into work and checked the schedule.

I found Keith in his office, thumbing through a catalog. I marched up to his desk and looked down. Two girls in micro-bikinis smiled up at me.

"Thinking of getting a two-piece?" I said.

He flapped the catalog shut and shoved it into his top desk drawer. Then he glared up at me and said, "You think you're real funny, don't you?"

"You know what's funny?' I said. "The fact that I'm only scheduled for two nights next week."

"So?"

"So, I usually work five."

He shrugged. "It's a slow time of year. What do you expect?"

"I expect you to live up to your end of the agreement."

"Oh yeah." He smirked. "What agreement is that?"

"You know which one."

"Oh stop griping," he said. "You haven't been fired. Have you?"

"No. But how am I supposed to make any money working only two days?"

"Sorry, not my problem." He glanced at his desk drawer. "Is that all?"

"No." Damn it. I really didn't want to do this. I leaned in close and lowered my voice. "Because you know damn well I could make it your problem."

He looked only mildly interested. "Really? How so?"

"Oh for Pete's sake, do I really need to spell this out?"

"I'm all ears," he said.

"Fine. That little picture of you and Brittney? I bet the district manager would just love to see it."

He nodded. "Yep. I bet he would." He put on a sad face.

"Except they won't. How sad for them."

"What do you mean?"

He gave me an oily grin. "Rumor has it, that cell phone of yours? Big memory problems. Missing pictures, wrong data. Oh well, that's the breaks, huh?" He made a shooing motion toward the door. "Back to work now."

Damn it.

I glared at him. "You broke into my locker. Didn't you?"

"Me? Why would I do that?"

"To delete that picture, that's why."

"Sounds like somebody's a little paranoid," he said.

This time, I was the one smiling. "You know what? You're right. I am."

His eyebrows furrowed. "What?"

"Yeah. Totally. That's why I texted that nice little picture to a friend of mine before it disappeared from my phone." I put on my own sad face. "Awwww. How sad for you."

His gaze narrowed. "You're bluffing."

"You sure about that?" I crossed my arms. "So. About that schedule?"

"Oh alright," he muttered. "I'll change it before your shift is done."

"Good. Because I'll be checking."

"But just so you know, it's not because you threatened me. It's because —" suddenly, his face brightened "—because you deserve this."

I squinted at him. That weasel was up to something. I just knew it. "When you change it," I said, "remember to give me more days, not less."

"Not a problem," he said.

Damn it. He still looked too happy. "Five days," I said. "Not three, not four. Alright?"

"Yup. Got it." He glanced toward his office door. "So, you gonna be waitressing any time soon?"

Wordlessly, I turned around and marched toward the door. Just before I got there, I stopped and turned around. "And none of those two-hour shifts either. I want full shifts, like I usually get."

"Yeah, yeah," he said, reaching into his top drawer for the catalog. "Shut the door, will ya? I got work to do."

Two hours into my shift, I still hadn't figured out his angle. I knew how Keith worked. He'd find some loophole, and I'd be screwed.

Thank God I hadn't been lying. I had texted the picture to Erika. But between our argument and everything else going on, I never confirmed she still had it.

She wouldn't delete it, would she?

I was still mulling this over when I hustled toward my next table and was hit by another unwelcome surprise.

Skank. Party of one.

CHAPTER 29

I stopped a few tables away and stared. What was she doing here?

I dashed back to the waitress station and caught Josie. "I need to trade tables," I said.

"Let me guess," she said. "The blonde at table nineteen?"

"Yeah, that's the one."

"Sorry, no dice. She asked for you personally."

"How do you know?"

"I was there when they seated her."

"Oh crap," I said.

I glanced out toward the table. I'd met only two of Lawton's groupies in person. One was Brittney, and the other one was sitting out there at that table.

I'd waited on Amber exactly two times. Both times, she'd been with Brittney. The first time they'd gotten drunk and danced on their table, hoochie style. The second time, they'd come for the sole purpose of giving me a hard time.

Well, I'd just about had it. Maybe she was the customer, but I was way past caring. She'd hassled me at work. She'd hit on my boyfriend. She'd planned – or at least gone along with – that so-called prank.

When I reached her table, she had the menu propped up in front of her and was looking around expectantly.

I skipped the usual greeting and got straight to the point. "What are you doing here?"

She blinked up at me. "Was that a real question, or a funny waitress question?"

I didn't crack a smile. "A real question."

"I'm here to apologize." She glanced down at the menu. "Hey, what are your specials tonight?"

"Are you serious?" I said.

"Yeah," she said. "The fish tacos, are they good?"

"We don't have fish tacos," I said.

"Oh, poo. I was really in the mood for them." She ran a manicured fingernail along the menu's appetizer section. "The crab cakes, are they made with real crab? Or fake crab?"

"Real crab."

"You sure?" She wrinkled her nose. "Because fake crab tastes way too fishy."

"Forget the crab," I tossed my order pad onto the table and crossed my arms. "I believe I heard something about an apology?"

Amber gave a breezy wave of her hand. "Yeah, but I figure I'll do that after dessert."

"Let me get this straight," I said. "supposedly, you came in here to apologize. But you're making me wait on you first?"

"Why not?" she said. "The food's good, and I'm totally starving."

"You know what?" I said. "This is the worst apology, ever. No." I held up a hand. "Make that the second-worst apology, ever."

She grinned up at me. "Brittney, right? She rolled her eyes. "Yeah, I heard how that went."

"From who?"

"Lawton's brother, who's totally luscious by the way." She

licked her lips. "I figure with Lawton off the market, I should probably go after him. What do you think?" She cocked her head. "Am I his type?"

"How should I know?" And then the full impact of her words hit me. "And what do you mean Lawton's off the market?"

"That's what I hear," she said.

"From who? Brittney?"

"No way. I'm totally over her." Her eyes brightened. "So you've gotta tell me, did she really apologize naked?"

"Semi-naked."

"God, what a slut."

I stared down at her. The statement seemed awful strange coming from someone who probably matched Brittney guy for guy.

"Did you hear?" Amber said. "Brittney's totally cut off."

"What do you mean?"

"No more parties, no more V.I.P. tickets, none of that stuff. She's out like a trout. Blacklisted, totally."

I shook my head. "I don't get it."

"Well, that was the deal," Amber said. "Brittney and me, we had to make things right with you. And if not?" Amber slit an imaginary knife across her throat. "Cut off. Like yesterday. Lawton's got a lot of friends too. So it's not just him neither."

"So let me get this straight," I said, "if you didn't apologize, he was going to turn you into some kind of social pariahs?"

Her eyebrows furrowed. "What do man-eating fish have to do with anything?"

"Not piranhas," I said. "Pariahs. You know? Social outcasts?"

"Ohhh. Yeah. That's it." She brightened. "So here I am!"

She glanced down at the menu. "Maybe I should have breakfast food, like French toast or something. What do you think?"

"I think," I said, "that this so-called apology isn't going so well."

"Oh, alright," she said. "Jeez, if you're gonna be all picky about it." She closed her menu and set it off to the side. "I'm sorry about our prank. We thought it would be funny, but obviously, it wasn't, and I'm really super sorry."

"Wow," I said, "that actually wasn't that bad."

"Thanks," she said. "I've had a lot practice."

"But I still don't understand how you'd call it a prank."

"Oh, it totally was," she said. "You know, like a steal-the-mascot thing. See?"

"No, I don't see. I'm not a mascot. I'm a person. And honestly? I don't think that stealing an animal is much better."

"Most of the time," Amber said, "it's just a statue or something. It's not like we'd kidnap a dog or anything. Jeez, what kind of people do you think we are?"

"Well, you tried to kidnap me," I said, "so I probably shouldn't answer that."

"Too bad we didn't get the chance to do your car. You might've found that funny at least."

I stared down at her. "What do you mean, do my car?" And then it hit me. Those two guys and their sedan. Their car had been vandalized, spray-painted with profanity. "Oh my God," I said. "You were gonna paint my car, too?"

Her eyebrows furrowed. "Paint? No way. That stuff doesn't come off. We use shoe polish."

"Shoe polish?"

"Yeah. One trip through the car wash, and it's gone."

"So your friends," I said. "Those two guys. Was their car

painted? Or was that just shoe polish too?"

"Shoe polish, totally," she said. "Their car's fine now. Joey and Paul are still pissed, but hey, that's guys for ya. No sense of humor."

I felt myself swallow. Pissed or not, their car was fine. My car was fine. The only car that wasn't fine was Lawton's. And he'd done that at my prompting, even if that hadn't exactly been my intention.

"So," Amber said, "do you accept my apology or what?"

"I guess so," I said.

"Awesome," she said, reaching for her menu. "Because I'm in the mood for pancakes. You serve them all day, right?"

An order of pancakes and a spiked orange juice later, Amber was gone. And she actually left me a pretty decent tip.

I still wasn't sure how I felt about her so-called apology, but I had to give her credit for trying. If nothing else, she had been wearing clothes at the time, which was more than I could say for Brittney.

When my shift was over, I went to the back room and checked the schedule, posted on the back bulletin board. Looking at it, I felt my blood pressure spike and my gaze narrow. Keith changed the schedule, alright – just not in any way that would make me happy.

"That little weasel," I said.

149

CHAPTER 30

Josie was passing through on her way to the back door. "What now?" she asked.

"That stupid Keith," I said. "Get this. I'm on the schedule for five days next week, but for three of them, I'm on training duty."

"Oh man, that sucks," Josie said.

"Yeah, and check this out. Wanna know who I'm training?"

Josie sidled next to me and looked. Her brow wrinkled. "Brittney Adams? Is that the blonde who came in to see Keith the other night?"

"Yup."

Josie winced. "Ouch. Poor you."

"No. Poor Keith," I said. "Because right after I'm done here, I'm gonna strangle him."

"Good luck with that," she said. "He left like an hour ago."

I looked around. "Then who's in charge?"

Josie shrugged. "Got me. The day shift manager starts at six."

"But that's not for another hour," I said. Even for Keith, this was beyond strange. "So there's no manager on duty?"

"Not anymore." She grinned. "Unless you want the job."

"Hell no," I said. "What I need is a real job."

SABRINA STARK

"Hey, you and me both."

"Do you know, I sent out like twenty resumes last month?" I said. "Not that it did any good."

"You think you got it bad?" she said. "My brother? He's got a master's degree. Wanna know where he's working?"

"Where?"

"Flannigan's. As a bartender."

"Really? He can't find anything better? What's his degree in?"

"Psychology."

I gave her a sympathetic look. "Not the best-paying field, from what I hear."

"Got that right," she said. "He's better off tending bar. With tips, anyway."

I could totally relate. It was the same dynamic that kept me waitressing. Probably Josie too. She had a bachelor's degree in something or other, for all the good it did her.

We said our goodnights, and I headed back to my locker. Twisting the combination, I thought of Keith tampering with my cell phone. Somehow that weasel had gotten into my locker, and I needed to find out how.

But in the meantime, I definitely needed a new lock, something with a key this time.

Pulling out my cell phone, I found a new voicemail from Erika. It was short and to the point. "Call me as soon as you get this. Or else."

I glanced at the clock. It was five in the morning. She didn't mean now, did she? I checked the time of her message. Three o'clock in the morning. Just two hours ago.

Well, she must've meant it, right? I gathered up the rest of my stuff and headed out to my car. While waiting for the engine to warm up, I gave her a call.

We were still talking by the time I pulled into the Parkers' driveway a half hour later.

Turns out, Erika's parents were cutting off her financial support, right after the current semester.

"Are you sure they won't reconsider?" I said.

"Not a chance." She gave a hollow-sounding laugh. "Guess I shouldn't have flunked that last history class, huh?"

Erika was on her fifth year at college, going into a sixth. She'd changed her major three times and was back to undecided.

"I'm really sorry," I said. "What are you gonna do?"

"I guess I'll have to find a job," she said.

"First time for everything, huh?"

"Yeah, I guess. So anyway, that's probably why I blew up at you. I'm really sorry."

"Nah, don't be sorry," I said. "I was a total crab-ass. I had it coming."

"That's for sure."

"Heeeey!"

Alright," she said. "Enough about me. What'd you decide about that man of yours?"

"Nothing yet," I said. "But we've got plans for Monday."

"What kind of plans?" she said.

"I don't know. He just said he had something to show me."

"I know what it is," she said.

"Don't say it," I warned.

"His massive cock."

I groaned. "I knew you were gonna say that."

"Oh c'mon," she said. "Give the guy another chance. You know you want to."

"Maybe," I admitted. "But just because I want to, it doesn't mean I should."

"This is what you should do," she said. "Go out with him, do whatever, have a good time. See what happens." Her voice turned serious. "I've known you a long time, Chloe. You haven't had a lot of fun in your life. Maybe it's time to just let go for once, you know?"

I did know.

Erika's life had been full of fun. Maybe too much fun, the way it sounded. But look where it had gotten her. If her parents didn't change their minds, she wouldn't be a whole lot better off than I was.

"Maybe," I said.

"Stop saying 'maybe.' Say 'I'm Chloe Malinski, and I'm a sex machine.'"

I laughed. "I'd never, ever say that."

"Then don't just say it. Do it."

"I'll think about it," I said. "But hey, before we go, here's a question."

"What?"

"Remember that photo I texted you the other night?"

"The one of that couple in the back seat? Yeah, I remember. The guy looked exactly like your boss. Same tie and everything."

"Actually," I said, "it was my boss."

"No way!"

"No lie," I said. "So anyway, you still got it, right?"

"The picture? Not anymore. I mean, I figured it was just a joke." She hesitated. "It wasn't?"

My heart sank. Here, I'd been counting on Erika to keep it. But had I actually told her to keep it? No. I hadn't. It wasn't her fault it was gone. It was mine.

"Yeah, just a joke," I said.

Too bad the joke was on me.

CHAPTER 31

Nervously, I paced the living room. It was just after two o'clock on Monday afternoon. Lawton had called me a couple hours earlier to finalize our plans. What those plans were, I had no idea.

All he said was to dress casually and be ready to see something he'd never shown anyone.

I knew exactly what Erika would say. That ruled out his massive cock.

Waiting for him, I wore jeans and a dark V-necked shirt. Not fancy, but nothing I'd be embarrassed to be seen in either.

Right on schedule, a car pulled into the driveway. Watching out the window, I felt my eyebrows furrow. It was a brown sedan with a rusty front bumper and dented hood.

As I watched, Lawton slid out of the driver's seat and started walking toward the front door. Still confused, I grabbed my purse and met him at the half-way point.

"What's that?" I said, glancing over at the car.

"Our ride," he said.

I gave him a dubious look. "You sure this thing runs?"

He grinned. "It got me here, didn't it?" He flicked his head toward the car. "C'mon." He walked around and opened the passenger's side. He waited.

I didn't move.

"How far are we going?" I said.

"Not far."

I still didn't move. I'd been stranded more than enough in my own piece of crap. I didn't need to be stranded in his piece of crap too. I glanced at my old Fiesta. It looked like a luxury ride in comparison. It was probably more reliable too.

"Wanna take my car?" I asked.

He laughed. "Not a chance."

I'm no car-snob, but I didn't understand what was going on here. He had a whole fleet of vehicles in his garage. Why on Earth would he want to drive this thing? More to the point, why on Earth would he want to drive this thing today? With me?

Was this some sort of payback for what had happened to his favorite hot rod?

"Trust me," he said, "it runs great."

I bit my lip. "I suppose you have a backup plan if we get stranded?"

"We won't."

"I must be insane," I said as I finally walked toward him and climbed into the car. He closed the passenger's side door behind me, and walked around to get in the driver's seat.

As I buckled up, I noticed something strange. The car's interior was obviously old, but not half as ratty as the outside. And it didn't have that old musty smell either. It smelled not exactly new, but definitely fresh.

When he fired up the engine, something else struck me. It didn't sound like an old beater either. I'm no car expert, but the way the engine roared to life and settled into a nice, steady purr, it made me wonder if there was more to this car than I'd originally guessed.

As soon as we pulled out of the driveway, I turned sideways in the seat to face him. "Alright. You know I'm gonna ask, so let's just get it out of the way. Why this car?"

"What," he said, "you don't like it?"

"Am I supposed to?"

Laughing, he gave me a sideways glance before returning his gaze to the road. "Alright," he said, "as much as I'd like to mess with you, I don't want you to worry."

"Too late for that," I said.

"So here's the thing," he said. "Where we're going, I'd never take any of my other cars."

"Why not?"

"'Cause they're not as safe." He turned to give me another glance. "And since I've got you here, I'm not taking any chances."

"Oh come on," I said. "Be serious."

"I am serious. My other cars, they draw too much attention."

"I don't want to be mean," I said, "but this car? It'll get plenty of attention."

"Yeah? Well don't let the exterior fool you. The engine, along with everything else under the hood, is in prime condition. And it's fast too. A lot faster than it looks." He lifted a hand and tapped the driver's side window. "And see this glass? Bullet-proof."

I laughed. "Oh stop it."

"I'm not kidding."

I studied his face. Either he was telling the truth, or he had one hell of a poker face. "You serious?" I said.

"Yup. And the wheels – "

"Don't tell me," I teased. "Also bullet-proof?"

"Not exactly. But close."

"Oh c'mon," I said. "How can something be sort of bullet-proof?"

"It's the way they're constructed," he said. "Even if they're punctured, they'll keep going, at least long enough."

"How?"

"Polymer rings."

"What's that?" I squinted at him. "Oh never mind. You're just messing with me."

He didn't confirm or deny it. Instead, he asked, "How good are you at keeping secrets?"

"Pretty good," I said.

Probably too good, at least according to Erika.

"Glad to hear it," Lawton said. "Because I'm counting on that."

CHAPTER 32

I watched the road ahead, looking for clues to our destination. "Is this where you tell me where we're going?"

"Call it a trip down memory lane," he said.

Considering his choice of car and his veiled comments about wanting to keep me safe, I should probably be been scared. But somehow, I wasn't.

It was like standing on the edge of some cliff and looking down, feeling the danger, but clinging to safety. I let my gaze shift to Lawton. He was sitting back in the driver's seat, one hand over the steering wheel as he navigated the afternoon traffic.

He was solid. And dangerous. I felt myself swallow. And that's when I knew. If this thing were a cliff, I was in big danger. Because so help me, I wanted to jump.

I turned sideways in the seat to face him. "C'mon, give me a hint," I said.

It wasn't quite the peak of rush hour, but it was getting close. We'd just made it out of the residential section and were pulling onto I-75. Lawton slid into traffic, and eased into the fast lane.

"You haven't guessed?" he said.

I had a rough idea of where he supposedly grew up. From the street signs, it was easy to see which direction we were heading. "Detroit?"

"Yup."

"Which part?"

As for me, I'd grown up in Hamtramck, a city almost completely surrounded by Detroit. But I'd been avoiding Detroit itself for years.

In high school, I used to spend a lot of time in Greektown or sometimes on the Riverwalk. And once, I spent an entire afternoon in the Institute of Arts, admiring the marble structure outside, and hundreds of paintings inside.

But after Kimberly Slotka, a girl from my American history class, got carjacked and pistol-whipped for her used Camaro, I guess I just stayed away from the whole area. Most of us did. Mostly we stuck to our own neighborhoods, or ventured out into the suburbs.

Downtown was supposedly on an upswing, with young professionals and hipsters moving in where others had left. In my few recent visits, I'd seen some of this firsthand. But then there were the parts I would never visit, places where pizza deliveries required an armed guard, if they delivered at all.

Today was a weekday, and it was still light out, so there were parts of the city that wouldn't be too bad. But other parts, they weren't good at any time.

The cars on the highway were an interesting mix. I saw late-model Cadillacs and even a couple of Lexuses, along with too many Fords and Chevys to count. Cars, trucks, SUVs. Some old, some new. Way too many were beat up or rusted around the wheels.

Motor City or not, Detroit was hard on cars. All of Michigan was. In the winter, rock salt fell in torrents from giant trucks that rumbled through snowstorms, dropping their payloads onto the slick pavement.

All winter long, the battle went on – the salt trucks on one side, snow and ice on the other. Caught in the crossfire were all those cars, screwed no matter who won. Either they'd slide, or they'd rust. Most did both.

It was early November. We'd see snow before the month's end. I was sure of it. My tires were bald, and my battery was iffy at best. If winter never came, I'd be a happy girl.

We spent a few minutes on Woodward, and then turned off on some side street, and then another, heading deeper into the guts of the city. I saw boarded up shops and burned-out buildings, and houses that looked like no one had lived there for decades.

"Welcome to Zombieland," Lawton said.

He had a point. I saw stately brick buildings with overgrown shrubbery and broken windows, burnt-out shells of others, and charred roofs falling over the brick-and-mortar remains of once-majestic structures.

The streets were nearly empty, with random, beat-up cars parked haphazardly along the curbs and almost no traffic at all. For such a large city, it was eerily quiet.

"Zombieland," I said. "Or a war zone."

"Yeah, and we lost."

I looked around. "Where is everyone?"

"Moved, holed up inside, still asleep. Hard to say."

The further we drove, the worse it got. I saw boarded up buildings covered in graffiti interspersed with bare fields of tall, scraggly grass and scattered tires. Telephone poles leaned at odd angles, and vines crept into the missing windows of vacant buildings.

Then, it got worse. The large, majestic structures gave way to tiny homes, some burnt, some boarded up, and others missing patches of siding and their front doorknobs.

"Is this where you grew up?" I asked.

"Almost," he said. "It's a few blocks up." He gave me a sideways glance. "We're gonna stop. But don't roll down the window, and don't open the door."

"Trust me," I said. "I wasn't planning to."

When we rolled to a stop a few minutes later, we were in front of a narrow, two-story brick house with a covered front porch.

Lawton flicked his head toward it. "My Grandma's house." ☐
☐

CHAPTER 33

He made a noise that probably was supposed to be a laugh, but didn't quite make it. "Nicest one in the neighborhood."

I glanced around. Actually, he was right. The home wasn't any larger than the neighboring houses, but it was definitely nicer, like someone not too long ago had actually cared. It had white shutters and a matching porch, peeling in places, but noticeably fresher than its surroundings.

"She loved that house," Lawton said, his voice quiet.

"Is she, uh –"

"Still alive?" Lawton shook his head. "No. She died a few years ago. I grew up here though."

"Just you and your Grandma?"

"Sometimes my Mom lived here too. But most of the time –" He shrugged. "She was off doing other things."

"Like what?" I asked.

He gave another bitter laugh. "Drugs, mostly. My Grandma, she was a school teacher at St. Mary's. She always said she should've done better, especially with Mom being her only kid."

He looked off into the distance. "But I dunno. Mom was just wild, I guess."

"Like mother like son?" I teased, trying to lighten his

mood.

"No." His gaze snapped in my direction. "I'm nothing like her. She never looked out for us, never gave a shit one way or another what happened to us when she was off doing fuck-knows-what."

I shrank back, surprised not only by his language, but by the venom behind his words. Sure, I cursed like a sailor, but – . No, I used to curse like a sailor. Now I just cursed like...well, Lawton, actually.

His gaze softened. "Sorry."

"It's alright," I said. "You said 'us'? You mean you and Bishop, right?"

Lawton shook his head. "No. I didn't even know about Bishop 'til I was a teenager. We're half-brothers. Same dad, different cities."

"So how many kids did your Mom have?"

"Two. Me and a sister."

"Where's your sister now?" I asked.

"College out East. Working on her master's in social work."

"And your Mom?" I asked.

"Dead."

"Oh, I'm so sorry," I said. "How?"

"Overdose. Finally. Best thing she ever did."

Even knowing more of his life story, his icy demeanor was a shock. What kind of guy was actually glad when his mother died? Even with my Mom, as crappy as she was, I'd still be sad if anything bad happened to her.

He studied my face. "I know what you're thinking."

"I'm not thinking anything," I said, "just taking it all in."

"Let me ask you something," he said. "Your brother. He's thirteen, right?"

I nodded.

"Well, I'm the oldest," he said. "My sister, she's maybe three years younger than me." He smiled. "Probably about your age, come to think of it." The smile faded. "When she was thirteen, Mom tried to sell her."

I felt my body grow still. "What do you mean?"

His gaze hardened. "You know what I mean."

I blew out a breath. I guess I did, but I was hoping that I'd just misunderstood him.

"That's when Grandma kicked her out for good," Lawton said. "Told Mom if she ever came back, she'd be dead before she hit the door. And Grandma meant it. She never said anything she didn't mean. She had this old Remington. She was a hell of a shot too. Took me deer hunting up north once."

"She sounds like an amazing person," I said.

"She was," he said with the trace of a smile. "She'd been a widow forever too. I never knew my Grandpa. Neither did my Mom, come to think of it. He died in some factory explosion a month after she was born. So I guess my Mom didn't have it so good either."

Lawton shook his head. "Anyway, even with Mom out of the house, I couldn't let the thing with Kara go. I mean, what kind of man does that? And why the hell should he get away with it? So I ask around, and I find out who the guy is."

"Then what?" I said.

"Then," he said, "I go after him."

I did the math. "So were you what, about sixteen?"

"Yup."

"So what'd you do?"

"I showed up at his house, knocked on the door, all nice and polite. And then, when he answered, I beat the piss out of him. The guy was in I.C.U. for a week."

"Good," I said.

He gave me a smile that didn't quite reach his eyes. "Oh c'mon," he said, "no warnings about vigilante justice?"

Thinking of my own brother, I could only shrug. I knew exactly what I'd want to happen if anyone tried that with him.

I glanced again toward the house. "At least you didn't kill him," I said.

"Yeah. But it didn't end there. The guy was a city councilman. Had a wife, a couple of grown kids." His voice grew sarcastic. "A regular pillar of the community."

"So he pressed charges?"

"Yup."

"What were they?" I said.

"Attempted murder."

My voice was quiet. "Wow."

"Yeah." Lawton shrugged. "But hey, it was true, right?"

"You wanted to kill him?"

"Wouldn't you?" he said.

"If you really wanted to kill him," I said, "you would've grabbed the gun. Right?"

"Maybe," he said. "Or maybe, shooting the guy seemed too easy."

"But with what happened to your sister, I mean, that had to count for something, right?"

He gave a bitter laugh. "Not when Mom wouldn't testify. And Kara, she didn't even know about it. And I was damned determined to keep it that way."

He looked out over the street, marred with potholes and weeds. "And let's say the thing with Kara got out. She'd be the girl who almost got molested by some forty-year-old. School was hard enough already. She didn't need that."

"What do you mean?" I said.

"Our school? It was the worst in the district. But it was the only one we had. And Kara and me, we got enough shit already because of the way we talked."

"I don't get it," I said.

"Like I mentioned, Grandma was a teacher. English mostly. And she didn't put up with any sloppy talk."

"You mean swearing?"

"Or bad grammar."

I felt myself smile. "But that's a good thing," I said.

"Yeah, well people didn't like it, especially other kids."

"Why not?" I said.

He looked around, taking in our surroundings. "Wherever you live, you gotta fit in, right?"

I thought of myself at the Parkers'. Slowly, I nodded.

"Well, we didn't fit in," he said. "It was a problem. And the older we got, the bigger the problem."

"So what'd you do?" I asked.

He shrugged. "I learned to blend. Or when I couldn't, I learned to fight."

"Well, you sure learned that good," I said. "But what happened with that councilman?"

"Officially, I was a minor. But at first, the guy worked like hell to see me tried as an adult."

"At first?" I said. "So he changed his mind?"

"Yeah."

"Why?"

"With that," Lawton said, "I had a little help."

"From who?" I said.

"Bishop."

"But he couldn't have been much older than you."

"He wasn't. But he was old enough."

169

"What'd you guys do?" I asked.

"That, I can't tell you."

"Why not?"

"Because," he said, "it wouldn't be right. My secrets are one thing. But his?" Lawton shook his head. "They're not mine to be giving out. Even to you."

"I can respect that," I said. And I could. Somehow, it made me think more of him, not less. "So tell me in general terms," I said. "What happened with the case?"

"Plea bargain," he said. "I spent a couple years in juvie, got out when I turned eighteen. And you pretty much know the rest."

I tried to smile. "I seriously doubt that."

"Wanna know something funny?" he said.

"What?"

Lawton's gaze took in the neighboring houses. It suddenly occurred to me that we hadn't seen a soul since we'd stopped. It was kind of eerie, actually.

Lawton returned his gaze to me. "Juvie was a cakewalk compared to this."

"Why didn't you guys move?" I asked.

"Because Grandma had a bad hip and a pension that barely paid for groceries. And besides, where would she go?"

I looked around. "Anywhere but here," I said.

Lawton gave a bitter laugh. "Easy for you to say. When I was born, Grandma owned that house outright. But when I got in trouble, she mortgaged everything to pay for my legal team, sorry as they were."

"But what about a public defender?" I said.

"That's what I told her. But Grandma wouldn't hear of it. She said I deserved better."

"She was right," I said, thinking of the worst-case scenario.

If things had gone badly, Lawton might be sitting in prison right now, as opposed to sitting with me.

"By the time it was done," Lawton said, "she owed more than the house was worth."

"Oh wow," I said, letting that sink in. "That's awful."

"And what's worse," he said, "it wasn't all to the bank."

"Who else did she owe?" I asked.

"This local guy, specialized in high-risk loans."

"You mean a loan shark?" I said.

"More or less. Though he didn't like to be called that. Don't ask me how I know."

"So who owns the house now?" I said.

"The bank, probably. When Grandma died, she still owed a lot of money."

"To the loan shark?"

"No. Him, I paid off."

"How'd you do that?"

"One day, he saw me mixing it up with a couple of guys in the neighborhood. Said he liked what he saw, offered me the chance to work off some of the loan."

"By fighting?"

Lawton nodded. "It was the one thing I was actually good at. And for whatever reason, people liked to watch."

This was totally unsurprising. All I had to do was look at him. His body was a work of art, and he had a face to match. I liked to watch him no matter what he was doing.

"I can see why," I said.

He turned to look at me, a smile tugging at his lips. "Yeah?"

"Yeah," I said, hearing the breathiness of my own voice. "Totally."

How Lawton had survived unscathed, I had no idea. Well,

actually, I did. I had never heard of him losing a fight. And the way he moved, it was deadly poetry. No matter what he did, he made it look easy. But the way it sounded, easiness was a foreign concept in his world.

"So anyway," he continued, "one fight led to another. Every time, the money got a little better. And then there was that fight video that made the rounds." He shook his head. "I still don't know that got out. The organizers weren't too happy about that."

"Because the fights were illegal."

"That and taxes," he said.

"Taxes?"

"Yeah. They didn't like to pay them."

"Oh."

Outside the car, I saw the first sign of life. A couple blocks in front of us, a lean, scruffy man with bushy hair weaved his way from one side of the street to the other. As he walked, he stopped every once in a while, peering into the few beat-up cars that dotted the oddly quiet street.

"You know him?" I asked.

"Not from before. And not from now either. I never come back here."

"So why today?" I said. "And why with me?"

"Because," he said, "there's something I need to say."

CHAPTER 34

He turned sideways in the car to face me. "It's about what happened. What I did to you."

I stared deep into his eyes and heard myself ask, "What about it?"

He looked down and shook his head. "It wasn't right. I'm not stupid. I know that. Shit, I knew it at the time. And why I couldn't stop myself—" He looked up again, meeting my gaze with an intensity so sharp that it hurt to watch. "I am so fucking ashamed of myself, I can't even tell you."

My breath was coming short and fast. This car, this place, him – it was all so surreal. And his voice was hypnotic. I wanted to fall into his arms and never let go.

He reached out for my hand. "You're my dream girl, Chloe. You've got to believe that." His voice got this far-off quality. "I wished for you, and here you are, everything I ever imagined. Yeah, I won't lie. I've been with a lot of girls. But there's been nobody like you."

"Really?"

He nodded, never breaking eye contact. "I mean it. I love you. I should've told you sooner. And I should've done a better of showing it. But if you just give me one more chance, I swear to you, you won't regret it."

I caught my breath, and my heart flip-flopped. I wanted to

believe it. But it was all so unbelievable. Girls had literally fought over him. Lots of girls. Did they all think they were something special too?

"I want to tell you something else," he said. "And I'm dead serious. The things I've told you today, I've never told anyone."

"Ever?" I said.

"Ever."

The admission was staggering. And still, the question lingered. Why me?

He was Lawton Rastor, and I was a waitress without a home of my own. And he'd been linked to so many girls, women actually. How could someone like me stand out in a sea of endless choices?

But I couldn't help it. Listening to him, my heart melted, and my eyes grew misty. When he squeezed my hand, I squeezed it back, too blown away to say much of anything.

"So when I thought you were just playing me," he continued, "pretending to be something you weren't, well, I guess I went a little nuts. But I swear to God, it will never, ever happen again."

I squeezed my eyes shut, trying to process what he just said. If I were completely honest, I was pretending, although not in the way he feared.

Here he'd just bared his soul to me, told me his deepest, darkest secrets. If I couldn't do the same in return, I didn't deserve to be happy. And I sure as hell didn't deserve someone like him, who would bare his soul just to say he was sorry.

I squared my shoulders. "You need to know something too," I said. "That house in your neighborhood? It's not mine. I'm just staying there, that's all." I looked down. "I don't really belong there."

"Baby," he said. "I know it's not your house, remember?"

I felt myself nod.

"And you wanna know where you belong?"

"Where?" I said.

"With me."

I felt myself smile. In my whole life, I'd never been wanted like this, not even from my parents.

"Now c'mon," he said. "No more serious talk. Whatever's going on, we'll work it out, alright?"

I nodded.

He leaned closer. "First, I just have a question."

"What?"

"Do you love me?"

My voice was just a whisper, but when I spoke, it seemed to fill the entire car. "Yes."

His leaned closer still. "Say it."

I looked deep into those breathtaking eyes, and said what he wanted to hear, the truth. "I love you."

Something in his expression eased, and he gave me a heart-stopping grin. "Baby, I love you too. More than life itself. I mean it."

When our lips met, it felt like coming home. Or rather, it felt like coming home to the home I never had. His lips were urgent and soft and everything I remembered. A half-sigh, half-moan escaped my lips, and I wanted to melt into him right then and there.

Too soon, with a visible effort, he pulled away and looked around, taking in our surroundings. "We'd better go," he said.

I looked around, too. "What's wrong?"

"Nothing yet. But it'll be dark soon." He settled back into his seat and started the car. "And trust me, the farther away we get, the better."

As he pulled away from the curb, I said, "So, this car? Is it really bullet-proof?"

"Pretty much."

"But why?"

"Why not? Haven't you ever wanted a bullet-proof car?"

"No." I laughed. "Not particularly."

"Eh, you're not a guy. Besides, I'm glad I have it." His voice softened. "Otherwise, I'd have never brought you down here."

"Yeah?"

He nodded. "I might take a lot of chances in life, but with your safety? No way I'm risking that. Not ever."

I felt myself smile. "You couldn't have bullet-proofed one of your nicer cars?" I teased.

"Nope."

"Why not?" I said.

"Let's say we drove the Lexus. We'd be taken for an easy mark." He shrugged. "Or a drug dealer. But in this thing, we're practically invisible." He looked around. "It's perfect for stuff like this."

"Stuff like what?" I said.

"Seeing things without being seen, watching without being watched. A car like this in Rochester Hills, yeah, it sticks out like a sore thumb. But a place like this, it's just part of the landscape."

"But why the bullet-proofing?" I said. I took one last look around. "It's practically a ghost town."

His tone grew serious. "Just because you don't see people, it doesn't mean no one's around. Besides," he said, "I use it for a few other things."

"Like what?" I said.

He turned to give me a heart-stopping grin. "It's a secret."

"What?" I sputtered.

He laughed. "No more serious talk. Remember? You hungry?"

I nodded. It suddenly occurred to me that it was dinner time, and I hadn't even had lunch. We turned off his street, away from his childhood home.

I hadn't had an easy childhood, but compared to Lawton's, mine was a cakewalk. What would it feel like to actually live in a place like this?

I never wanted to find out.

As we left his old neighborhood behind, I watched the urban landscape change from worse to better with every mile.

He took me to a little Tai place in the business district. I had to work in just a couple of hours, so we didn't have a lot of time, but the time we did spend together made me remember why I'd fallen for him so hard in the first place.

We held hands over dinner and laughed over dessert. I talked about Josh and Grandma and the time I'd let Erika bully me into piercing my naval.

His eyes smoldered into mine. "Is it still pierced?" he asked.

I laughed. "You know the answer to that. No."

"You sure?" he said. "I could check."

"You could," I said, "but we'd probably get kicked out of here."

He grinned.

I found myself grinning back. "What are you so happy about?" I said.

"You didn't say I couldn't check, ever. You just said I couldn't check now."

I thought of Erika's words. Just have fun, let it go.

I looked across the table at him. I loved this guy. And he made me laugh. True, he'd also made me cry, but that was part of life, right? And he did love me. I could see it in his eyes.

And I loved him too. So much it almost hurt.

Maybe I was a fool. But I'd rather be a fool in love than a fool with regrets. And I knew one thing for certain. If I walked away now, I'd regret it forever.

Before we left, he leaned in close, ignoring the dirty plates and empty glasses. "Tell me something," he said.

I was lost. Lost in his eyes. Lost in his presence. "What?" I said.

"Are you still my girl?"

There was no way I could stop myself. For better or worse, I felt myself nod.

He practically dove across the table, wrapping his arms around me and pulling me close. I heard his voice, tender in my ear. "Baby, I promise you. You're not gonna regret this."

What I really regretted was that I had to work that night. So instead of spending the night in his arms, or even an hour in his bed, I'd be spending the night at the diner, delivering food, pushing drinks, and worst of all, training Brittney.

We were sitting in the Parkers' driveway when I told him that Brittney was my new co-worker.

"Want me to take care of it?" he asked.

"How?"

He shrugged. "However."

I thought about it. It was tempting, but ultimately, I couldn't say yes. I didn't want anyone to fight my battles for me, no matter how easy it sounded. So, with a certain amount of regret, I told him no.

There was barely enough time to walk Chucky and get ready. From the driver's seat, he turned to face me. "I don't wanna let you go," he said.

"You mean to work?"

"No," he said leaning toward me. "I mean anywhere." He wrapped me in his arms, and our lips met in one final urgent kiss.

I stifled a groan as our tongues danced and my core ignited. Desperately, I tried to justify calling in sick, or at least showing up late. Or maybe skipping Chucky's walk.

I wanted Lawton so bad that I felt like I'd melt away to nothing if I didn't have him this instant. I wanted to feel him inside me, to have his tattooed skin pressed against my own unmarked stomach and breasts, to feel his hands on my back, and his pelvis grinding into mine in that special way that drove me insane.

I heard myself sigh. I just couldn't.

I'd been on the other side of this equation too many times. I'd been the person let down or left hanging because someone was off doing something they wanted, and letting others pay for their fun.

I wasn't going to be that person. Not now, and not ever.

With another groan, I pulled away. I looked toward the house, and saw the curtains move. A moment later, Chucky's face appeared in the window.

Lawton laughed. "Our chaperone."

"Yeah." I blew out a breath. "I've gotta go."

"I was afraid of that."

Before I got out of the car, I leaned into him and asked, "When do you fly out?"

"Tomorrow morning. Six o'clock."

"So early?" I said.

He nodded. "Are you sure don't wanna come with me?" He leaned his forehead against mine. "Tell ya what, you don't even have to wake up. I'll carry you onto that plane myself."

I laughed in spite of myself. He would too. "I wish," I said. "But I've got Chucky. And work."

"When I get back," he said, "we'll have to talk about that."

He'd be gone a whole week. It seemed like a week too long. "And just so you know," I said, "I want to do a whole lot more than talk."

CHAPTER 35

Brittney smirked. "I've just got to be rude to people. How hard can it be?"

"Funny and rude aren't the same thing," I told her.

"Why not?" Brittney gave a toss of her golden hair. "I've seen you do it. And you get good tips, right?"

The uniforms aside, there was a reason my tips were good, and it had nothing to do with rudeness. The place was like a dinner show, with everyone playing a part. As for me, I played a big-haired, big-mouthed waitress with attitude.

"Attitude and rudeness aren't the same thing," I told her.

"Oh shut up," she said. "You're just trying to sabotage me."

"I'm serious," I said. "You can sass them, but you can't insult them."

She frowned. "Now you're just trying to confuse me."

"It's not that complicated," I said. "Sass them too little, and they feel cheated. But sass them too much, they'll get insulted."

"Oh whatever," she said. "You're not the boss of me, so stop acting like it."

I wanted to strangle Keith. It was bad enough he'd hired Brittney in the first place. But to assign me as her trainer? It was sheer stupidity.

I should've shrugged it off. But this time, there was more to it. A lot more. He was goading me, plain and simple. It was just one more thing to drive me out. Just like his constant nitpicking.

Keith's game wasn't exactly subtle. I'd seen it before. That weasel wasn't going to fire me. He was going to make me quit, the same way he'd gotten rid of my favorite cook.

Now, I was stuck training Brittney. I wanted to blow it off, but I couldn't afford to. If she gave bad service, it would hurt me a lot more than it hurt her, at least while she was under my guidance.

We were sitting at a tiny table in the back room. I'd been reviewing the job duties, along with the basic customer service procedures.

"Listen," I said. "I'm telling you, you can't be mean to people. That's not what this job is about."

"Sure it is," she said. "I've eaten here. Lots of times." She shrugged. "You come up, you say something funny, and then deliver the food. What's so hard about that?"

I gave her a look. "Have you ever even waitressed before?"

"Oh please." She raised her eyebrows. "Do I look like a waitress?"

I gave her appearance the once-over. Somehow, she'd missed the mark entirely. The look was supposed to be retro, with big hair, bright lipstick, and dark eye-shadow.

Somehow, Brittney had gotten it all wrong. Her long blonde hair was too sleek, her lips too pink, and her eye shadow far too subtle.

And then, there were her clothes. She'd opted for spiked high-heels instead of the low-slung saddle-shoes the rest of us girls wore. On her tight white blouse, she'd skipped the top two buttons, opting to show an amount of cleavage that was borderline obscene, even by the diner's dubious standards.

"Well?" Brittney gave yet another toss of her hair. "Do I?"

I shook my head. "Definitely not."

She grinned. "Got that right."

"You look like some bit player in a porno."

Her eyes narrowed. "Bit player?"

"What? You wanna star in it?"

"Well, I sure as hell wouldn't be a bit player." Her lips curled. "I've got standards."

"Yeah?" I said. "Is that why you're doing Keith?"

A hint of color rose to her cheeks. But then she leaned forward and lowered her voice. "He's not the only one I did."

I felt my own cheeks grow warm. I knew exactly who she was referring to. Lawton. "Yeah, but you're ancient history," I said, looking down to sift through the training procedures.

For the next half hour, we reviewed every step in the waitressing guidebook, from greeting the customer to delivering their bill. Through the whole process, it was pretty obvious that Brittney was only half-listening.

She studied her nails, touched up her makeup, and at one point, even pulled out her cell phone to tap out a series of texts to who-knows-who.

At last, something got her attention, the tip-splitting arrangement while she was in training. Hearing the details, her eyes snapped to attention. "But that's not fair!" she said.

I shrugged. In truth, I'd felt the same way when I'd been in training. But now that I'd been working here a few years, I had a totally different perspective.

"Look," I explained, "it's just the way it works. You. You're in training. So you're getting a regular wage, just like the cooks. Me, I'm not in training, so I'm getting the waitressing rate, which as we all know, is a lot lower."

She pouted. "But Keith said I'd be getting tips too."

"Yeah," I said. "And you will. Once you're out on your own. But until then, your trainer, whoever that is, gets the tips. It's just the way it works."

She gave me a dirty look. "What a total crock."

Honestly, I could relate. When I'd been in training myself, it had hurt like hell to watch my trainer scoop up all that cash while I got nothing except the hourly wage.

But now, I totally got it. Even with tips, the trainer took a huge pay cut when working with a new girl. Saddled with someone who didn't know the ropes, the trainer couldn't get nearly as many tables, especially if she had to stop every five minutes to explain things along the way.

Training was a major bummer. But we all had to take our turns. Unfortunately, my turn was with Brittney.

"That's just the way it is," I said. "Someday, you'll see."

"Now you sound just like my mom."

I raised my eyebrows. "So you're mom's a waitress too?"

"Hell no," Brittney said, straightening in her seat. "She's a bank president."

"Right," I said.

"She is!"

Regardless of what her Mom did for a living, I had Brittney pegged right from the get-go. She was just another star-struck girl who thought the job was all fun and no work. If she lasted more than a week, I'd be surprised.

Later that night, my worst fears were confirmed when Brittney greeted our very first table. Seated at that table was Mr. Bolger, a regular customer who had requested me personally.

He was a squat, middle-aged man with two ex-wives, wandering hands, and more money than class. I'd been waiting on him for a couple years now. I knew his quirks, and I knew his tipping habits, which in truth, were pretty darn impressive.

As I watched, Brittney plopped down beside him. "Hiya Tubs," she said, looking down at his stomach. "Lemme guess. You want one of everything, right?"

Mr. Bolger set down his menu. "What?" he said.

"Oh Brittney," I said, keeping my tone light. "Stop teasing the man." I gave him my best flirty smile. "Brittney's in training," I told him, adding just a little more spice to my voice than necessary. "So you get both of us for the price of one."

The innuendo was obvious, and I felt just a little dirty using it. But it didn't take a genius to know that calling a customer fat wasn't gonna make them feel all warm and fuzzy, especially when it came time to leave a tip.

Mr. Bolger leaned back in his booth. "Oh yeah? I'm liking the sounds of that." His gaze dipped to Brittney's cleavage. "So tell me, Blondie, am I gonna be your first?"

"Hell no," she said, giving a playful slap to his arm. "I've had lots of guys." She eyed his hairline. "But none with a toupee before."

His face froze.

"So," Brittney continued, "when you shower, do ya take that thing off, or what?"

As it turned out, I didn't need to worry so much about the tip-splitting arrangement, because there wasn't a whole lot of money to go around. Even Mister Bolger, who usually tipped like a mogul, ended up stiffing us.

I guess I couldn't blame him. He had no idea who was getting the tip. For all he knew, it was going to Brittney, who'd insulted him from one side of the restaurant to the other.

And it wasn't just him. Brittney had this annoying habit of calling customers by nicknames based on their appearance. Over the course of the night, we'd waited on Horse Face, Thunder Thighs, Chicken Lips, and too many others to count.

I couldn't tell if she was truly that dense, or was doing it on purpose because she knew it would hurt me a lot more than her.

When I complained to Keith, he said it was my fault for not training her better. And when a disgruntled table of two, also known as Bucky and Snaggletooth, refused to pay for their meals, Keith threatened to dock my pay to compensate for it.

I thought of all the things I could've been doing tonight instead, naked things with the guy of my dreams. I should've called in sick, because when push came to shove, I'd been screwed tonight after all, just not in the way I wanted.

The next afternoon, as I headed to my Grandma's house, I was feeling even more screwed. But this time, it had nothing to do with Brittney.

It had to do with three official letters I found waiting when I checked my post office box.

Bad news. Surprising news. Whatever kind of news you called it, it had me cursing all the way to Grandma's house.

CHAPTER 36

Grandma glared down at the letters. "Those sons-of-bitches," she said.

I bit my lip. "Maybe it's just a bank error."

Grandma snorted. "Bank error my ass."

"Or maybe just an honest mistake?"

Grandma was still looking at the letters. "You just got these today?"

"Yeah, but it's been a couple weeks since I checked my box." I sifted through the envelopes, looking at the date stamps. "Oh shit," I said.

Grandma looked up. "What?"

"These aren't even the latest ones. I've deposited two more since these. Do you think they bounced, too?"

If they did, I was in deep trouble. Before the Parkers had left for Costa Rica, they'd left me a series of post-dated checks. Those weekly checks covered everything – regular expenses, my house-sitting salary, incidentals, whatever.

That salary wasn't a fortune, but it still had me worried. Because my salary was nothing compared to the other expenses those checks were supposed to cover. Those were a fortune, at least by my standards.

For starters, Chucky ate only the best dog food, some custom organic stuff from a specialty shop. Pound for pound, it probably would've been cheaper to feed him prime rib and be done with it.

And then, there were the countless other things related to the house itself – the lawn service, the pest control, some guy who came once a week to trim their hedges and trees. It all seemed beyond wasteful to me. The hedges and trees had stopped growing weeks ago. It was nearly winter, after all.

The Parkers probably spent more money on yard care than I spent on groceries and gas.

Except – oh God – it wasn't going to be me paying for their lawn care. Was it?

"You call 'em yet?" Grandma asked.

"I tried. I couldn't get through."

"I knew it!" Grandma said. "Those fuckers bailed on you."

I shook my head. "They couldn't have bailed. They've got a house, a dog, family photos, the works. " Again I sifted through the letters. "This has to be just some, I dunno, bank thing or something."

Grandma gave me the squinty eye. "What kind of degree you got again?"

"You know perfectly well what it is."

"I just wanna hear you say it."

"Fine," I said. "Accounting."

"Uh-huh. And you believe that horseshit you're shoveling at me? Well, then you better call that school for a refund, because they did a shitty job of teaching you."

"Sorry. They don't offer refunds." It was too bad in a way. They hadn't done a shitty job, but my degree wasn't exactly paying off.

"Here's what you do," Grandma said. "Go back there tonight, and clean 'em out. Take everything. The china, the fancy artwork." She leaned closer. "In that house of theirs, they got copper pipes?"

I gave her a look. "I don't know. And it doesn't matter, because I'm not gonna clean anyone out."

"Why the hell not?"

"I dunno. I mean, it's probably just some snafu with their bank transfers or something. They are in Costa Rica. Remember?"

"Calling it a snafu don't make it right," Grandma said.

"Besides," I said, "I'm watching their dog."

"Shit, take the dog too. You said he's a pricey one, right?"

I rolled my eyes. "I'm not gonna steal their dog. Besides, if Chucky were mine, I wouldn't sell him." I leaned back and crossed my arms. "I'd keep him."

That mutt was growing on me. Except technically, he wasn't a mutt. He was a purebred Yorkie, descended from national show dogs on both sides. But he acted like a mutt. That had to count for something, right?

"Alright," Grandma said, "Just threaten 'em."

I stared at her. "What?"

"Yeah. Tell 'em if they don't pay up, their dog's gonna be dog food."

"See?" I said. "This is why I never discuss money with you."

Grandma was a smart lady, but she had her own ideas of justice. Of course, she hadn't been quite so bloodthirsty when someone had cleaned out her life-savings a few years earlier.

Then again, that thief had been her daughter. My mom. Of the absentee variety.

"I'm not gonna kill their dog either," I said.

"Did I say you should kill him? No. I said you should threaten to kill him. Big difference."

"I'll think about it," I said.

"Your ass. You're not gonna think about nothin'."

"Besides," I said, "what if the Parkers are hurt or something?"

"They're gonna be hurt if they don't pay up."

A few feet away, the cottage door opened. I glanced over to see Josh, my younger brother, come through the door with a book bag slung over his shoulder.

I glanced at Grandma's kitchen clock. "Three o'clock already?" I said.

"What do you mean 'already'?" Josh said, "I've been busting my hump since nine o'clock."

"Oh. My. God," I said. "You didn't just say you've been busting your hump."

"Hey, I have," Josh insisted. "It's not like I'm in grade school anymore."

"Alright, fine," I said with a laugh. "You're officially a hump-buster."

"Damn straight," he said.

"Oh God," I said. "Not you too. I thought we all agreed not to swear anymore."

"You agreed," Grandma said. "We agreed it was fuckin' stupid."

"Yeah," Josh said, "and besides, you talk that way all the time."

"Not all the time." I gave him a serious look. "Please tell me you don't talk this way in public."

"Hell no," he said. "I'm not that stupid."

I smiled in spite of myself. "You're not stupid at all, and you know it."

Josh was in the gifted program, and he needed to stay there. This meant he needed to stay at his current school, which also meant he needed to stay exactly where he was –

living with my Dad and Loretta.

And Grandma? Well, she needed to stay in the cottage. As long as she lived there, Josh had at least one place close by where he felt welcome.

I couldn't help but notice that Josh had come straight to the cottage after getting off the bus. He hadn't gone to where he supposedly lived.

Grandma's place was rented, and it was tiny – one bedroom, one bathroom, a cozy kitchen, and small living area with windows overlooking an elaborate rose garden, now dormant.

Across the garden loomed a much larger home, where my Dad lived with Loretta in a two-story brick house, much like the Parkers'. Everything was Loretta's – the house, the cottage, the gardens, and probably all their possessions.

This meant that Loretta wasn't just mine and Josh's stepmother. She was also Grandma's landlady.

It was all so complicated that I had a hard time keeping it straight sometimes. But it worked as long as Grandma thought she had a job.

Reminded of this, I stood and reached for the bin of envelopes she had stuffed during the last week. I said my goodbyes and headed out to my car.

I was loading the bin into my trunk when I heard that dreaded voice somewhere behind me call out, "Up to your usual tricks, I see?"

CHAPTER 37

I glanced behind me and stifled a groan. Sure enough, there she was, an overly thin woman with short, brown hair – Loretta.

Today she wore tailored slacks, a cream-colored blouse, and her usual scowl as she barreled down the driveway toward me.

With a sigh, I turned back to the car and slammed the trunk before leaning against it. She came closer, holding an official-looking clipboard.

Her scowl deepened. "Well, are you?" she said.

Up to my usual tricks? Honestly, I had no idea. "What tricks?" I asked.

"Do I really have to spell everything out for you?" She gave a dramatic sigh. "Fine. I'm referring to your leaving without stopping by."

"I tried to stop by," I said. "No one answered."

It was true. After the hassle Loretta gave me last time, I had literally forced myself to knock on their front door first, before setting one foot inside Grandma's cottage.

"Besides," I said, "aren't you supposed to be at work?"

"Aren't you?" she said.

"No. I work nights, remember?"

She pursed her lips. "There's no need to get snippy."

We could go around like this for hours. I so didn't have the time or energy. I glanced at the house. "So, uh, you want me to stop by, now?"

Please say no, please say no, please say no.

"Not necessary," she said. "Your father isn't home."

If it wasn't necessary, why was she giving me grief? Oh yeah, because she could. That's why.

"Oh," I said.

"Is that all you have to say for yourself?"

"What am I supposed to say? That I'm sorry?"

"Not if that's the best you can do." She looked down at my clothing. "Please tell me you're not wearing that for Thanksgiving."

I glanced down at my jeans and turtleneck. I looked respectable enough. "Are we dressing up?" I asked.

"Is that a rhetorical question?"

"No. It's a real question. Are we?"

She gave a little sniff. "Well, we certainly are. Out of respect for this house, I would think you would want to do the same."

What I wanted to do was grab her by the hair and slam her face into my trunk. What I did do was nod. "Alright, I'll dress up."

"And you will be bringing the salad?"

"Wait a minute," I said. "I thought I was bringing the dessert."

She gave a long, drawn-out sigh. "Must we do this again?"

"What again?"

With a shake of her head, she raised the clipboard and ran a long finger down a printed spreadsheet. Halfway down, she stopped. "Here," she said with a decisive finger-tap. "Chloe, salad." She looked up and raised her eyebrows. "Are you

Chloe?"

"I dunno," I said. "Is that a rhetorical question?"

"Oh for Heaven's sake," she said. "Must everything be a joke with you?"

"I wasn't joking," I said. Well, okay, I was. But nothing about this seemed remotely funny to me. When it came to Loretta, I'd lost my sense of humor years ago.

"So," I said, "you want me to bring a salad?"

"Yes," she said in a tone of forced civility. "A salad would be lovely. Thank you."

Too bad the salad wasn't only for her. I'd have Chucky take a big crap in it. Then I'd feed it to her with a shovel. Now, that would be lovely.

"And what," she said, "is so funny now?"

"Nothing," I said. "Salad. Got it."

"I'll believe it when I see it," she said, before turning on her heels and heading back toward the house.

I was driving home when my cell phone rang. Desperate for a return call from the Parkers, I lunged for it and checked the display.

Lawton. Today was Friday, and he'd be home in three days. He'd been calling me every night. I loved hearing from him, and things would be even nicer when we could do more than just talk.

Still, as happy as I was to hear from him in the middle of the day, I'd be lying if I didn't admit that this wasn't the call I'd been desperate to receive.

I pressed the button. "Hello?"

"What's wrong?" he said.

"Nothing."

"Alright." He was quiet for a beat, and then said, "Got any plans for tonight?"

I had the night off, not that it would do any good. He was in Vegas, and I was here. "Not really," I said. "Why?"

"Because I've gotta be honest. I couldn't wait to see you."

"You came back early?" I said.

"You might say that."

I laughed. "What does that mean?"

"It means," he said, "that I'll be landing in a couple hours. I've got to be back in Vegas tomorrow morning, but I remembered you had tonight off, so—"

My trouble with the Parkers suddenly faded into the background. "So you want to get together?" I said.

"Yeah. But listen, no more hiding out in secret. You're my girl, and from now on, I'm doing things right. How about I'll pick you up at seven?"

I smiled into the phone. "Sounds good. But hey, what should I wear?"

"What kind of night are you in the mood for?" he said. "Casual, formal?"

As far as clothing, I preferred nothing. Just the thought of his naked body gyrating against mine was enough to make my mouth water. But he was right. Hiding out in secret hadn't gotten us very far.

"How about casual?" I said.

"Casual, it is." His voice lowered. "And Chloe?"

"Hmm?"

"I don't care what you wear. I'm dying to see you."

CHAPTER 38

I spent most of that afternoon trying to reach Mrs. Parker. Even with them out of the country, this had never been a problem before.

At least once a week, she'd been checking in from Costa Rica, just to see how things were going. And every once in a while, I called her too, always on her cell phone, and usually with mundane, but time-sensitive questions about home maintenance.

Now, every single call was going straight to her voicemail. I told myself this was a good sign. It was better than hearing a disconnection notice, right?

Out of desperation, I pulled out our original paperwork and scoured the documents for emergency contacts. I ran my finger down the long list and came up with nothing useful. If I needed to reach Chucky's vet, I was home-free. But if I wanted to reach Chucky's owners, I was totally screwed.

If I didn't hear back from them soon, I'd have to come up with some sort of plan.

Until then, I vowed to push it out of my mind. I had a guy who loved me flying halfway across the country just to take me out on a date. If that wasn't a better thing to think about, I didn't know what was.

Lawton picked me up right on time, driving some exotic sports car that I didn't recognize.

First, we hit an authentic Greek restaurant owned by a friend of his. What they brought us, I had no idea, at least not by their official names. But there was something delicious made with spicy chicken and homemade bread, and an amazing dessert with nuts and honey.

We talked about plays and politics, and local landmarks that we both had visited, even if not with each other. He talked about his sister, his Grandma, and a little about Bishop, who I was relieved to hear was out of town.

As for me, I told him a little more about Grandma and a lot more about Josh, trying not to brag, as much as I wanted to.

I didn't talk about the Parkers. And this time, it wasn't because I was ashamed, and it wasn't because of that agreement. Mostly, it was because when it came to house-sitting, things weren't exactly going so well.

Tonight, I only wanted to only think about good things. And that didn't include bounced checks or missing home-owners.

By the time we hit dessert, I'd pushed the Parkers completely out of my mind. They were gone, and Lawton was here. Being with him, even after all that had happened, was like a dream.

Sometimes people recognized him. Sometimes they didn't. But no matter who was around us, he only had eyes for me. We left the restaurant a little after nine and hit a comedy show at one of the downtown casinos.

In the car afterward, Lawton was navigating the city streets when he turned to me and said, "Want to hit a club or something?"

I looked down at my jeans and simple blouse. "I'm not really dressed for it."

He laughed and glanced down at his own clothing. "Like I am."

I gave him a good, long look. His left hand rested loosely on the steering wheel while his right elbow rested on the center console. Even in relaxation, the tattoo-covered muscles shifted with the smallest movement of the vehicle, showing off the lines and ridges of his amazing physique.

His clothes were simple, just dark jeans and a black T-shirt, but his appearance was anything but.

His clothes didn't have to be satin, silk, or some designer brand. His mere presence spoke for itself, making Lawton look like a million bucks in what could've been a ten-dollar shirt for all I knew.

I recalled what was under that shirt. I'd pressed my face against his naked chest how many times now? However many times it had been, it didn't feel like enough.

As if feeling the heat of my gaze, he turned his head in my direction. His gaze was electric, and he gave me a grin so heart-stopping that I felt my lips part as if waiting for a kiss.

"Baby," he said. "It doesn't matter what you wear. You'll be the most beautiful girl in that place." He turned his attention back to the road. "And you know what? If anyone gives you shit about what you're wearing, they'll have me to answer to."

I couldn't help but laugh. "What are you gonna do?" I said. "Beat 'em up if they tell me no jeans allowed?"

In profile, I saw him smile. "Depends."

"On what?"

"How nicely they tell you."

I rolled my eyes. "Yeah, well the fashion police can be

really brutal."

I was only half kidding. It was part of the reason I shopped at consignment stores. The clothes might've been secondhand, but they were almost always the right cut and label.

"There's this new place off Six Mile," he said. "A friend of mine's a bouncer there." He gave me a sideways glance. "And I'll tell you what, if he doesn't agree that what you're wearing is the sweetest stuff he's ever seen, I'll personally kick his ass."

I pretended to give it some thought. "I dunno," I said through laughter I couldn't quite contain. "He's not a big guy, is he? Because I sure don't want you getting hurt on my account."

As we pulled up to a red light, Lawton put a hand to his heart. "Now I'm hurt." He made a strangled, choking sound as the car came to a stop. "Might. Be. Fatal." He groaned. "Need. Mouth. To. Mouth." He flopped his head back onto the headrest and closed his eyes.

I glanced at the light. It was still red, but for how long. "Very funny," I said.

He didn't move.

"C'mon," I said with another nervous glance ahead, "the light's gonna turn."

He gave a low groan. "Almost. Gone."

"You are such a –" I laughed as I tore off my seatbelt and moved toward him. "Damn it, I don't know what you are." When our lips met, he came magically to life, moving his lips against mine in a way that sent a bolt of heat straight to my core.

I felt his hand in my hair and his tongue against mine. The next strangled moan was my own, as I felt my insides combust and my knees tremble.

A car horn sounded behind us, and I nearly jumped out of my skin. I pulled away and looked toward the light, now green. There were several cars behind us. The horn sounded again, followed by another, probably from the vehicle behind them.

I jumped back into my seat. "Go!" I said.

"Not 'til you buckle up."

I fumbled for my seatbelt, listening to the cacophony of horns behind us. When the seatbelt snapped shut, Lawton floored it, leaving the other vehicles in the dust. I glanced behind us. The light was red again, and the horns were still blaring.

The driver of the car behind us was giving us the middle-finger salute. Lawton rolled down the window and gave the driver a casual wave.

"Oh my God," I said through choked laughter. "You're trying to get us killed."

He turned to give me a grin. "Never," he said. "The club's up here on the left. What do you think?"

I thought of how it would feel to have Lawton pressed up against me, our bodies grinding to the beat of whatever – slow song, fast song, hell, a damn polka. I wanted to feel him against me. And I didn't want to wait until we got back.

"Count me in," I said.

CHAPTER 39

The club was jam-packed with a line out the door – not that we waited in it. Whether it was because Lawton knew the bouncer or simply because of who he was, we bypassed the line and were ushered straight inside.

Behind us, I heard a few muttered grumbles of those left waiting, but Lawton took my hand, and we just kept going. A flash of cash and a few words from Lawton netted us a newly placed table right near the dance floor.

We ordered a couple of drinks from a harried-looking waitress, and Lawton turned to me. "Wanna dance?"

I looked around. "Shouldn't we wait until we have our drinks?"

"Why?" he said.

"So no one steals our table."

He laughed. "Baby, no one's gonna steal our table."

"How do you know?"

"Because I paid 'em an extra fifty to keep it free."

"Who's them?" I asked.

He pointed toward a beefy guy standing with arms crossed a few feet away. "Him."

"I didn't see you talking to him."

"I worked it out with my friend."

"The bouncer?"

"Yeah."

I vaguely recalled them sharing a greeting and a few hushed words, but mostly I remembered Lawton introducing me as his girl with a look of such pride that I practically melted.

"I don't want you to worry about anything tonight," Lawton said. He stood and reached for my hand. "Now c'mon. Ready?"

I looked up at him, a silhouette of absolute perfection. His body, his face, and the way he looked at me sent a jolt of electricity straight through me. Nearby, a couple of girls in slinky dresses whispered to each other and pointed. One of them licked her lips.

I stood. I was more than ready.

A few second later, we were moving against each other on the dance floor. I felt his hands on my hips and his gaze on my face. The song was slow, with a rhythmic beat that suggested sex on the beach under a full summer moon.

I moved closer, feeling our hips touch and then grind against each other as his hands moved slowly up my back. I moved my hands to his sides, feeling the sinewy muscles surrounding his stomach shift and contract in time with his movements.

I threw back my head and looked into his eyes. The floor was packed, but from the look on his face, there was nobody but us. I knew the feeling.

When the song ended, and a faster one took its place, we didn't change position. I leaned closer and rested my head against his chest. It felt so strong, so permanent, and so amazing that I knew I'd never want to leave. Not when the song ended, and not ever.

We stayed that way for a long time, oblivious to everything

but each other as songs came and went, just like the dancers around us.

Finally, thirst got the better of me. I glanced through the gyrating bodies toward our table and saw our drinks sitting there, waiting. With a sigh, I pulled away and pointed toward the table. "Look. Drinks."

But he didn't look toward the table. His eyes looked thirsty, but not for the beer he'd ordered however long ago. "Yeah? Ready to sit down?"

When I nodded, he took my hand and led me to the table. I took a sip of my drink and choked as the fire burned down my throat.

He eyed me with concern. "What's wrong?"

I was still coughing. "I think they made it a double. Wait. Scratch that. Make that a triple."

He grinned. "Probably thought they were doing you a favor."

I laughed. "Maybe. But it's not exactly thirst-quenching, if you know what I mean."

"Want me get you a new one?"

I looked around. I didn't see our waitress. In fact, I didn't see any waitresses. No surprise, given how crowded the place had become. "Nah, that's alright," I told him.

"You think so, huh?" He stood and reached for my drink. "Wait here. I'll be back in five minutes."

I watched his back disappear into the crowd, thinking of how nice it was to have a guy who'd go to this much trouble without my even asking. A glance at our neighboring tables told me I wasn't the only one. Girls, guys – it didn't seem to matter. Something about him commanded their attention.

Did they recognize him? Or was it merely his appearance that made people sit up and notice? I tried to think of him as a stranger might. I recalled that first day, near the Parkers', when I'd walked past him, standing there wearing no shirt.

Back then, he was sex and danger. Now he was that, and so much more.

That day, I hadn't even recognized him. But something inside me had definitely responded. Lawton was just that way. People loved to look at him. I felt myself smile. Of course, they could look all they wanted, but I knew who would be touching him tonight, and it wasn't any of these people.

Still smiling, I stood to go to the ladies room, hoping to make the most of the time he was gone. I glanced at the beefy guy near the dance floor. He had barely moved since Lawton had first pointed him out to me. The way it looked, he took his table-watching seriously.

When he saw me looking, he gave me a quick nod, and glanced toward the table as if to assure me that everything would still be there when I returned.

I started weaving my way through the crowd. When I glanced at our table the next time, the guy had his back to me, watching over the table like he feared it might escape if he took his eye off it for one second.

The whole thing was oddly surreal. I wasn't used to people doing things for me, even something so small as this. It felt weird and wonderful all at the same time.

Unfortunately, the next person I ran into wasn't quite so accommodating.

CHAPTER 40

I was still looking back at the table when I bumped into someone. Hard. I looked up. It was a massive guy, at least seven feet tall, with a gold earring and a thick, tattooed neck.

"Sorry," I said, shifting to move around him.

But when I moved, he moved in exactly the same direction, blocking my path with a low chuckle. Something about it sent an odd shiver down my spine.

I glanced around. There were too many bodies and no easy path to get around him, so I put my hands on my hips and glared up at him. "What's your problem?" I said.

He looked down on me and smiled, revealing gold grillwork over his front teeth. "So you're the new one?" he said.

"The new what?"

"The new chick." He said "chick" like it was a social disease. "Lawton's squeeze."

"Hey!" I said, "I'm no one's squeeze."

Slowly, his gaze traveled down the length of me, stopping way too long in certain places. "No? You can be my squeeze, once he's done with you." With a deranged smile, he sidled forward. "Or maybe you don't wanna wait."

Without thinking, I took a step backward, bumping someone behind me. I spun around and jostled a tall girl with big hair and too much lipstick. She was holding two drinks. One of them hit the floor. The glass shattered against the hard surface. "Hey!" she hollered. "Look what you did!"

"Yeah," said the big guy. "Look what you did."

Ignoring the girl, I whipped back around to face him. I craned my neck upward, trying to decide of I should back up slowly, or run like hell.

But suddenly, a wall appeared in front of my face. I recognized that wall.

It was Lawton's back.

I'd never been so glad to see anything in all my life. The lean, corded muscles in his neck and arms were a stark contrast to the hulking guy in front of him. Still, I felt myself swallow. The guy in front of Lawton was so much bigger. Scary bigger. I didn't know what to do. Find a bouncer? Call for help?

Frantically, I looked around.

"Baby," Lawton said over his shoulder. "Go back to the table. I'll meet you there in a minute."

And leave him alone? No way. I mean, I knew I was no use in a fight, but no way I'd just run away like I didn't give a crap what happened to him.

Because I cared. I cared a lot.

Behind me, I heard the girl's other drink hit the floor. "Oh my God," she said. "Is that Lawton Rastor?"

The big guy obviously heard, because he bellowed out, "Hey, everyone! It's fucking Lawton Rastor! And his fucking squeeze! Aren't we so fucking lucky?"

At my back, I felt a sudden drop in temperature, like the bodies around me were sidling away. Was everyone leaving? If so, that sounded like a damn good idea. I reached toward Lawton's shirt, hoping to pull him away before things got any worse.

But then, like lightning, Lawton threw back his head. Immediately, a fist flew past his face.

But it wasn't from the guy in front of him. It was from some new guy off to our right, a big muscle-bound guy with complicated facial hair.

The fist had barely disappeared when Lawton's right arm shot in the guy's direction. His fist slammed into the guy's ear.

"Motherfucker!" the guy yelled, staggering backward, and then off to the side, like he couldn't quite keep his balance.

"Chloe," Lawton said in a warning tone, "you'd better not still be there."

From the tone of his voice, he knew exactly where I was, and he wasn't happy.

Slowly, I began to back up. I didn't stop until I felt the warmth of the crowd at my back. My heart was racing. I looked around. Where was the bouncer? Where was anyone? Should I dial 911?

Ahead of me, the first guy took a swing at Lawton's face. Lawton swatted the fist away, leaving the guy's face wide open. That's when Lawton's right fist shot out, slamming hard into the center of the guy's face.

He staggered backward, and his hands flew to his nose. A river of blood poured between his fingers. "My nose! You fuckin' broke it, you asshole!"

With a guttural roar, the guy off to the right charged toward Lawton. Without changing direction, Lawton gave him a hard elbow to the neck. The guy dropped to the ground, wheezing. With barely a glance, Lawton kicked him in the side, sending the guy rolling onto his back.

The first guy, his face a bloody mess, barreled toward Lawton head-first. Lawton's fist flew out toward the guy's mid-section, hitting him hard enough to double him over. With a half-moan, half-wheeze, the guy dropped to his knees.

Finally, the bouncers made their appearance. I recognized one of them as Lawton's friend, a black guy in a black T-shirt with the club's logo. He looked down at the second guy, still lying on his back. "Snake, you dumb-ass. Not again."

With something like a sigh, Lawton's bouncer friend grabbed one of Snake's booted feet in each hand and started dragging him toward the exit.

The first guy, now on his hands and knees, raised his head and muttered, "That son-of-a-bitch broke my nose!" He glared at Lawton. "Third fuckin' time. You cock-sucker."

Lawton took a step toward him and grabbed him by the collar of his shirt. His voice was quiet, but it carried over the now silent club. "You wanna fuck with me? Fine. Fuck with me all you want. But if you ever fuck with my girl again—"

He leaned close to the guy's ear and said something that only they could hear. The guy glanced at me, and I almost heard him swallow. When Lawton finally released him, the guy looked around the quiet crowd. "What the fuck are you lookin' at?" he said as he rose unsteadily to his feet and stumbled toward the exit.

And then, somewhere behind me, I heard a girl's voice, a different one from the first, say, "Holy shit, was that Lawton Rastor?"

CHAPTER 41

Five minutes later I fell, laughing, into the passenger's seat of his car. I never did get my drink, which was probably a good thing. My head was spinning so fast, my body could barely keep up.

I should've been horrified. Hell, I was horrified. But I was something else too. And it had me rubbing my thighs together as I settled into the passenger's seat.

Lawton closed my car door and strode around the front of the car. I watched him through the window. With a soft sigh, I watched him move.

That long, easy stride, those wary eyes, the way his muscles shifted in time with his movements. It was a visual symphony that had me wanting more than just a look.

He was every girl's fantasy.

He was my fantasy. And he was mine in real life too. For how long, I had no idea. I knew it wouldn't be forever. In real life, things like that didn't happen. He'd go on to marry a movie star or a socialite, or no one at all. And I'd – I bit my lip – I didn't know what I'd do.

But I knew what I wanted to do now.

I turned sideways in the seat to face him. I watched as he settled into the driver's seat and slammed the door shut behind him.

"That was interesting," I said.

He gave me a look. "That's one way to put it."

I felt my eyebrows furrow. "Are you mad at me or something?"

He turned straight ahead, studying the dimly lit parking lot. "No."

"Are you sure?"

Cast in shadows, I watched him in profile. He didn't answer, and he didn't move so much as a muscle.

"You are," I said.

Slowly, he shook his head.

I reached out, placing a hand on his thigh. "Then what is it?"

He turned to face me, and his hand closed over mine. "You could've been hurt," he said.

"But I wasn't."

"But you could've been."

"So that's why you're mad at me?"

His hand tightened. "No. Baby. Not you. Me."

"Why you?" I kept my tone light. "You rescued me. You're the hero of this story, not the villain."

"You sure about that?"

"Definitely."

"Oh yeah?" he said. "Well, let me ask you something? You ever have that happen before?"

"What?" I said.

"You ever have some stranger come up and give you crap for no good reason?"

"Well, I am a waitress," I said. "So, yeah. It happens to me all the time, actually."

"You know what I mean." He leaned toward me, over the

center console. "I shouldn't have left you alone."

"Why not? I don't need a bodyguard."

"That place," he said. "I mean it's nice enough." He shook his head. "But the crowd. Shit." He reached over, brushing a stray lock of hair from my face. Something in his voice changed. "I wanted to kill him."

"Which one?"

"Both."

"Well, you did a pretty good job of half-killing them, so that's gotta count for something, right?"

He gave me a look. "I can laugh at a lot of things, Chloe. But seeing you hurt isn't one of them."

"Except I wasn't hurt." I grinned over at him. "I wasn't even touched. So there."

He closed his eyes as if shutting out an image too painful to watch. "But you could've been."

"Hey," I said. "I want to ask you something, and I hope you'll be honest with me."

His eyes opened, and he met my gaze with an intensity that was almost too painful to bear. Slowly, he nodded.

I leaned very close. "By any chance," I whispered, "are you Lawton Rastor?"

His face froze. The moment seemed to go on forever, and then, his lips twitched. He gave me that crooked smile of his, the one that made my breath hitch and my heart melt. "Me?" he said. "Nah. I'm the guy with Chloe Malinski."

"Oh her?" I said in a disappointed tone. "But she's just a nobody."

"Baby," he said, "she's somebody, alright." Slowly, he moved his lips closer to mine. "Matter of fact, she's everything to this guy I know."

"Oh yeah?"

"Oh yeah."

CHAPTER 42

He closed the distance between us, crushing his lips onto mine in a kiss that seemed born of half relief, half desperation.

I raised my hands and brought them to his head, feeling the tousled strands of his hair dance around my fingers as our lips, our tongues, and our breaths combined. The center console dug into my side, but I barely noticed.

My voice was breathless as I said, "I want you."

His lips drifted lower, leaving a trail of soft kisses down my jawline and toward my shoulder. "Ready to go home?" he said.

Home. It was a funny word. "I feel like I'm home right now," I said. I glanced toward the rear of the car. "Hey, look a back seat."

I felt his muffled laugh against my shoulder. "No way."

"Aw c'mon," I said. "I know you want to."

I reached out toward his leg. I trailed my hand across his jeans, starting at the knee and working my way up, slowly and surely. When my hand hit a definite bulge, the muffled laugh turned into a muffled groan.

"Baby, you're killin' me over here."

"Then you should just give in," I teased. "It'll be so much simpler."

He pulled his head back and gazed into my eyes. "Not

gonna happen. Not here. As tempting as you are."

"Why not?" I said.

"A place like this," he said, looking around the dim parking lot, "bad things can happen. And if anything bad happened to you—" he shook his head "—I'd never forgive myself."

"With you here?" I said. "I'm not worried."

Funny, I meant it too. Wrapped in his arms, and feeling him close to me, I felt like nothing bad could ever happen, not to me, and not to him.

"Here's the thing," he said. "Yeah, we could climb into that back seat, but I'd have to keep an eye out."

I felt a hand on my knee, mirroring my own motions from just a moment earlier. His hand drifted higher up my thigh, and higher still, going so slow I felt like I'd combust right then and there.

When his hand finally reached the intersection of my thighs, my eyes drifted shut, and my lips parted. The sound that escaped might've been a sigh, and it might've been a moan.

"Or," he said, rubbing his thumb in a slow, circular motion across that perfect spot, "I could take you home, where the only thing I have to think about is you."

"Home," I said. "Now."

By the time we reached Lawton's estate, I was burning for him, feeling the heat of that brief touch simmer and grow with every turn and every mile. When we finally roared through his gate and skidded to a stop in the turnaround, he cut the engine and jumped out of his car.

He strode around to the passenger's side, flung open my door, and threw me over his shoulder, barbarian style.

I couldn't help it. I squealed and giggled all the way up the front walkway. He pushed through the front door and slammed it shut with a haphazard kick.

Without breaking a sweat, he headed up the wide stairway with me, still laughing, slung over his shoulder. I lost one shoe halfway up and the other when we hit the top step.

He strode down the long hall, heading straight to his bedroom. When he reached it, he hoisted me up and flung me onto his bed, where I landed with a fit of laughter that made my insides ache.

He stood at the foot of the bed, looking down on me with a smile so wicked, and a body to match, that my breathless laughter quieted to mere breathlessness.

He was so damn beautiful. And he loved me. And I loved him. I was living a dream, and I never wanted to wake up.

He leaned over the bed, and unbuttoned my jeans with one hand, and then went for the zipper. He straightened up, and took a pant leg in each hand, tugging slowly and surely until I wore only my shirt and underpants.

When he leaned down to tug at my panties, I said, "No fair. You're still dressed."

"Who said anything about fair?" he said, giving my panties a slow tug downward. "Baby, you are so beautiful," he said. "It hurts just to look at you."

"So are you," I said, motioning him toward the bed. "But you're too far away."

With a small chuckle, he grabbed my ankles and pulled me toward him, until my pelvis rested at the edge of the bed. Slowly, he ran a hand up my thigh. "Better?" he said.

I crooked my finger, motioning him to come closer. When he did, I gripped the hem of his shirt and tugged upward until he gave in, lifting his arms, and letting me tug it, hard, over his head and toss it onto the floor.

Leaning over me with his bare chest, with all those

217

muscles, ridges, and tattoos, I could almost envision him as a conquering warrior, come to claim his prize. I felt my knees tremble and my breath catch. He knelt at the foot of the bed and lowered his head, kissing the inside of my thigh just above the knee.

That small kiss ignited a flame, sending a quiver of heat straight to my core. I felt his tongue on my skin and his hands on my thighs, caressing the skin with slow, steady strokes. His mouth moved higher with every kiss until I felt his lips brush my opening and his tongue giving me a long, sweet stroke.

I was panting now, squirming against him and gripping the bed coverings with both fists.

"I love the way you taste," he said. "And feel."

I felt a finger slip inside me, and I ground my hips upward, wanting more. So much more. Soon, a second finger joined the first, and he took my hot, swollen clit into his mouth. He sucked, lightly at first, and then harder, making me moan and sigh in time with the motions of his mouth and fingers.

I lifted my torso, resting my weight on my elbows, to look down at him. His eyes lifted, meeting mine, and something in my heart gave way. Because what I saw there, it wasn't just a gorgeous guy who knew exactly what he was doing.

It was a guy who made me feel whole in ways I'd never imagined.

And damn, I loved watching him. When his eyes dipped down again, I let my gaze soak up the rest of him, those powerful shoulders, those strong arms, the neck I loved to caress when we kissed on the couch.

When my head drifted backward, my body followed. Soon, my eyes drifted shut too.

The movement of his fingers and the motions of his tongue were sending me closer and closer to that sweet abyss.

Then I fell over with a series of shudders and sounds that I wouldn't want the neighbors to hear.

When he lifted his head, I couldn't stop quivering as he stood, and finally unzipped his jeans. "I love you so damn much, Chloe," he said. "I never wanna let you go."

"Then don't," I said, "because I love you too."

I lifted my head, and made a motion to get up. I wanted to taste him too, to have him in the same way he had me.

"No," he said. "Stay right there. I want you just like this. You're so damn beautiful."

When his jeans reached the floor, and his navy briefs followed, I felt a shudder of anticipation. His body was a work of art, and not just the parts that had graced all those magazine covers.

Still standing, he pressed the tip of his massive erection to my opening, and then with one slow steady movement, he surged forward. My slickness welcomed him, closing around him as our two bodies became one.

Through heavy-lidded eyes, I watched him. The muscles of his abs shifted and moved in time with his hips, and I felt my own stomach contract, at first a little, and then a lot. His body was magnificent, and he knew how to use it.

Every thrust, sometimes slow, sometimes fast, was reaching places I almost didn't know existed, and not just with my body. It had never been like this. Not with anyone. Not ever. I ground against him, feeling him move inside me and relishing every motion.

Almost before I realized it, I was clutching the bedding yet again, moving my own hips faster in time with his, faster and faster, until with a symphony of shudders and moans, we reached that glorious peak and floated back to Earth.

Except it didn't feel like Earth. It felt like Heaven. And

when he settled down next to me a moment later, it felt like home.

It felt like I belonged.

CHAPTER 43

When I woke the next day in the Parkers' guest room, reality hit like a cold fish to the face. Last night had been a dream, a wonderful dream. But today, I had to face reality.

At five o'clock in the morning, Lawton had left for the airport. He'd urged me to stay, to sleep in his bed, to stay at his house. The invitation included both me and Chucky, who we'd retrieved from the Parkers' later that night.

But as I watched Lawton get dressed, I knew that delaying my departure wouldn't really help. It would only postpone the inevitable. So when he left for the airport, I asked him to drop me and Chucky off on the way with the anticipation of his return in just a couple of days.

As we said goodbye in the Parkers' driveway, I soaked up that final feverish embrace like my sanity depended on it. In a way it did, because if things continued to go downhill as far as house-sitting was concerned, I might not be his neighbor very much longer.

If I didn't hear back from the Parkers within the next day or two, I'd have some tough choices to make. Would I need to check with their bank? Leave their house? Call the police?

I sure as hell hoped not. It was exactly the kind of thing I tried to avoid, especially if I ever wanted to work again as a house sitter.

My day improved considerably when I arrived at work that evening and learned that Brittney had called in sick. Keith gave me the news personally, not looking too happy about it.

"Is it the flu?" I asked.

"Wouldn't you like to know?" he said.

"Not particularly," I said. "And just for the record, she really is terrible at this. Like I already told you, she insulted every single customer."

"And like I already told you," he said, "maybe she wasn't adequately trained."

"Hey, I tried," I said. "She never listens. You know what I think? She's trying to sabotage me."

"Chloe," he said, "not everyone is out to get you."

"I'm just saying, it's a problem."

"Wanna know what the real problem is around here?"

"What?"

"Your boyfriends."

I stared at him. "What do you mean?"

"Well, first, you've got one of them beating the crap out of his own car in our parking lot, and then you've got this other one coming in every day asking for you. What do you think? This is some kind of dating service?"

"I don't even know who you're talking about," I said.

"Sure you don't."

"I don't," I said. "Whoever he is, he's not my boyfriend."

"Funny, that's not what he said."

I felt my eyebrows furrow. "What'd he look like?"

"Heavyset guy, longish hair, said his name was Chester."

"Shaggy?" I said. "He's not my boyfriend. He's not even my friend."

Keith crossed his arms. "Oh yeah? Well from what I heard, you were all over him the other night in our parking

222

lot."

"I was not!"

"Oh really? Well Jordon said he saw you on the guy's shoulders, making a regular spectacle of yourself. Got anything to say about that?"

"I was taking video," I said. "And it wasn't even my idea."

"Just so you know," Keith said, "if he comes in here again, I'm writing you up."

"You can't write me up," I said. "It's not my fault if he comes in here."

Keith pointed to his name tag and cleared his throat. "What does this say?"

I gave him a look. "You don't know your own name?"

"Very funny," Keith said. "Go on, read what it says below my name."

I rolled my eyes. "Manager."

"Exactly. I'm the manager, and if I say you're getting written up, you're gonna get written up. End of story."

"Okay, fine write me up. Whatever. Are we done here?"

He pointed his thumb at his name tag. "We're done when I say we're done."

I looked at him expectantly.

He glanced at the clock, and then toward the dining area. "Alright, we're done. Now get out there, and remember what I said."

About Brittney? About Shaggy? About his name tag? Honestly, I had no idea what the guy was referring to. But I was used to that. I headed out toward the waitress station, just glad for the chance to make up for lost ground.

Without Brittney, I had a decent chance of making some money tonight, and I wasn't going to let the opportunity slide just because Keith was up to his old tricks.

By midnight, I'd actually made some progress when I heard someone at the bar call my name. I turned, and there he was, Shaggy, his cell phone in one hand and a beer in the other.

I stalked over. "What do you want?" I said.

He frowned. "Why do you gotta be so mean about it? Or, uh, is this part of your waitressing act?"

"No," I said, "I actually meant to be mean."

"Jeez, what'd I ever do to you?"

"Well for one thing," I said, "you're lying about being my boyfriend."

"You're one to talk," he said. "You gave me a fake name." His gaze narrowed. "Betty."

"Look," I said, "I'm really busy. Just tell me what you want, so then you can leave."

"When I tell you," he said, "you're gonna feel really bad."

"Oh yeah? Why?"

"Because the only reason I'm here is to do you a favor."

My gaze narrowed. "What kind of favor?"

"Here's the thing." He glanced around. "I saw you with Lawton Rastor."

"So?"

"So, he seems to really like you."

I made a forward motion with my hands. "And?"

"And I do some video work on the side, weddings and stuff."

I shook my head. "So?"

He lowered his voice. "You know that sex tape of his? If you wanted, I could set up a sequel."

My mouth fell open. "Are you saying you did the first one?"

He glanced around. "I don't like to brag."

"Oh trust me," I said, feeling a cold rage sweep over me. "It's nothing to brag about."

"But I'm guessing you want to be famous too, right?"

I gave him look. "Does Lawton know about this?" Of course, I knew the truth, but his answer would tell me a lot.

Shaggy reached up to scratch his ear. "Not yet. But I mean, he'd find out eventually, right?"

I crooked my finger, inviting him to come closer. When he did, I moved my head close and whispered in his ear. "Listen, if you ever ask me something like that again, you're gonna be real sorry. And you wanna know why?'

He leaned back and gave a nervous look around the restaurant. "What are you gonna do? Tell Lawton?"

"No." I smiled. "I'm gonna tell Jen."

His eyes widened. "Jen, my girlfriend?"

I nodded.

"You wouldn't."

I crossed my arms. "I would."

Again, he looked around. "She's not here now, is she?"

I shrugged.

"I gotta go," he said. A split-second later, he was heading for the exit.

I gave him a cheery wave. "Don't come back soon!" □
□

CHAPTER 44

That next day was Sunday. I had the next day off and was determined to make the most of it, especially with Lawton still out of town. When he returned Monday, I wanted to be all caught up on chores and ready to make up for lost time.

I spent most of that Sunday catching up on things I should've been doing all along – doing loads of laundry, creating a new flyer for Grandma's non-existent job, and spending some quality time with Chucky.

But no matter what my hands were doing, my brain seemed to be doing something else entirely. I still hadn't heard back from the Parkers, and I was trying not to panic.

As the hours dragged on with no answer and no return phone call, I couldn't help but consider the worst-case scenarios.

This was a slow-motion train wreck waiting to happen. Mrs. Parker had written me checks, and I'd written my own checks against those checks. It had never occurred to me that her checks wouldn't be good. The first few had cleared just fine.

Eventually my own checks would bounce, but not right away, only because my account had overdraft protection. Still, it wouldn't be cheap. It was tied to a scarily small line of credit with a scarily big interest rate. If I needed to tap into that line,

I'd have virtually no way to pay it back – unless, of course, I wanted to take Shaggy up on his sex tape offer.

And no way was that going to happen.

Still, I couldn't get it out of my head, and not only because of the ick factor. Lawton had seen Shaggy that night in the parking lot. He'd even yelled at Shaggy to stay away from me.

Assuming Shaggy's implication was true, shouldn't Lawton have warned me that Shaggy was the guy behind that original sex tape? When Lawton returned tomorrow, I'd definitely be asking about it.

Late that afternoon, I returned from walking Chucky to find a white van in the driveway and a strange man on the porch. The man wore some kind of brown uniform and carried a clipboard gripped loosely in his right hand.

When I approached the front entrance, with Chucky on his leash, the man turned to face me. He was a lean man about thirty years old and a serious demeanor. "Mrs. Parker?" he said.

I hesitated. "No. But I can give her a message if you'd like."

"I'm from the cable company," he said. "I'm here to disconnect the service."

"Excuse me?"

He cleared his throat. "For non-payment. Final notice should've come last week."

"We didn't receive any notice," I said.

He consulted his clipboard. "It must've went to your post office box. Third notice."

I didn't have access to the Parkers' post office box. In truth, I didn't realize they had one. But as someone who used a post office box myself, I didn't see anything all that unusual about it.

Of course, it did seem unusual that they wouldn't be asking me to retrieve their mail.

About the cable, I really didn't care. I didn't have time to watch anything, anyway. But the Parkers might care if they returned to find it out of service.

"This seems awful odd for a Sunday," I said.

"You're telling me," he said, not looking too happy about it.

"Can't it wait a few days?" I said. "See if I can't clear it up?"

"Sorry," he said. "I'm just the messenger. Of course, if you wanna give me a check, I'll take it back to the office, cancel the cancellation."

The dog food was one thing. The cable, now that was something else. No way was I paying for that. So a half hour later, I was officially without cable TV.

I wouldn't have cared, except for what it said about the Parkers. Were they having money trouble? Or was it just some weird fluke with their bank account?

Sitting in their house – some might call it a mansion – I couldn't help but notice all the luxury surrounding me. I'd been living in their home so many weeks now that I barely noticed. But when I looked at it with fresh eyes, it was pretty obvious that some serious money had gone into whatever look they were going for.

Even all those exotic plants of Mr. Parker's, they couldn't have been cheap. Their plant food wasn't, that's for sure. It arrived once a week by mail from some horticulture shop in San Francisco. In my old neighborhood, I knew kids who weren't treated half as well.

What if the Parkers were deadbeats? Would I be out all that money? To them, it might be a pittance, but to me, it was a fortune.

And then something worse hit me. What if they were dead, period? They were in a foreign country. Would I even hear about it if they were?"

As the day progressed to evening, I was having a hard time thinking about anything else.

When my cell phone rang just before midnight, I dove straight for it and answered without looking at the display. "Hello?"

"Hey," Lawton said.

"Oh," I said. "It's you."

There was a long pause. Then, he said, "Is this a bad time?"

"No. Not at all. Just waiting for a phone call."

Longer pause. "You need to go?"

"Nah, I have call-waiting."

"So…" Lawton's tone was carefully casual. "Who'd be calling you so late?"

"No one. It's just a business thing."

"You mean from the restaurant?"

"No. Something else."

"Anything you wanna talk about?"

Actually, it was the last thing I wanted to talk about. I'd been obsessing about it all day, and I was desperate to think about anything but that. Besides, Lawton didn't need to hear about my problems.

"Nah, it's nothing," I said, trying to push the worry out of my voice. "Are you still coming home tomorrow?"

"Yup. Tomorrow morning. You still have the day off?"

"Oh yeah."

We made plans to meet around noon. At my suggestion, we agreed that I'd swing by his house with Chucky, and then go for a walk. "For old time's sake," I said, thinking of how we'd first gotten to know each other in the first place.

"Don't forget new time's sake," he said. "And Chloe?"

"Yeah?"

"I've gotta tell you, I'm missing you like crazy. The other night–"

My phone beeped.

I pulled it from my ear and looked at the display. Mrs. Parker. Finally.

Lawton was still talking, but I didn't catch a single word of it. Desperate to get the incoming call, I cut him off. "I'm really sorry, Lawton, I've gotta go. See ya tomorrow, alright?"

Without waiting for a response, I disconnected him to switch over to the new call.

My voice was breathless as I said, "Hello? Mrs. Parker?"

And to my infinite relief, I heard her voice loud and clear. "Hey Chloe, I just got your messages."

CHAPTER 45

Well, at least she wasn't dead.

I'd already left most of the details in a long voicemail. But for some reason, I felt compelled to repeat them, trying hard to keep my tone neutral and use inoffensive words like "bank snafu" and "technical glitch" as opposed to more interesting words like "deadbeat," and "where's my damn money?"

I even told her about the cable guy and yesterday's disconnection.

When I finished, Mrs. Parker made a noise of sympathy and said, "Chloe, I am so sorry. I can only imagine what you must think of us."

Me? She should've heard what Grandma thought of them.

"Well," I said in a carefully neutral tone, "I didn't know what was going on, so I figured I should call and see if you knew anything."

"Oh yeah," she said with a little laugh. "Do I ever."

I waited.

"Okay, she said, "the good news is this. I just got off the phone with our financial manager, and he knows exactly what happened."

"What?" I asked.

"Long story, but if you think I'm embarrassed, you should talk to him. He's got this new assistant, wife's brother, if you can believe it. Anyway, this brother-in-law of his missed a whole series of bank transfers, including ours."

"What do you mean missed them?"

"He didn't make them. He went out to lunch or something, who knows?"

"Oh wow."

"Wow is right. But don't worry," she said. "The money should be there the day after tomorrow, or the day after that at the latest. I'm glad you called. Otherwise, it might've been days before we figured it out."

"Oh. That's good."

"And listen," she said. "I know this must've been a major inconvenience for you. And I feel just terrible. So does my husband. Tell you what. I'm going to send you a little bonus, not just for the bank fees, but to buy yourself something nice – like a day at the spa. And don't you dare say 'no.' "

I wasn't planning on it.

But I did thank her, trying hard to banish the lingering worry. In a couple days, this would all be over, right? And the way it sounded, I might actually come out ahead in the long run.

But somehow, until the money was actually there, it felt like a burden more than anything.

It wasn't until later that night that something struck me as kind of odd. During our whole conversation, she hadn't asked me one thing about Chucky.

At eight o'clock the next morning, the doorbell rang, sending Chucky into his usual spaz attack, barking and running up and down the stairs.

Since I worked nights, I almost never woke up before ten, mostly because it tended to majorly screw up my sleep schedule the next time I worked. But when I peeked out the guest room window and saw a sleek red sports car idling in the driveway, I felt myself smile.

I didn't recognize the vehicle, but considering Lawton's travel schedule, I had a pretty good guess who it belonged to. I dashed to the bathroom and gargled some mouthwash while I ran a quick brush through my hair.

Eager to catch him before he drove off, I snapped on Chucky's leash and answered the door in what I'd slept in – a thin yellow tank top and black silky shorts.

Except it wasn't Lawton.

It was some slick-looking guy in his mid-forties. He wore dark sunglasses, expensive looking slacks, and a designer sports coat.

His eyebrows furrowed. "Mrs. Parker?" he said.

My smile faded. I was getting a little tired of people calling me that.

Plus, I felt like a major dumb-ass. Whenever I thought it was Lawton at the door, it turned out to be someone else. And whenever I expected it to be someone else, it turned out to be Lawton.

If this kept up, I was going to develop a serious door-opening phobia.

Near my feet, Chucky had his tongue hanging out and his head cocked to the side. It was almost like he was also trying to figure out what some stranger was doing on our doorstep, particularly a stranger without doggie treats or bacon.

The man's gaze dipped to my attire, making me feel all the more stupid for answering without looking. But in my defense, my brain was still asleep, even if my body wasn't. The guy was lucky I hadn't answered the door in a ratty bathrobe.

"Did I come at a bad time?" he said.

Hell yes, it was a bad time. What kind of person showed

up on someone's doorstep unannounced at eight o'clock in the morning?

I pulled out my best upper-crust voice. "May I ask what this is about?"

"Well, quite honestly," he said, "I'm a little surprised you're still here."

I raised my eyebrows. "Pardon?"

"I was under the impression," he said, "that the house would be vacant."

"I'm sorry," I said in a distinctly unapologetic tone. "But why on Earth would you think that?"

"Because according to our agency, the lease ends tomorrow." He craned his neck as if trying to peer into the house.

Lease? So the Parkers didn't own the house? This had to be some kind of mistake. But all these so-called mistakes were adding up. And in spite of Mrs. Parker's assurances, I'd be incredibly naïve to believe this was all some weird coincidence.

Looking at the man, I had no idea what to say. So I said nothing.

"Did you decide to renew?" he asked.

Oh, screw it. "I wouldn't know," I said, "because I'm not Mrs. Parker."

"Oh." His brow wrinkled. "Is she home?"

"Not at the moment."

"How about Mr. Parker?"

"Nope."

He reached into the lapel of his coat and handed me a business card. I gave it a quick glance. It identified him as Chad Flemming of Executive Properties.

"Will you please have one of them call me the moment

they return?" he said.

"Oh, it'll be before that," I assured him with a smile that felt stiff enough to crack my face.

When that shiny red sports car disappeared down the road a couple minutes later, I tried to call Mrs. Parker again. Somehow, I was incredibly unsurprised when it went straight to voicemail.

CHAPTER 46

Distraught by this latest weirdness, it was impossible to fall back asleep. So instead, I spent the next few hours alternating between anger and worry. Something very wrong was going on here, and I had no idea what to do about it.

The more I thought about it, the more I decided that Mrs. Parker's explanation was a steaming pile of crap. It was pretty obvious that no money was coming, at least not in the near future, and I couldn't afford to support things on my own.

If this kept up, I'd be feeding Chucky out of my own money. Forget buying groceries for myself.

And Lawton was back in town. We were spending the day together. It was every girl's dream. My dream. But my house-sitting nightmare kept intruding.

A little before noon, I got dressed in casual clothes and grabbed Chucky's leash. With Chucky lunging ahead of me, I trudged to Lawton's house feeling so weighed down, I could hardly move.

If I were someone like Brittney, I'd probably just ask Lawton for some money and be done with it. To be all nicey-nice about it, we'd probably call it a loan. But we'd both knew the truth.

And then, what exactly would he be paying me for? Sex? Companionship? Obviously, he could get all of that for free.

But I didn't want to be one of those girls, a dependent, a hanger-on, a groupie. I wanted to be something different.

When I reached Lawton's front door, I rang the bell and waited. Chucky was already going berserk, straining at his leash and pawing at the door like he couldn't wait another minute to get inside. I knew the feeling.

Although I'd never want to burden Lawton with my troubles, the thought of feeling his strong arms around me was almost enough to keep me going.

But when a minute went by, and he still hadn't answered the door, I looked around, feeling awkward as hell. It was such a contrast from that one night, when he'd answered before I'd even touched the bell. Had the newness worn off? So soon?

I gave it another minute, and then reluctantly rang the bell again. A couple minutes later, Lawton finally answered. But instead of a face filled with anticipation, what I saw was so different and foreign, that I took a small step backward.

Oblivious to Lawton's demeanor, Chucky bounded forward. Whining and yipping for attention, he pawed at Lawton legs. With a half-smile, Lawton crouched down to ruffle Chucky's fur.

"Hey Buddy," he said. "I know what you want." Standing, he reached into the pocket of his jeans and pulled out a silvery bag. He shook it at Chucky, who went absolutely nuts. With a low chuckle, Lawton pulled out a handful of treats and let Chucky devour them down to his heart's content.

And then, as he crouched down with Chucky, he looked up. Our eyes met.

"I'm glad you're here." he said.

Funny, he didn't sound glad. And he didn't look glad either.

"Is something wrong?" I said.

He stood and brushed Chucky's crumbs off his jeans. "Nope."

I waited for him to elaborate. He didn't.

I glanced back toward the street. "Still up for a walk?" I looked around. "Or maybe you wanna do it another day?" I tried to sound like this was no big deal, even though the thought of trudging away alone was almost more than I could bear. "I mean, if this is a bad time for you—"

"It's not. Wanna come in?"

In spite of his words, the tension was radiating off him in waves. As for me, I'd been tense long before I'd even touched that doorbell. I looked down and spotted Chucky quivering with excitement. The way it looked, we all had some energy to work off.

"I'd like to come in," I said. "But do you care if we walk first?"

"Nope." Lawton held out his hand, palm up.

I looked down. My eyebrows furrowed.

Lawton broke the silence. "Leash?" His mouth tightened. "Unless you want to take him."

"Oh," I stammered. "Sorry." I placed the leash in his open palm. Our fingers touched. His hand was warm and solid, but oddly unresponsive.

It was a brisk fall day with leaves skittering around our feet. By unspoken agreement, we headed out on the usual route.

"So," he said, "you got your call last night, huh?"

"What call?"

"Never mind," he said. "Forget it."

"Oh," I said as realization dawned. "You mean that business call?"

"Yeah," he said in a cold, flat voice. "The business call."

I glanced at his profile. There it was again, that studiously neutral expression.

"You don't believe me?" I said.

"I never said that."

"But you're not saying you do, either."

He shrugged. "What do you want me to say?"

I was so not in the mood for this. "I don't want you to say anything," I said. "Not if you're gonna be like that."

"Alright. If that's what you want." And then, true to his word, he didn't say a single word for the next two blocks.

I gave him a sideways glance. This was so not how I imagined today going. Between the visit from that property manager and Lawton's odd demeanor, this whole day was feeling like a bad dream.

Maybe it was a bad dream. If I was lucky, I was still in bed. Maybe I'd wake up to find money from the Parkers and Lawton back to his normal self.

Then again, Lawton was anything but normal no matter what kind of mood he was in. And it wasn't just his amazing body or movie-star face. It was that lethal dose of unbridled energy and raw power. It should've made me run. Not to him. From him.

Today, that energy felt nearly explosive, like too much heat was confined in too little space. I'd seen him fight. I'd slept with him, loved him, laughed with him, and yeah, more than once, cried over him.

But the energy falling off him now, I couldn't place. Obviously the late-night phone call had set him off. I tried to see it from his point of view. The call was late, sudden, and unexplained. If I were being honest, I had to admit, I might feel the same way.

I softened my voice and tried a new approach. "You're mad about that call last night, aren't you?"

He shrugged.

"Okay." I blew out a breath. "You know I'm just staying in that house, right?"

He nodded.

"Well, that call last night. It was from the home-owner, just some financial thing that couldn't wait."

"At midnight," he said, more a statement than a question.

"It wasn't quite midnight," I said, trying to keep my tone light.

"Uh-huh. And how about this morning?"

"What about this morning?"

"Forget it."

Ahead of us, Chucky was straining at the leash. I spotted a chipmunk darting across a brick walkway. Chucky went berserk, trying to reach it for about five seconds, until he spotted a big gray housecat lounging on the other side of the street.

Chucky lunged toward the cat with all his tiny might, straining at his leash and barking his fool head off. The cat looked oddly unconcerned.

I raised my gaze to Lawton and caught him looking in my direction. Still walking, I gave him a smile, the secret one we always shared when Chucky spazzed out.

Except this time, Lawton didn't return the smile.

And then, something else caught his attention. His gaze left my face, and his expression darkened. I turned and saw exactly what had caught his attention.

In the Parkers' driveway sat a slick black Mercedes.

Up ahead, on the Parkers' porch was an unfamiliar man in a flashy business suit. I wasn't expecting anyone. Then again, I hadn't been expecting a lot of people who'd been showing up lately.□

□

CHAPTER 47

I glanced at Lawton. His face was stony, but he said nothing. Chucky, meanwhile, had given up on the cat and was straining toward a group of elderly power-walkers coming toward us.

I glanced back to the porch. In one hand, the man held a briefcase. In the other, he held a large manila envelope.

I turned to Lawton and said, "I'll be right back."

Before he could respond, I dashed ahead, jogging down the Parkers' long driveway and hurrying up to the house.

The stranger, an overly tanned man with poufy blonde hair, stood legs apart, hands on his hips. He lifted a wrist to study his watch. It looked like a Rolex.

"Can I help you?" I said.

Slowly, he turned to face me. "Chloe Malinski?"

"Yes?"

"I assume you have I.D.?"

I froze. When someone comes to your door and demands I.D., it was never a good thing, especially when they looked like a parody of some celebrity lawyer.

"Do you have I.D.?" I said.

His gaze narrowed. "Are you the house-sitter or not?"

I glanced at Lawton, suddenly wishing I'd asked him to come with me. Something was definitely off with this guy.

The guy followed my gaze. He spotted Lawton, who was watching us with an expression I could only describe as hostile.

The man cleared this throat. "Sorry," he said, "it's been a hell of a week."

"You have no idea," I said.

"Anyway," the man said with another quick glance toward Lawton, "the Parkers sent me."

"Why?"

"Because I've got your money, and I'm supposed to deliver it."

"What money?" I said.

The man looked at me like I was a world-class moron. "Bounced checks, bank problems, any of this ringing a bell?"

"Of course it's ringing a bell," I said, "but I wasn't expecting someone to show up here in person."

"Yeah? I wasn't expecting to be running my ass all over town today, but here I am. So I guess we're both surprised now, aren't we?"

"By any chance," I said, "are you the brother-in-law?"

His gaze narrowed. "What's that supposed to mean?"

"Never mind," I said.

"Yeah? Well, don't believe everything you hear," the guy said. "I did everything I was supposed to. It's not my fault if it got all messed up."

"Of course," I said.

"So like I said, I've got your money." He gave me a deadpan look. "But obviously, I can't just fling it at whoever comes up the driveway claiming to be the house-sitter. I need to see some I.D. Got it?"

Grudgingly, I reached into the back pocket of my jeans and pulled out my slim travel wallet. I retrieved my driver's license and handed it over.

He gave it barely a glance before handing it back. Then, he pulled the envelope from under his arm, undid the clasp, and reached inside to remove a small sheet of paper.

That done, he held out the envelope toward me. "Your money," he said.

I took the envelope and peered inside. I saw a neat stack of bills. I was thrilled to get it, but utterly confused by the method. "Cash?" I said.

"Yeah. The Parkers were pretty ticked. They figured you wouldn't trust a check. By the way, this covers the next month's expenses too, so don't be trying to cash any of those old checks."

"Should I count it, or—"

"Yeah, and I've got to watch, because if any of it goes missing, I'm not getting the blame this time. Besides, you've gotta sign a receipt." He glanced toward the front door. "Wanna invite me inside?"

"Not particularly," I said.

"Suit yourself," he said, "but that's a big wad of money to be counting out here in the open."

"Yeah, well I'm not exactly alone," I said with a quick glance toward the street, where Lawton still watched with an ever-darkening expression. Obviously, this was taking way too long.

I pulled out the money and started counting, adding as I went. Mentally, I compared the amount of cash to the total of all those bad checks.

When I was done counting, I felt myself smile. It covered everything – the checks, the overdraft fees, and, as Mrs. Parker had promised, a nice bonus. I wouldn't be splurging on a spa treatment, but a new car battery was definitely in my future.

I felt like a huge weight had lifted from my shoulders. And to be honest, I felt more than a little guilty for not giving the Parkers the benefit of the doubt.

"By any chance," I said, "do you know anything about their lease?"

"Yeah, that got all screwed up too," he said. "That'll be my next stop. Lucky me."

I pulled the money from the envelope, rolled it up, and stuffed it in the front pocket of my jeans. Still smiling, I handed him back the empty envelope. "Got a pen?" I said.

He pulled a shiny gold pen from his lapel pocket. He handed it over along with the receipt. I checked the amount, signed on the dotted line, and then handed it back.

With raised eyebrows, the man glanced down at my front pocket. "You really planning to walk around with that?" he said. "Seems to me, you'd want to put it inside. Someplace safe and all."

I couldn't help it. I laughed. I pointed toward the street. "See that guy out there?"

The man looked and then gave a short nod.

"That's my bodyguard." I patted my pocket. "I think I'll be fine."

"Yeah. But who's gonna guard you from him?"

"Well, there is the dog," I said.

In unison, we turned to look. Chucky was flopped over Lawton's shoes, staring up at the clouds.

"Um, yeah. Good luck with that," the man said, turning to walk back to his car. A moment later, he got inside and drove off.

I shoved the cash deeper into my pocket and jogged back to where Lawton waited, his posture stiff and his expression stony.

"Sorry about that," I said.

Lawton didn't respond. He was still looking toward the house. His gaze narrowed.

"Ready to finish our walk?" I said.

"First," he said, turning to face me. "Tell me something. What's the money for?"

CHAPTER 48

I looked up at him, taking in his tight jaw and hard eyes. I looked down at Chucky. He was still flopped on Lawton's feet like all that spazzing had worn him completely out.

Perfect. Just when I could use a good distraction, Chucky decides to roll over. Didn't he have a squirrel to chase or something?

Then again, I shouldn't need a distraction. It's not like I'd done a damn thing wrong.

The mental whiplash was making me crazy. First, I was mad at the Parkers and happy to see Lawton. Now, I was fine with the Parkers, and unhappy with whatever Lawton's problem was.

Did I ask him about his financial arrangements? No. Not even once. Even though his stuff had to be a whole lot more interesting than mine.

I lifted my chin. "I don't really like the tone of your question," I said.

"Alright," he said. "Then how about this one? Who do you live with?"

"What?"

"It's a simple question, Chloe."

"I already told you, I don't live with anyone."

He pointed toward the Parkers'. "So that's your house."

"No," I said in a tone far more patient than I felt. "And I've already told you that."

"Uh-huh." He moved his hand in a forward motion. "Go on."

"With what?" I said.

"Your explanation."

"What's gotten into you?" I said. "It's a job. That's what the money's for. There. You happy?"

His expression didn't change. I looked to the sidewalk. Chucky looked up at me as if he was also were waiting for some sort of explanation. Or maybe he just wanted a treat. That made two of us.

I threw up my hands. "What do you want me to say? That this house is beyond my price range?" I felt my face grow warm. "Well, obviously it is. Is that what you wanted to hear?"

Erika's words echoed in my brain. Was she right? Was I ashamed of being a paid interloper?

Growing up, I'd been a poor kid in a rich district. But it had never held me back. I still had friends. I got good grades. It was totally fine.

So what if I never hosted sleep-overs or went on field trips? And so what if my clothes were shabby and I had to cut my own hair? I didn't care, and neither should Lawton. It's not like he'd been born with a silver spoon in his mouth.

"All I want to hear," he said, "is the truth."

I reached up to rub the back of my neck. Everything was getting all jumbled. If this conversation kept going, we'd both end up saying something we'd regret. I didn't want that to happen. And if it did end up happening, I sure as hell didn't want that happening on the sidewalk in front of the house.

"Can we talk about this somewhere else?" I said.

"If that's what you want," he said, turning away from me.

As if sensing the movement, Chucky jumped up and bounded forward, ready to torment the next squirrel or mail truck or whatever.

Lawton started walking, and so did I. We walked in silence, step after step, passing house after house. Of course, calling them houses was a vast understatement. They were houses in the same way that Erika's first Porsche had been just a car.

Silently, I sorted through my thoughts, trying to decide who I hated more, Lawton or myself – him for the unexpected attitude or me for not understanding why he was so mad.

Up ahead, I spotted his estate. It was our starting point and our final destination. I gave Lawton a sideways glance. His jaw was tight and his gaze remained straight ahead. The hand that held Chucky's leash was fisted so tight, it was practically a death grip.

Too soon, we were at his front door. He opened it up, but made no move to go inside. Supposedly, we were spending the day together. But somehow, I didn't see that happening.

He turned toward me and held out the leash. Silently, I took it. Our gazes met. What he saw in mine, I had no idea, but his own eyes were so cold that I stifled a shiver.

Apparently, the script called for me to slink away, dismissed like some gardener who had accidentally uprooted the begonias.

Screw that.

I put my hands on my hips. "Lawton," I said, "what the hell is your problem?"

"My problem?"

Suddenly, I felt a tug on my hand. A split second later, Chucky bolted past Lawton and into the house. I spotted the tail end of the leash, dragging along the tile floor as Chucky disappeared from sight.

"Chucky!" I yelled. "Damn it."

In front of me, Lawton didn't budge, and he didn't turn around. He was focused on me.

"Wanna know what my problem is?" he said. "Alright, here it is. When I think of someone else holding you, touching you –" his voice caught. "– being with you in the ways I'm with you, it makes me want to tear their fuckin' throat out."

CHAPTER 49

I stared up at him. "What someone? Who the hell are you talking about?"

"You tell me."

"I can't," I said. "Because he doesn't exist."

"Alright. Then who was that guy?"

"Which one?"

He shrugged.

I stared at him in disbelief. "You mean the guy on the porch?"

"That'd be a good start," he said.

"You've got to be kidding me. That guy? You seriously think he's my boyfriend or something?"

He shook his head. "That's not what I said."

"Then what are you saying?"

"I'm saying that I don't get it."

"Get what?"

"Alright," he said. "I'll spell it out. I don't get why some guy in a fancy car would be showing up on your doorstep and handing you a pile of cash. I don't get who you live with, or why you've never asked me inside."

His voice rose. "I don't get why you're getting 'business' calls at midnight on a Sunday night or why I'd happen to drive by early this morning and see some guy in a sports car leaving your house."

I wanted to shrink back, surprised by the simmering rage brought to the surface. Instead, I took a step forward and glared up at him. "You're twisting everything around, making it sound worse than it is."

"Is that so?" He crossed his arms and waited. "Then go ahead. Tell me how you'd say it."

"I already told you." I gestured vaguely toward the Parkers' house. "I get paid to stay there. What don't you get?"

I threw up my hands. "Yeah. I do it for money. Big fucking deal. And the reason I didn't tell you right from the start is because that's part of the deal. I'm supposed to look like I actually belong here."

In front of me, Lawton was a mass of coiled muscles and stony features. He said nothing, and I kept on going.

"Yeah." I made a scoffing sound. "I've got the dog, I've got the plants. Hell, I've even got some stupid lawn guy coming once a week to trim shit that doesn't need trimming." My voice cracked. "But it's all about the money, because I don't have any of my own."

I looked down at my pocket, bulging with cash mostly already spent. Here, I'd been so happy to get it, and for what? For a new car battery and a whole lot of grief from someone richer than God?

I swallowed a sob. "I'm broke. There, you happy?"

His eyebrows furrowed. "What?"

"Yeah. You want the whole story? Well, here it is. I've got a Grandma who gets all her rent money from this fake job I had to make up. I've got a kid brother who thinks our mom gives some sort of a crap, even though she doesn't. I've got student loans from a degree that as far as I can tell, probably cost me a lot more than the damn thing's worth."

My voice rose. "And now, I've got you ragging on me like I'm some kind of horrible person."

His eyes softened. "Chloe—"

"Don't 'Chloe' me," I said. "What the hell? Have you been rich so long that you've forgotten what it's like to live in the real world?"

He took as step toward me. "Chloe, you need money? I mean, shit, why didn't you say something?"

He reached a hand toward his back pocket. An image flashed in my brain, the memory of Brittney plucking cash from his outstretched hand.

I wasn't a Brittney. I lifted my chin. "I don't want your charity. As you so aptly observed, I just got paid. So I'm practically rich, right?"

"But you just said—"

"I know what I said. Quit rubbing my nose in it, alright?"

His eyebrows furrowed. "But what about your waitressing job?"

"What about it?"

"So you do that for the money too, not–?"

"For the ego trip?" I gave a bark of laughter. "You ever work as a waitress? It's fucking hard work. I take shit all night long from people who act like they're better than me just because they're sitting down, and I'm standing up. I dress like some bimbo and act like I'm stupid, for God's sake."

I tugged at a strand of my hair. "You know how many times I've got to wash this to get the hairspray out? You think I'm doing this for some sort of ego trip." I made a sound of disgust. "That's rich."

I glanced around the neighborhood. "At least with this job, I get to dress how I want. And I get to live in a nice place where people treat me half-way decent."

His voice was very quiet. "And that's good enough for you?"

"It's gotta be. I've just got to keep doing what I'm doing, that's all."

"But Chloe," he said, "you don't need to. Not anymore."

"Oh yeah? Why not?"

"You just don't."

The way he was looking at me, I'd seen it before. Too many times, in fact. I'd seen it on the faces of the rich girls in my class who went to Disney every winter. I'd seen it on the faces of my friends' parents when they offered me rides to places I couldn't afford.

It was that awful combination of surprise and pity. And I knew exactly what came next.

Lawton pushed a hand through his hair. "So, you want a loan or something? I mean, if you won't take money –" He blew out a breath. "All I'm saying is, you don't have to do this. Don't go back there, alright?"

I thought of my other options. My mom's shitty apartment? Yeah, because I just loved to listen to her and some random loser screw like monkeys in the apartment's only bedroom while I covered my head with a couch pillow.

Or how about my Dad's house? The place had four bedrooms, but none I was welcome in. Loretta had hated me from day one. She still hated me. And my Dad was a giant, pussy-whipped bastard who'd rather see his daughter sleep in the basement than make a ripple with his psycho second wife.

Or what about my own place? Oh, that's right. I couldn't afford one.

I felt something warm encircle my body. Lawton's arms. He was holding me tight against his chest. "Baby, don't cry," he said. "I'm sorry. We'll work it out. You can move in with me, alright?"

I heard a sob. Oh, God, it was coming from me. I was crying. I almost never cried, and now, it seemed like I was crying all the time.

And I couldn't help it. I leaned into him, soaking up his strength and the soothing sounds he made in my ear.

We stood like that for what seemed like a long time until my tears were spent and his shirt was soggy. And yet, I couldn't seem to make myself move.

Even through the soft cotton fabric, his chest was rock-hard against my cheek. I felt the muscles in his arms and the tightness of his stomach. It felt like a slice of heaven wrapped up in a perfect package, delivered just to make my life complete.

Erika was right. I should've been honest with him all along. Well maybe not all along, but certainly after we'd become intimate. I vowed that as soon as I got the chance, I'd call her and tell her how right she was.

"I've been such an idiot," I said. "I should've told you sooner." I gave a little laugh. "Like it's such a big deal, right?"

His body stiffened, as if the memory of our argument – correction, multiple arguments – were something he'd rather forget. And then, he clutched me tighter.

"Baby, I don't want you to do this with anyone else. Not ever."

I smiled through the tears. "Yeah?"

I felt him nod. "I mean it. Move in with me. Right now, today. This'll be our home. Together, alright?"

I clung to him, soaking up his strength and the unexpected offer. A real home. I couldn't even imagine. Then again, I guess I could. When I was with Lawton, I didn't feel like some sort of interloper. I felt like I belonged.

It had nothing to do with the size of his house or the opulence surrounding us. It had to do with him. Just him. We clicked in ways that had nothing to do with fame, fortune, or heart-stopping good looks.

It was a tempting offer, and would solve so many of my problems. But part of me was still old-fashioned. Moving in wasn't exactly the offer of my dreams, even if it was pretty spectacular.

Still, I felt myself smile against his chest. "I'll think about it," I said.

"Don't think. Just do it." And then, he pulled away. He looked down at me an expression bordering on desperation.

"You don't want to take money from me," he said. "I get that. And I respect the hell out of that, honest. But baby, please. Come on. Stay with me. Or shit, I'll buy you a house of your own if that's what you want. Just no more other guys anymore, alright?"

I felt my eyebrows furrow. "What do you mean?"

"I mean," he said, "I love you."

"I love you too."

He reached out, gathering me into his arms once again. I felt his grip tighten and heard his voice, a low whisper in my ear. "You don't have to sell yourself anymore. From now on, let me take care of you, alright?"

Slowly, his words sank into my brain. I felt myself stiffen. I pulled back and gave him a hard look. "Sell myself?" I said.

☐ ☐

CHAPTER 50

He leaned close, trying once again to pull me into his arms. I pushed away and looked up at him. "Just what are you implying?" I said.

"Baby," he said. "I don't want to judge you. I mean, the things I've done for money–" He blew out a breath. "In a way, I guess I sold my body too, right?"

Slowly the pieces started to click. And once they did, they clicked so hard and so fast that I had a hard time staying upright. "Oh my God," I said, stepping away from him.

"Hey," he said, his voice filled with sympathy. "Like I said, I don't wanna judge you for doing what you had to do, but—" He shook his head. "It stops now, alright? You've gotta promise me."

I closed my eyes, feeling all the color drain from my face. When I opened them again, he was staring at me with a look of such pity, I wanted to slap that look right off his face, and then kick him in the balls for good measure.

"Let me get this straight," I said. As I stared up at him, my body trembled, and my voice rose. "You think—" I felt myself swallow. "You think I'm some kind of hooker?"

"Chloe." His voice was soft. "I didn't call it that."

"But that's what you think?" I stumbled backwards. Breathing hard, I pushed my hands through my hair. It was official. This day was a nightmare.

"Baby," he said. "What is it? You okay?"

I glared up at him. "Okay?" I shook my head. "Nope. Definitely not okay here."

I cupped my hands around my mouth and hollered toward the interior of the house. "Chucky! C'mon! We're leaving!"

"What?" He reached for my hand. "Why?"

I slapped the hand away. "Don't touch me."

"Why not?"

"Because, you idiot, I'm not a hooker." I spoke very slowly and clearly, enunciating every word. "I'm a house-sitter!"

His jaw dropped. "What?"

"Oh yeah." When I tried to laugh, it came out half-crazed. "Big difference there, huh?" I turned away and shouted out again, "Chucky, where are you?"

With muttered curses, I stalked toward the kitchen. I felt a hand on my elbow. I shook it off and whirled to face him. "I already told you, stay away from me!"

Lawton stared at me with a pained expression. "So those guys—"

"Who?" I said. "The property manager who stopped by this morning?"

He swallowed. "Property manager?"

"Or maybe," I said, "you meant the financial guy?"

"Financial guy?"

"Yeah. The guy on the porch." I gave Lawton a cold smile. "And just so you know, when I say financial guy, I mean someone who manages the home-owner's accounts, not for example, some fucking pimp!"

As I spoke, Lawton's face grew paler and paler, until he looked white as death.

"And the call last night?" he said.

"It was just what I said. And in case you're wondering, she's a woman. And she called me last night because their accounts are all screwed up, which, in case it hasn't escaped your attention, is a whole lot different than screwing for money!"

His brow furrowed. "So she's the home-owner?"

"Renter, owner, hell, at this point, I have no idea. But she definitely lives there." I crossed my arms. "Except, I guess, when she's off in Costa Rica with her husband."

Lawton shook his head. "But the guy who lives in that house, he's not married."

"Oh yeah? How do you know?"

"Bishop told me."

"Yeah? Well, maybe he's wrong."

"No. He's never wrong."

I gave him an icy smile. "Then maybe you should ask Bishop whether or not I'm hooker. I mean, he knows everything, right?" I threw up my arms. "Why am I even discussing this with you?" I turned to call over my shoulder. "Chucky!"

Lawton reached out for me. "Baby, c'mon, don't go. Not like this."

I slapped his arms aside. "Look, let me make this really clear. Whatever we had, it's over."

He shook his head. "Don't say that. C'mon. I'm sorry, alright?"

"No," I said. "It's not alright. What is it with you? Why do always assume the worst about me?"

"I don't."

"You do." I turned and stalked through the house, looking for Chucky, and beyond eager to leave.

"C'mon, Chloe." Lawton's voice broke. "Don't go like

this."

I whirled to face him. "You've got to promise me something."

"Anything," he said.

"Don't call me. Don't talk to me. Don't–"

"Baby, c'mon—"

"Don't write me. Don't email me. Don't text me. And, if you see me on the street, don't fucking wave to me." I choked down a sob. "Just leave me alone, alright?"

He reached out, trying to gather me in his arms. Again, I slapped his hands aside. "What part of leave me alone don't you understand?"

"But Baby, you're upset."

"Of course I'm upset! My boyfriend—" I raised my hand. "No. Make that my ex-boyfriend, thinks I'm a damn hooker!"

"Chloe, c'mon, don't say that. That's not the way I thought of it."

"Yeah, right," I said, taking a deep breath and wiping my eyes with the back of my hand. "Now, promise me."

"To leave you alone?" His lips parted, and his eyes were glassy. "I can't."

"If you ever loved me," I said, "you can."

"Don't ask me to," he said. "Beat me, yell at me, whatever, but don't make me do this. Please."

I made a scoffing sound. "Look," I said, "All the time I've known you, I've never asked you for one fucking thing. And I know damn well that other girls have. So now, this is it, the first thing I've ever asked, and you can't even say 'yes'."

"Baby—"

"Promise me. I mean it."

I needed a promise, because there was one thing I'd learned the hard way. The guy was impossible to resist, and I was too tired to try.

"And if I do promise you?" he said. "What then?"

I looked away. "I don't know."

His voice was ragged. "Are you saying there's a chance?"

"Yeah," I said. "Slim to none."

"I am so fucking sorry," he said.

"You already said that."

Just then, Chucky skidded around the corner, one of Lawton's socks dangling from his teeth.

For Chucky's sake, I tried to keep my voice calm. "C'mon Chucky, time to go."

Lawton's voice was just a whisper. "Don't go. Please?"

I gave him a deadpan look. "Where's my promise?"

"I can't."

"Alright, fine. Whatever. I guess it's all about you, huh? Heaven forbid you do anything you don't want to."

He was silent, and so was I. Chucky looked from me to Lawton and back again.

The seconds stretched, and then Lawton spoke as if the words were torn from his throat along with his heart. "Okay."

"Say it," I said.

"I promise."

I gave him a slow nod, and turned toward the door.

"Wait," he said.

I turned around.

"I'm not giving up," he said.

"Well so much for your promises," I said. "What'd that last? Two seconds?"

"I'll keep it," he said, "even if it kills me."

"I mean it," I said. "Even if you see me in the supermarket, just keep on going. Alright?"

Instantly, it struck me as an incredibly stupid thing to say.

Did billionaires even visit supermarkets? Whatever. As long as he got the point, right?

Slowly, he nodded. But then he spoke, a strangled whisper in the quiet room. "You call me. I'll be waiting."

"Then you'll be waiting a long time," I said.

"I don't care," he said. "Call me anytime. Day, night, middle of the night. I don't care. Just call me. Okay?

"Don't count on it," I said. And then, with Chucky in my arms, I headed toward the front door, opened it up, and walked out. When I hit the front walkway, I set Chucky down. He plopped down on the walkway and refused to budge.

"Damn it," I muttered and scooped him up. He wriggled the whole time I walked toward iron gate, still open from when we'd arrived. The short walk seemed to take forever. But when the gate was finally behind me, I stopped and turned around. Chucky gave a long, plaintive whine.

Lawton stood, framed in his doorway, looking out at me with an expression of such anguish that the lump in my throat grew to epic proportions. I choked it down and turned away, hugging Chucky close as I made my way along the smooth sidewalk.

"Time to go home," I said.

Of course, the home might be Chucky's, but it wasn't mine, because, let's face it, I didn't have one.

CHAPTER 51

Work, sleep, mope, walk Chucky – the days dragged on with very little change.

At work, Brittney finished all the required training and went out on her own. She was still rude and barely competent, but at least she wasn't my problem anymore. True, I saw her more often than I liked, but she barely spoke to me, and I was happy to return the favor.

Slowly, but surely, those with the flu were returning back to work. I kept waiting for the axe to fall, but somehow it never did.

Instead, I kept getting the worst shifts on the worst nights. I was the first to get sent home and the last to be called in when someone else was sick. I should've cared, but somehow, I couldn't make myself give it more than a passing thought.

Slowly, but surely, I was sinking deeper into a financial hole. But I'd been sinking so long that I was almost used to it. So I did what I always did. I sent out resumes, went on interviews, and curbed any expense I could think of.

At the Parkers, I worked hard to keep myself busy, cleaning, organizing, and consoling Chucky as best I could. For both our sakes, I'd started walking him along a different route, avoiding Lawton's place like the plague it had become.

To my surprise and relief, he kept his promise. I missed

him. I thought about him every day. I longed to feel his arms around me and hear his voice in my ear. But wanting him so bad that it made my heart ache didn't mean I should go back to him.

I was on my third week of moping when the sound of the doorbell woke me from a nap on the couch. With weary resignation, I dragged myself up and stumbled, still half asleep, to the door and peered out the peephole.

Who I saw there didn't make me happy. I opened the door and glared at him. "What do you want?"

If Bishop was surprised by my rudeness, he gave no indication. "Got a minute?"

"No."

"That's too bad," he said. "Because I came to apologize."

When I didn't respond, he added, "From what I hear, girls like that sort of thing."

I narrowed my gaze. "Is this some kind of trick?"

"No trick," he said. "I'm assuming you're not gonna invite me in?"

"Got that right."

"Figured as much. Wanna talk outside?"

"Not particularly," I said.

"But you will anyway."

"What makes you say that?"

"Because you're curious what I'll say." He flicked his head toward the interior of the house. "Go ahead, grab a coat. I'll wait here."

"Yeah, you do that," I said, slamming the door in his face.

I stalked back to the couch and threw myself down on it, determined to go back to sleep. Whatever he was planning to say, I didn't want to hear it. What would he say, anyway? Was he really going to apologize? And if so, for what, specifically?

I closed my eyes and tried to drift. That lasted less than five minutes. It was no use. I was curious. "Damn it," I muttered and got up to retrieve my coat.

I went outside, slamming the front door behind me.

He was still there.

"You got five minutes," I told him.

"Alright," he said. "But just so you know, I'm going to save the actual apology for the end, so you don't run off before."

"Fine. As long as you're within five minutes." I made a show of looking at my wrist.

Bishop glanced down at my empty wrist. "That only works if you're wearing a watch."

"Not if you got the message."

"Fair enough." He glanced past me to the Parkers' front door. "A while back, I went into that house when you weren't home."

I made my eyes obnoxiously wide. "You did? I had no idea." I put a finger to my chin. "Gee, did you do anything else, by any chance?"

"I went through your purse. I checked out your license." He shrugged. "Gave the dog a few snacks. He seemed to like the bacon ones best."

"Is there an apology coming any time soon?" I asked.

"Alright. I shouldn't have done it. And I apologize."

"So," I said, "Lawton told you that I knew about that, huh?"

"Yup."

"Let me ask you something. If I had never found out, would you still be apologizing?"

"Nope."

"And why is that?

"Because I'm not stupid."

"You really are a dick, you know that, right?"

"Hey, have I ever denied it?"

"No. But I kind of wish you would. You really know how to take the fun out of it."

"I'll keep that in mind."

I narrowed my gaze. "Did Lawton make you do this? Because it seems to me, you're a little late to the whole apology parade."

"No. And he doesn't know I'm here."

"So why are you?"

"Because he loves you, and I don't want to be the one standing in the way of that."

"Don't worry," I said. "It's not you. For starters, he thinks I'm a damn hooker."

Bishop grinned. "I think you set him straight on that."

"Oh, shut up." I crossed my arms. "So, tell me, why'd you do it? Why'd you go through my things?"

"You got a younger brother, right?"

I nodded.

"Let me ask you something. What would you do to protect him?"

I didn't even bother lying. "Just about anything," I said.

"Well, there you go."

"But he didn't need protection from me," I said.

Bishop only shrugged.

"How'd you get in here, anyway," I said.

"Now that, I'm not gonna answer."

"Why not?"

"Trade secret," he said.

"Oh for crying out loud. Fine, let me ask you something else. Those guys who attacked me, what happened with that? Why wouldn't they report you to the police?"

"Because they know better."

"And why would you do that, anyway?"

"Do what?"

"Oh for crying out loud. You undressed them. You –"

"Technically," Bishop said, "they undressed themselves."

I gave Bishop a dubious look. "Willingly?"

"Sort of."

"Uh-huh," I said. "So then, you shove them in a trunk and drop them off in a public place. And the way it sounds, you threaten them on top of it."

"Is that a complaint?" Bishop said. "You think we should've let it go? Pretend it didn't happen?"

"I don't know what I think," I said.

"Want my take on it?"

"Not really."

"I'll take that as a yes," he said. "Whether you admit it or not, you're glad we did it. For what they did, they deserved it. So we gave it to 'em. But now that it's all done, and some time has passed, you want the luxury of feeling bad about it."

"I don't feel bad for them," I said.

"You're right. You don't. Not deep down. But it makes you feel good to think you do."

"You're so full of it," I said.

"Hey, I'm not complaining," he said. "It's the way it works. Some people, they do the things that need doing. And others, they get to sit back, nice and safe, with clean hands and a cleaner conscience." He shrugged. "I'm alright with that. And so is Lawton."

"But you beat the hell out of them," I said.

"No," he said. "Lawton beat the hell out of 'em. And you know damn well he could've hurt 'em a hell of a lot worse."

"Maybe he didn't need to hurt them at all," I said. "I mean, you guys embarrassed the crap out of them. Wasn't that enough?"

"Lemme put it this way. You're the girl he loves. Those guys? They scared you. They hurt you. You remember that night, right?"

I nodded, swallowing the fear and desperation I'd felt at the time.

"Yeah," Bishop said as if reading my mind. "There was two of them and one of you." Slowly, he shook his head. "Lawton couldn't let that go. And if you don't get that, maybe you don't know him as well as you think."

I heard myself ask, "How's he doing?" Probably, I shouldn't care. But I did care. I cared so damn much, I could hardly stand it.

Bishop shook his head. "Not good. But you didn't hear it from me."

I didn't know what to say to that, so I said nothing except a brief goodbye and headed back inside, closing the door behind me.

Inside the house, I sat on the couch for the longest time. Maybe Bishop was right. Maybe I didn't know Lawton at all. Or maybe I did, and I just didn't want to face it.

Either way, I wouldn't figure it out today. I trudged upstairs and got ready for work.

CHAPTER 52

"Guess what?" Josh said.

From the look on his face, it was obviously good news. "You got all A's again?"

"No." He gave me an aw-shucks smile. "Yeah, well, I did. But this is even better."

I gave Grandma a sideways glance. She hadn't said one word about the so-called good news since I'd arrived. Her lips were pursed as she crammed another flyer into its envelope.

The flyer – an advertisement for some fictional cat-training video – showed two fluff-ball kittens surrounded by loose yarn and shredded bed pillows.

"This is bullshit," Grandma said as she folded another flyer and crammed it, hard, into its envelope. "Everyone knows you can't train a cat. Whoever did this flyer is a dipshit."

As the dipshit designer – even if Grandma wasn't aware of this fact – I felt compelled to disagree. "Sure you can." I pointed to the promotional text. "Nine out of ten vets agree. See?"

Grandma gave a dismissive snort. "Then they're dipshits, too."

"Vets are never dipshits," I said.

"Yeah? Then the company's full of shit. Probably made the whole thing up. Bet they wouldn't know a real cat if it bit 'em

273

on the face." She frowned. "In fact, I wish a cat would bite 'em on the face. Would serve 'em right."

Without thinking, I reached a hand up to my face. When Grandma looked up, I pretended to scratch my nose.

Actually, there was no such company, and no such product. But that was my little secret, along with the fact that Grandma's so-called job was a sham. She refused to accept charity of any sort, even from me.

She was a smart lady, but had no real job skills, no car, and no driver's license or interest in getting one.

So a couple years ago, I'd invented this little envelope-stuffing job. It wasn't much, but it paid her rent, and kept her entertained. Today, the entertainment seemed more of the kill-the-graphic-designer variety.

I glanced at the flyer. "I thought you liked cats."

"Yeah, and I like 'em too much to subject 'em to this horseshit." She glanced down to the paper in her hand. "Precocious to perfect, my ass."

"Hey," Josh said, "doesn't anyone care what I have to say?"

Oh, I cared alright. But not in the way Josh thought. He was happy. Grandma was mad. And soon, I'd be in the middle. And there was only one person who caused this particular dynamic.

My mom.

I turned to Josh. "Sorry," I said. "What's your news?"

He grinned. "Mom's invited us over for Thanksgiving."

It was official. Thanksgiving was my least favorite holiday, ever. "Oh that's really nice," I said. "But we already have plans."

"That's the best part," Josh said. "She said we could do it on Friday. You know, the day after?"

I blew out a breath. Two days of family fun. How did I

ever get so lucky?

Josh's smile faded. "Aren't you happy?"

"Yeah. Totally." I summoned up a smile of my own. "But you know how hectic her schedule is."

Boozing, sleeping all day, hanging out with random losers, it was a real time sink. It didn't just keep her away from her kids. It kept her away from gainful employment, which was probably just fine with her.

"I mean, it sounds like fun," I said, "but we probably shouldn't get our hopes up."

"She's not gonna cancel this time," Josh said. "She promised."

I gave a small nod. "That's good."

"Remember that last apple pie?" Josh said. "Oh man, that was the best, ever."

I nodded. I remembered the pie perfectly. I was the one who made it. Mommy Dearest? She was too busy being passed out on the kitchen floor. It was three o'clock in the morning, and I'd come home from waitressing find her lying there with a half-empty bottle of apple schnapps.

It would be funny if it weren't so pathetic.

"Maybe she'll make it again," Josh said as he got up from his seat and headed off toward the bathroom."

"Or maybe," Grandma muttered after the door closed behind him, "some cat'll chew her face off first."

I felt myself nod. Better hers than mine.

On my way out, Grandma handed me a huge white envelope containing something flat and stiff. "Just in case," she said.

I looked down. "Just in case what?"

"In case they don't pay. You know, the house-sitting people."

"But they did pay," I said.

"Yeah, but you got another payment due next week, right?"

I felt my eyebrows furrow. "Yeah?"

"So, if they don't pay, you give 'em that."

I made a move to open the envelope.

"Hey, not in front of the kid," Grandma said.

I glanced past her, into the cottage, where Josh still was still sitting at the kitchen table. He caught my eye and grinned. The way it looked, Grandma's secret message wasn't as secret as she seemed to think.

"I'll open it when I get back," I assured her.

"Good girl."

When I pulled into the Parkers' driveway twenty minutes later, I couldn't wait a second longer. I opened the envelope and pulled out what was inside.

As I looked down, I couldn't help but smile.

It was a single sheet of lined notebook paper. Pasted crookedly across the sheet were a series of capital letters, obviously cut from the local newspaper.

Unable to resist, I read the ransom note aloud in my best tough-guy voice. "Pay up, or the dog gets it."

I was still laughing when I walked into the house. ☐

☐

CHAPTER 53

It was just two days before Thanksgiving and almost a month since I'd seen Lawton. My days hadn't changed much, but at least I had other things to worry about.

The Parkers' next payment never arrived, just like Grandma predicted. And even after multiple phone calls, I hadn't heard a single word back from either Mrs. Parker or her so-called financial manager.

In a desperate bid to forget all my troubles, I loaded up Chucky and took him to the park. It was freezing cold and gloomy as hell, but it was better than sitting around someone else's house moping all day. Or at least, if nothing else, it was a change of scenery.

I was walking Chucky around the nature trail when I spotted a familiar form up ahead. My heart flipped, and my breath caught. I'd recognize him anywhere, even in the dark long-sleeve shirt and silky black running pants.

Lawton. He wasn't walking. And he wasn't running. In fact, he wasn't moving at all. He stood, utterly still, in the middle of the trail.

I stopped in my tracks. He met my gaze, his expression anguished. I glanced over my shoulder, back toward my car. I could scurry back to it and leave right now. But then what? I'd have to face him sooner or later. So I squared my shoulders and marched forward.

His dark hair was a tousled mess, and his eyes were haunted as he watched me approach. He said nothing, but his gaze said it all.

Desperation radiated off him in waves. I'd seen him in virtually every scenario, not just in person, but on the Internet too. I'd seen him flirty. I'd seen him sexy. I'd seen him beat some guy twice his size to a bloody pulp.

I'd never seen him like this.

Out in front of me, Chucky was going nuts, straining at his leash and whining for Lawton's notice. Slowly, Lawton's gaze dipped to Chucky, and I saw the barest hint of a sad smile.

When Chucky barreled into Lawton a moment later, there wasn't much I could do, short of yanking Chucky backward and prying him loose.

But somehow, I just didn't have the heart. So I stood, silently off to the side, while Lawton crouched down and ruffled Chucky's fur.

A moment later, I heard the crinkle of packaging and joyful yips that somehow managed to tear my heart out. He still carried doggie snacks, even after all this time?

But true to his promise, Lawton didn't say a single word or give me so much as a wave.

Gently, I picked up Chucky and cradled him against me, meeting Lawton's gaze one last time before continuing down the trail with Chucky in my arms and his leash dragging behind us.

When I rounded the bend a few minutes later, I saw Lawton out of the corner of my eye. He still hadn't moved. He stood, facing the same exact same direction, the empty doggie-treat bag hanging loose from his fingers.

When I'd moved beyond the line of sight, I set Chucky

down and trudged forward once again, feeling hot tears slide down my cold face. When I completed the circuit, Lawton was gone.

When my phone rang later that afternoon, I couldn't help but dive for it. I wasn't sure what I expected. A return-call from the Parkers? A call from Lawton after all? Or maybe just Keith, calling me into work or threatening to fire me again.

But when I checked the display, what I saw there made me groan aloud. It was Loretta, again.

She'd been calling me every few days, switching what I was supposed to bring and pretending it was my fault for the mix-up. Salad, dessert, salad, dessert – I was getting whiplash just thinking about it.

In the end, I'd decided to play it safe. I'd purchased everything for both, not that I could truly afford it. But I needed a peaceful Thanksgiving, not just for my sake, but for Josh's.

Still, I couldn't bring myself to answer that call. Not this time. Seeing Lawton today had sucked all the juice right out of me, and I seriously doubted my ability to take her crap without giving some right back in return. So I let it to go voicemail and listened to the message as soon as the phone beeped.

"Chloe," she said. "This is Loretta. I know you're there. But fine, if you've got nothing better to do than disrespect my time, I guess I'll just relay everything in a message."

She sighed loudly into the phone. "One – you're bringing salad and dessert. Don't forget. Two – try to be on time, will you? It's not fair to the rest of us when you keep us waiting. Three – you mentioned bringing a guest, but I haven't heard a single word since then, so I'm assuming you're coming alone. Four – for God's sake, don't dress like a slob, alright? I want a nice Thanksgiving dinner for once, and I won't have you ruining it by not taking it seriously. And don't bother calling me back. I'm busy too, you know."

When the message ended, I tossed the phone onto the sofa. Chucky, stretched out on the easy chair, lifted his head and gave me a baleful look.

"Yeah," I said. "I know."

CHAPTER 54

Call me anytime. Day, night, middle of the night. I don't care. Just call me, okay?

Sitting in my car, I replayed Lawton's words. I pulled out my cell phone and checked the time. Only three minutes had passed since the last time I'd checked.

It was three minutes too long.

Remembering Loretta's warnings, I wore a semi-formal green dress with long sleeves and a scooped neckline. No jeans today, not if I knew what was good for me.

My Thanksgiving salad sat in the passenger's seat, wedged in a cardboard box to keep it from tipping. A prepackaged cheesecake sat on the passenger's side floor, with an apple cobbler balanced on top of it.

One salad, two desserts, and twenty minutes to get there. I glanced again at my phone. Another minute gone. If I wasn't on the road in like two seconds, I'd be late.

It shouldn't be a big deal. But I knew all too well that it was. With Loretta, everything was a big deal.

I turned the ignition key yet again, praying for some sort of miracle. Why, I had no idea. In at least a dozen attempts, the car hadn't given any sign of starting.

All it gave was an empty clicking sound that told me that unless I was planning to dine in the Parkers' driveway, my odds of a Thanksgiving dinner weren't looking too good.

If it weren't for Josh, I wouldn't care. Going to my Dad's house – correction, Loretta's house, where my Dad lived – was never my idea of a good time.

But I had to go. It was stupid, really. Loretta didn't truly want me there. Even my Dad was indifferent at best. Still, there'd be hell to pay if I cancelled or worse, didn't show at all. And the person paying would be Josh.

I ran through my options. Call Erika? No, she was off skiing. Call a tow truck? What for? Even if they got here in time, and were able to start the car, there'd be no guarantee it wouldn't stall along the way. Besides, I couldn't afford a tow truck, especially at holiday rates.

I tried the ignition another time. "C'mon," I said. "Just start, okay? Please?"

It didn't.

Again, I thought of Lawton's words.

I couldn't do it. I couldn't call him.

Instead, I picked up my cell phone and dialed a number that was only slightly less scary. Thankfully, it was my dad, and not Loretta, who answered the phone.

"Hey Dad," I said, "I ran into a little problem, and I'm hoping you can do me a favor?"

Long pause. "What kind of favor?"

"Nothing big," I said. "It's just that my car won't start."

Silence.

I cleared my throat. "But I'd really like to make it out there."

More silence.

"So," I continued in a rush, "do you think you might be able, if it's not too much trouble, come and pick me up?"

Long pause. "Now?"

"Well, yeah. I mean, actually the sooner the better." I tried to sound chipper. "I'm all ready, and I've got the salad and desserts. It's just that –"

"Hang on," he said.

In the background, I heard muffled voices. I could almost see him, covering the phone like he used to when my parents were still married, and another bill collector had tracked them down at our latest rental.

It was nice to know I rated in the same category as collection agencies.

A moment later, I heard jostling on the other end, followed by Loretta's clipped voice. "I should've known you'd pull something like this."

Oh God. Why had he put her on?

I closed my eyes and took a deep breath. "Like what?"

"Don't sigh at me," she said. "You know exactly what I'm talking about."

"What?" I asked.

"You still can't stomach the thought of sharing your Daddy, can you?"

Daddy? I hadn't called him that since – well, never, at least not that I remembered. "No," I said. "It's nothing like that. It's just that my car won't start, and –"

"And what?" she said. "You want to pull him away? You want him all to yourself? Is that it?"

"No," I stammered. "Of course not."

"Well, I'm not falling for it."

"Honest," I said, hearing a hitch in my voice that made me feel about five years old. "I wouldn't be calling if I had any other choice."

"Chloe," she said, in that overly patient tone of hers. "In life, there are always choices."

What the hell did that mean? If I chose to shove a turkey up her ass sideways, was that a choice? Even in the relatively cool car, my face was burning. From rage or embarrassment, I didn't know. Desperately, I searched for a solution that wouldn't send Loretta over the edge.

Obviously, my dad wouldn't be coming, and I knew better than to ask Loretta. Other than Josh, who was way too young to drive, this only left one person – Lauren, Loretta's natural daughter.

Lauren was about my age. We'd never been friends, but we weren't exactly enemies either. I'd once given her a ride to the airport. That had to count for something, right?

"Is Lauren there?" I said.

"Are you forgetting? She goes by Lauren Jane now."

"I'm sorry. But maybe she could come get me?"

"Oh, so now you want to pull her away too? Well let me tell you something. I'm not sending my daughter out on a day like this."

"A day like what?" I looked around. The air was cool, but the sky was sunny. "It's the warmest Thanksgiving I can remember."

"Thank you, Chloe, for that weather report."

I choked down the bile and tried one more time. My voice sounded very small as I said, "Can't anyone come and get me?"

"The only person left is me," she said. "And I've been cooking since the crack of dawn. So now you want me to run a taxi service too?" She made a sound of disgust. "I told your Dad you'd try something like this." She sighed into the phone. "What have I ever done to deserve this?"

I held the phone away from my ear as if the physical distance could keep the poison of her words from invading my skull. I didn't know what to say. I should've called a cab. No amount of money was worth this.

Like I could afford a cab on Thanksgiving, assuming they were even running.

"Here," Loretta said to someone on her end. "You talk to her. I shouldn't have to deal with this."

A moment later, I heard Josh's hesitant voice. "Chloe?"

"Yeah?"

"You're still coming, aren't you?"

"Sure," I said. "Definitely." I closed my eyes. "It's just my car isn't exactly cooperating."

He lowered his voice so low, I could barely hear him. "You mean it?"

"Yeah. Of course."

In the background, I heard Loretta's voice off somewhere in the distance. I couldn't make out the words, but her tone was all too familiar.

"How mad is she?" I asked. "Scale of one to ten."

"A hundred," Josh said without any trace of humor.

I should've known. My call had only made it worse. Stupid, stupid, stupid. "Don't worry. I'll be there," I told him. And I would be, even if I had to walk there, food and all.

"I'm supposed to tell you," he said in a shaky voice, "that if you can't make it here by noon to not bother."

"She's kidding, right?"

"I don't think so."

"Shit," I muttered.

His voice was quiet. "Yeah."

Don't worry, I'll be there." I swallowed. "But I've gotta go. Alright?"

"That's good. Because remember the thing with Mom? You know, tomorrow?"

"Yeah. I remember. Don't worry. I'll be there too." I tried to sound cheerful. "Just like we talked about, okay?"

"Actually," he said, "she called a couple minutes ago. She's got this other thing she forgot about, so you don't need to worry about tomorrow. I just thought you'd want to know."

"Oh," I said. "Well, I'm sure she really wanted to see us."

"Yeah. I guess."

I was mad as hell at my mom, but what did I expect? She did this all the time. Still, poor Josh. I hated that she'd gotten his hopes up yet again, only to cancel last-minute. As for me, I'd lost hope years ago. The way I saw it, I was the lucky one.

When Josh disconnected, I checked the clock on my phone. The call had cost me five precious minutes. Even if by some miracle, my car started now, I was still totally screwed.

More accurately, Josh was screwed.

Well, so much for Plan A.

My heart racing, I scrolled through my contacts, and found Lawton's name. I pressed the call button and held my breath.

It rang once, then twice, and then, I heard his voice, nearly breathless. "Chloe?"

"Yeah. Listen," I said. "I've got a question."

"Yeah?"

"You still want that beating?"

CHAPTER 55

A couple minutes later, Lawton's hot rod squealed into the driveway, looking only slightly better than it had the night he'd taken a crowbar to it.

He'd obviously replaced the headlights and both side-view mirrors, but the car body itself was still a mess, with a cracked windshield and big, ugly dents all over the hood.

I was standing near the trunk of my own car, holding the giant serving bowl of salad with both hands. Resting by my feet were the two desserts, sitting in their boxes on the hard concrete.

Breathlessly, I watched Lawton get out of his car, leaving the engine running, a low rumble that carried over the cool air.

Lawton looked just like I remembered – hot as sin, but distinctly underdressed in tattered jeans and a white T-shirt. The shirt had dark grease stains down the front and sides, like he'd been leaning over an engine or changing a stubborn tire.

The jeans had similar streaks, possibly handprints, just above his knees, where the fabric was torn and worn to the point where I saw the hint of bare skin showing through.

Whether his bare arms had similar streaks, I had no idea. Between the outlines of his muscles and intricate tattoos, I was having a hard time seeing much else.

Silently, I drank in the sight of him, watching him watch me as he moved with the kind of intensity that should've made me run.

He stopped and looked down at the boxes by my feet. "We taking those?"

I nodded.

Wordlessly, he picked them up and strode toward the passenger's side of his car. Shifting the boxes to one arm, he opened the car door with his right hand, and set the boxes on the floor just behind the passenger's seat.

Salad in hand, I joined him. He held the car door open while I climbed inside and settled the salad onto my lap.

Before he closed my car door, I looked up. Our eyes met and held. It was hard to breathe, much less speak.

But somehow, my mouth opened, and words tumbled out. "Boy, are you gonna be sorry."

He grinned. "Not a chance."

Looking at him, I felt my mouth go just a little bit dry. When he closed my door and walked around the front of the car, his smile was still there.

Reluctantly, I felt myself smile too, just barely, but enough to ease some of the tension.

Our conversation on the phone had been brief to the point of rudeness, on my part, anyway. But he'd come. Just like he'd promised. And obviously, he'd taken my words seriously, maybe too seriously for his own good.

I'd asked him – no, begged him, actually – to drop everything and come right now. Twenty seconds into my sorry excuse for an explanation, he was on the way.

I watched him settle into the driver's seat, all long legs and sinewy muscle.

"I wasn't kidding," I said. "This is gonna suck." I glanced

288

down at his clothes and winced. "Especially for you."

He shrugged. "I think I can handle it."

"That's what you think."

He flicked his head toward the street. "Which way?"

I gave him general directions to my Dad's house, and he backed out onto the street. When he hit the accelerator, the car's engine roared, and the seats vibrated with its raw power. Good thing he hadn't taken a crowbar to anything under the hood.

I settled into my seat, pretending that my eyes weren't starving for a good, long look at him. I tried looking straight ahead. Then I tried looking out my own window. But over and over, my gaze kept drifting back to where he sat, close enough to touch, but miles away in all the ways that mattered.

We were going fast, well above the speed limit. Houses and mailboxes passed in a blur as he navigated the nearly empty streets.

His dark tousled hair framed his chiseled face as he watched the road. He had one hand draped loosely over the steering wheel and the elbow of his other arm resting on the center console.

"So," he said, giving me a sideways glance, "this wasn't exactly the beating I expected."

On the phone, I'd given him only the briefest of details, telling him I needed a ride, and I needed a distraction. I hadn't lied then, and I wasn't going to lie now.

Whether we were together or not, I was done with secrets, and done with surprises. Besides, this thing would go a whole lot better if he knew up front what he was getting into.

"Trust me," I said, "by the end of the day, you'll be wishing for the other kind."

"I don't care. I'm just glad you called."

"Oh, that's what you say now," I said.

"Ask me later," he said. "I'll say the same thing."

I still couldn't believe I'd caught him at home. "You didn't have plans today?" It was a holiday, after all.

He shrugged. "I had invitations. None I wanted."

"Yeah," I said. "I know the feeling."

Given the choice between having someone handcuff me in a basement or spending a single holiday Loretta-style, it was no contest.

I'd take the basement.

I leaned back and closed my eyes, feeling the vibration of the seat course through me. Oh, Lawton would regret this, alright. Maybe he didn't think so now, but he would. A couple hours with Loretta, and he'd be begging for a nice crowbar to the face.

CHAPTER 56

"For someone who's about to put me through the ringer," he said over the engine's roar, "you don't look too happy."

I opened my eyes and stole another glance in his direction. "That's because I can't just send you in my place."

Still holding the salad, I fumbled for my cell phone to check the time. "We've got ten minutes," I said. The next road sign passed in a blur. If we'd been going the speed limit, we'd be at least fifteen minutes away. I didn't need to look at the speedometer to know we were going quite a bit faster than that.

"Oh c'mon," Lawton said. "What are they gonna do? Lock the doors?"

"You don't think they wouldn't?" I tried to keep my tone light, but somehow missed the mark. "You poor, misguided fool."

I leaned down to shove the cell phone back in my purse, and before I knew what was happening, the salad toppled off my lap. The clear wrapping came loose and half of the lettuce spilled onto my shoes.

"Oh my God," I said. "Stop the car! No. Wait. Keep going." Desperately, I righted the bowl. With the lost lettuce, the salad looked way too small. This was bad. Maybe if fluffed it up or something—"

I glanced over at Lawton. His gaze shifted briefly in my direction. His brow wrinkled.

And then it hit me how rude I was being. "Oh jeez, sorry about your floor mat," I said. I pushed a hand through my hair. "I guess I should've apologized first, huh?"

"Don't worry about it," he said. "It's just lettuce. No big deal."

"Yeah, I guess," I said in a distracted tone. "Good thing it wasn't soup, huh?"

"Salad, soup, whatever, it all cleans up." He turned briefly to look at me, and his tone grew serious. "Baby, what's wrong?"

I glanced down at the salad. I shook my head. "It's too small." I reached up to rub my forehead. "This is bad. What am I gonna do?"

"Chloe," he said in a low, soothing voice, "it's just a salad."

"No," I snapped. "It's not just a salad. You don't get it. This? It's a big deal. Because everything's a big deal."

Still driving, Lawton reached for my hand. "C'mon, what is it?"

I couldn't bring myself to pull away. And for once, it had nothing to do with my crazy, mixed-up feelings for him.

His hand felt big and strong, and so much steadier than my own was. Between the car trouble and my own clumsiness, I was feeling a growing sense of dread. What if things went downhill from here?

"Nothing," I said with a shake of my head. "It's fine. Watch the road, alright?"

It wasn't fine, of course. If the salad turned out to be the thing that sent Loretta over the edge, I'd be kicking myself all the way there and back. I took a deep breath and tried to steady my nerves.

I dealt with Loretta all the time. But today, she was already on the warpath. I'd be inside that house for at least a couple hours, tripping over land mines everywhere I stepped. If one of those things blew up, it wouldn't be just me getting hurt.

Our last holiday had been so awful. What if this one went the same way?

I couldn't let it. No way. I wouldn't let it happen. Not this time. I leaned back and shut my eyes as tight as I could, and not because of our decidedly unsafe speed.

"Aw c'mon," Lawton said, "it can't be that bad."

"I hope you're right," I said. "And this time, you'll be there, so—" I shrugged and let the sentence trail off.

"So? Go on."

"Well, normally they're a lot nicer in front of strangers." I opened my eyes to look at him. "And you're a stranger to them, so—" I shook my head. "Crap, I don't know. What if it backfires?"

"Chloe?" His voice was low. "Are you scared?"

I turned to look out the window. "No."

He was quiet for a moment, and then he said, "Baby, what is it?"

I remembered my vow. No more lies, no more secrets. "Okay, here's the thing." I blew out a breath. "I almost never go there, and when I do, it's always awful."

"What's so awful about it?"

"Like my dad," I said, "Whenever he has company over, he starts talking funny."

"How so?"

"Well, he's a commercial real estate broker–"

"A salesman?"

"Basically," I said. "So he's always trying to bond with whoever he's talking to, but he never gets it quite right."

293

"What do you mean?"

"Well, one time, Loretta had this Australian couple over for dinner, and by the time we hit dessert, my dad's talking in this weird accent, more English than anything."

Lawton's brow wrinkled. "But you said they were Australian, right?"

"Yeah, and the harder my dad tries to show that he's exactly like them, the worse everything gets. They start talking less. He starts talking more." I shook my head. "I'm pretty sure they thought my dad was making fun of them."

Lawton laughed. "Aw c'mon, that's not so bad."

"I guess," I said. "And actually, it's a lot better than how he acts when it's just family."

"How so?"

"Well, when no one's there except us and Loretta, he's either giving me and Josh a hard time or kissing Loretta's butt."

"Who's Loretta?"

"My stepmother, who totally hates me, by the way."

"Oh yeah? Why?"

"Mostly, she hates everyone, well, except for her own daughter." I paused. "And my dad. Sometimes."

"What about your brother?"

"That's the worst part," I said. "She doesn't loathe him quite as much as she does me, but she still has this way of tormenting him, even when she's pretending to be nice."

Lawton said nothing as he down-shifted to pass an oversized pickup truck. We blew past him like he was standing still.

"Oh, I know what you're thinking," I said. "You think I'm exaggerating, right?"

"I never said that."

"Uh-huh." I felt my stomach churn at the memory of my last holiday there. "You'll see. It doesn't take anything to set her off."

"Like what? Gimme an example."

"Well, a couple of Easters ago, it was oyster gravy."

I glanced in his direction. The look on his face said it all. Disgusted. And he was right.

Our shared loathing of seafood was just one of the many reasons I loved him. Correction – one of the many reasons I used to love him, before everything had gotten so messed up.

Before he locked me in his basement. Or assumed I was a hooker.

He shook his head. "That's just wrong."

No kidding. If I were willing to have sex for money, my life would've been a whole lot simpler.

"So," he said in a prompting tone. "The gravy?"

Oh, right. Loretta. Gravy.

I nodded. "Supposedly, it's a delicacy. Or at least, that's what Loretta keeping telling us."

Lawton's tires squealed around the next turn. "I've got this friend from Texas," he said. "Know what he'd say to that?"

"What?"

Lawton assumed a Western drawl. "You can call it Nancy and put a dress on it. But I'm still not gonna eat it."

"Say that to Loretta, and you're a dead man." I felt the corners of my mouth lift just a fraction. "As much as I'd totally love to see that."

"So about Easter?" Lawton said. "What happened?"

"Anyway, Loretta made this special batch of oyster gravy, and then flipped out when we didn't want any."

"You and your brother?"

"Yeah. And Lauren Jane too, except she didn't get in

trouble for it."

"Who's Lauren Jane?"

"Loretta's daughter."

"Ah."

"And then there was my dad, no help as usual. I lowered my voice in a decent imitation of him. "Loretta spent all morning in the kitchen making this for us, and the least you kids can do is have some."

"So did you?"

I nodded.

"How was it?" he asked.

I shuddered. "Awful. Like fish-barf."

"But your dad likes it?"

"Nope."

"So he doesn't eat it."

"Nope."

Lawton was shaking his head. "I don't get it."

"Don't get me wrong," I said. "He'd probably eat a smoking turd if Loretta asked him to."

"Better than fish barf," Lawton said.

"On second thought," I said, "you know what? He wouldn't eat it. He'd make us do it. That way, he gets the credit, and we get the shaft."

I glanced again at Lawton. His expression was stony, but his tone was carefully neutral as he said, "So Loretta likes the gravy?"

"I dunno," I said. "Couldn't tell you either way. She's always on a diet. So it's not like she actually eats the stuff herself. Mostly, she just picks at a salad or something and goes straight for dessert."

Lawton's eyebrows furrowed. "So this gravy, who exactly was supposed to eat it?"

I shrugged. "Me and Josh, I guess."

There was no trace of humor as he said, "Go on."

"So like I said, there's no getting out of it. At least not for me. So I put some on my potatoes, and take a bite."

"And?"

"Like I said, it's awful." I swallowed at the memory. "Worse than awful actually. But I know what I've got to do, so I smile and tell her it's delicious."

"Was she happy?"

"Loretta?" I said. "Never. But at least she's not throwing plates. So I keep shoveling it down, figuring that once it's gone, the whole thing's over, right?"

"It wasn't?"

"No," I said, glancing out the window. "It was just beginning."□

□

CHAPTER 57

His voice was very quiet in the noisy car. "What happened next?"

"So Josh," I said, "he's a picky eater. Always has been. And no matter how many times my dad tells him that something's a delicacy, he still doesn't want anything to do with it."

"Smart kid."

"You have no idea," I said, feeling the hint of a real smile. "So anyway, Josh keeps saying 'no thanks' to the gravy, but Loretta won't take no for an answer. So she shoves at this vase, and it tips over. Flowers spill, the vase cracks, and my dad gets mad."

"At Loretta?"

I gave a derisive snort. "Dream on. No. At Josh. So my dad grabs a ladle and starting slopping all this gravy onto Josh's plate, one scoop after another. And this crap gets on everything, not just the potatoes either." I shook my head. "The chicken, the corn, even the salad."

I closed my eyes as if I could somehow block out the memory. Someday, Josh and I might be able to laugh about it. But someday seemed a long ways off.

I glanced at Lawton. Any trace of good humor had had long since vanished. "Keep going," he said.

"So," I continued, "my dad tells Josh that he's not getting

another thing to eat 'til he finishes what's on his plate, even though it looks like some fish threw up on it."

"What happened? Did he eat it?"

I shook my head. "No. Josh just sits there, looking down at his plate, and my dad keeps hassling him, saying what a great cook Loretta is, and how lucky Josh is to be living under her roof. And the whole time, Loretta's just sitting there with this half-smile on her face, like everything is turning out exactly like she planned. And Josh, he doesn't eat anything else. Not one bite. And I can tell he wants to cry."

I blew out a breath. "But he's in fourth grade. Or at least he was back then, so he's too big to cry. And he's too little to take on my dad, obviously, or Loretta for that matter. So he doesn't do anything but stare at his plate until everyone else is done."

"But what'd you do?" Lawton said. "You were there, so–"

"Yeah. I was there. And I knew I'd be smart to stay out of it."

Lawton sounded confused. "Because you didn't need the trouble?"

I turned sideways to face him. The salad wobbled precariously. I grabbed it and held on for dear life. "No," I said, "Because I know better, or least I should've. Because every time I try to help, I just make it worse."

"Is that what happened this time?"

"Oh yeah. Because stupid me, I couldn't just let it go. But doing the thing I want to do is completely out of the question."

"What was that?"

"Breaking that damn vase over her head."

"Sounds good to me," he said.

"Yeah, but I don't want to make everything worse. So as

nice as I could, I suggest letting Josh get a new plate. I say stuff like, 'I think we've all learned a good lesson here.'" I shook my head. "What a load of crap. Anyway, I get Josh to say he'll try some gravy on his potatoes if we can just start over."

"So that's what happened?"

"Hell no. Because by now, my dad's all worked up. He gives us this big lecture on how we don't appreciate how much Loretta's done for us. Then one thing leads to another, and I'm so stupid that I actually give an honest opinion on why Loretta made that stupid gravy in the first place."

"And what happened then?"

"Well, before I know it, Loretta takes Josh's plate and crashes it onto the floor, food and all. Then she goes after the serving dishes, the gravy boat, the chicken platter, a couple of wine glasses. It totally sucks, because everyone's freaking out. But part of me's thinking 'So what? At least Josh won't have to eat a bunch of fish barf.'"

I pushed a hand through my hair. "And in the end, Loretta storms off to her room, and my dad gives us yet another lecture, this one about how we ruined Loretta's favorite holiday."

"Easter?"

"Supposedly. But they say that about every holiday, so I dunno. Talk-Like-a-Pirate-Day could be her favorite for all I know. Anyway, after my Dad tells me to get the hell out, Josh is stuck dealing with the fallout."

I looked down at my lap. "And as far as that gravy? Loretta made another batch, special just for him. And they wouldn't give him anything else to eat until the whole thing was gone. And they wouldn't him eat anyplace else either."

I swallowed a lump, and continued. "And I knew it was all

my fault. Because if I hadn't said something, it would've ended at dinner, one way or another. Swear to God, I'd have eaten that whole bowl myself if I could, but after I was kicked out, I wasn't allowed inside at all for at least a year."

"When you left, you couldn't take him with you?"

I shook my head. "I didn't have my own place, still don't. Besides, he's a minor. My dad has full custody, so, well, you know how that goes."

Lawton said nothing, and I glanced in his direction. I took in his clenched jaw, his narrowed eyes. The silence stretched out.

"It's not like we were abused or anything," I assured him. "Lots of kids have it worse, right?" I tried to smile. "And at least Grandma lives next door. So Josh spends a lot of time at her place."

Lawton's voice sounded carefully controlled. "How much time is that?"

"Well, pretty much all of it actually, except for when he's sleeping, or when Grandma's out of town."

"On that Easter," he said, "was your Grandma there, too?"

"No. She's my mom's mom, which puts her way down on Loretta's guest list."

"But they're neighbors?"

"Sort of. Grandma rents Loretta's guest cottage."

"So renting the cottage is okay, but coming to dinner isn't?"

"It's complicated," I said. "The cottage is nice, but it's not a real rental. It's got no driveway of its own, and besides, their neighborhood isn't zoned for that sort of thing."

"So it's all done on the sly. That's what you're saying?"

"Yeah. Grandma can't drive anyway, so there's no car. And since she's a relative, the neighbors think she's just a guest."

"But she's paying?"

"Yeah. All cash, so there's no zoning trouble."

"You ever think of renting the cottage for yourself?" he asked.

"I tried. But Loretta wouldn't let me. She still won't let me stay overnight there, even as Grandma's guest."

"Why not?"

"Because," I said in a mocking tone, "I need to learn real responsibility." I looked out the window. "Just as well. I work most nights anyway. But Grandma, she's works from home, so–"

"Are we talking about that job that isn't real?"

"Oh," I said. "Yeah. I guess I did mention that huh?" I nodded. "Yup. That's the one."

I glanced up, surprised to realize we were almost there. I reached out, putting my hand on his arm. "Lawton, no matter what she does, don't set her off, alright? She'll probably be pissy about what you're wearing. But that's okay, because it'll keep the focus off Josh."

I looked over at him. For all my vows to make Lawton pay, it suddenly occurred to me that this was an awful lot to ask of anyone, even him. "I'm sorry," I said. "You don't mind, do you?"

"Nope," he said. "This'll be fun."

"I'm serious," I said. "She's a total psycho."

"Yeah?" He gave me a crooked grin. "Haven't you heard? I am too."

CHAPTER 58

We squealed into the driveway with one minute to spare. Glancing at the house, I caught movement in the front window.

Josh.

"C'mon," I said, shoving open my car door. Salad in hand, I jumped out and watched as Lawton circled the car and retrieved the two desserts from the back.

By the time we reached the front door, it was already open. Josh stood just inside the doorway, his hand on the doorknob and his gaze troubled.

"You made it," he said, stepping outside and shutting the door behind him.

For his sake, I summoned up a smile. "Told you I would."

Josh glanced briefly over his shoulder, and then lowered his voice. "She was just about to lock you out."

He didn't need to say who she was.

For Josh's sake, I kept the smile in place. "Good thing I found myself a fast driver then." I cleared my throat. "Speaking of which, this is Lawton, my, uh, friend." I turned to Lawton. "This is Josh."

Lawton held out his free hand. "So you're the genius Chloe's always talking about."

"Aw, I don't know about that," Josh said, looking down at

305

his shoes. He wore dark slacks, a white dress shirt, and a grey neck tie with tiny polka dots.

"You look good," I said.

Josh looked up. "Thanks. So do you." Absently, he reached up to tug at the knot of his tie. "I wanted to wear jeans." He shrugged. "But you know."

I did know. And then, as if we were thinking the same thing, we slowly turned to look at Lawton.

He stood with his legs shoulder-width apart. He had the dessert boxes cradled in one arm, and the other arm loose at his side. But even relaxed, the muscles and tattoos of his bare arms were hard to ignore, not to mention his greased-stained white T-shirt.

But Josh wasn't looking at Lawton's shirt, or his tattoos. He was looking down at Lawton's jeans, taking in the shredded fabric and grease stains.

Josh blew out a low whistle. "She's gonna totally chew you up," he said.

"Who?" Lawton said.

Behind Josh, the door swung open so fast and hard, it hit the doorstopper with that weird, clangy noise I knew so well.

"Her," I muttered under my breath.

Loretta gave me a cold, withering look. "You think I can't hear you?"

Oh crap. Time to shape up fast, starting with an apology.

But before I had the chance, her cool gaze swept to Lawton. She gave him a long, disapproving look, taking her time as if cataloging everything, from his tousled hair to his tattered jeans.

Her lips pursed.

In spite of my nervousness, or maybe because of it, I wanted to laugh. Loretta prided herself on impeccable manners, at least in front of strangers – except, I knew, when the stranger in question was deemed beneath her notice.

Her opinion of Lawton was pretty obvious. She already had him categorized somewhere between the guy who mowed her lawn and the panhandlers she was always complaining about.

She leaned around him to look at the driveway. "Who are you?" she said. "The tow truck driver?"

Loretta knew damn well that Lawton wasn't a tow truck driver. For one thing, there was no tow truck, a dead giveaway in my book.

But there was his car. I followed her gaze and tried to see it like she'd see it – an ancient muscle car with chipped paint and ugly dents.

I cleared my throat. "Loretta," I said, "I'd like you to meet Lawton. My friend, and uh, my ride."

"I see." She pursed her lips. "Lorton, is it?"

"Close enough," Lawton said, holding out his hand.

Loretta looked down at the hand, but didn't take it. "Are you some kind of mechanic?" she said.

Lawton grinned. "You could say that." With a shrug, he put down his hand. "Just part-time though. You know how it is."

"No," she said with a little sniff. "I'm afraid I don't." She glanced again toward the driveway. "I assume you're also providing our Chloe with a ride home?"

Lawton grinned. "Definitely."

Loretta consulted her watch. "Fine. But don't be later than two o'clock." She turned to me. "Will you be waiting for him in the driveway? Or shall he knock on the door?"

"Actually," I said, "he's my guest. You said I could bring one?"

Just then, Lauren Jane's face appeared behind Loretta's shoulder. "Oh my God," she said. "Is that–? Are you?" She turned toward me. "Is that Lawton Rastor?"

Loretta whirled around to face her daughter. Standing outside, I heard her voice, hushed and urgent as she asked, "Who's Lawton Rastor?"

CHAPTER 59

Ten minutes later, we were all settled around the long, oval table, with my dad at the head and Loretta at the foot.

With a smooth, practiced move, Loretta settled the cloth napkin onto her lap and gave me her sweetest smile. "We're all so glad you could make it, Chloe."

With a tittering laugh, she looked around the table and added, "We were just about to send out the cavalry." She gave my dad a significant look. "Weren't we, Dick?"

Nodding, my dad pulled out the booming voice he used only in front of company. "Anything for our little Chloe," he said. "It sure wouldn't be a family dinner without her."

Resisting an eye-roll of epic proportions, I glanced at Lawton across the table. Either he had one heck of a poker face, or he didn't see the humor.

He'd been seated between Josh and Lauren Jane. Josh was looking at Lawton with undisguised awe. Lauren Jane was all teeth and eyes, studying Lawton like a wolf studies a mutton chop.

Lauren Jane reached over and ran a finger along Lawton's forearm. "I like your tattoos," she said. "Do you have more?"

I wasn't sure whether to laugh or rip Lauren Jane's arm off and beat her over the head with it.

So instead, I stood. "Who's ready for salad?"

At Loretta's insistence, we were eating the meal in courses. Salad first. And the way it looked, it was time to get the show on the road.

My heart racing, I stood and retrieved my salad from the sideboard. The salad plates were already on the table, so all I had to do was pass the bowl around and pray that no one noticed it was already half empty. With a shaky smile, I handed the bowl first to Loretta.

Her brow wrinkled. "Where's the rest of it?" she asked.

I bit my lip. "Well, you see, on the way here—"

"I ate it," Lawton said.

She turned toward him. "Pardon?"

"I thought it was a snack." He shrugged. "Sorry."

Loretta's gaze narrowed. I was still holding the bowl. She looked up at me. "Is that true?"

"Oh Mom," Lauren Jane said, "of course it's true." She licked her lips. "I mean, just look at this guy." She gave Lawton a long, appreciative look. "You don't get a body like that on cheeseburgers."

I stifled a laugh.

"Is something funny?" Loretta said.

I shook my head. "Nope. Sorry."

With a little sniff, Loretta started serving herself some salad. She nodded toward my chair. "Sit. Please." She gave me a stiff-looking smile. "We'll just pass the courses around, family style." She looked around. "Now, isn't this nice?"

"Mmm…it sure is," Lauren Jane said in a low, husky voice.

I looked over and spotted Lauren Jane's hand wrapped around Lawton's right bicep. The way it looked, she'd caught him in mid-motion of sipping from his wine glass.

The glass, still poised at his lips, was nearly full. This wasn't good. A few more minutes of this, and he'd be needing the whole bottle.

Matter of fact, I should've gotten him drunk on the way. Better yet, I should've gotten myself drunk. Lawton was driving, after all.

Lauren Jane gave the bicep another squeeze. "You must work out like crazy," she told him. "Just how much can you lift, anyway?"

"Wait," Josh said, "I know this. Three-hundred pounds."

We all turned to look at him.

He shrugged. "I read it on the internet."

"Chloe dear," Loretta said, "Will you be taking your seat any time soon?"

I looked around the table. Was I still standing there? Oh crap. I was.

Silently, I returned to my seat. I watched as the salad was handed from person to person around the table. When it got to Lawton, he passed it along without taking any.

"You don't want any?" Josh said.

"Nah. I'm good," Lawton said. "Since I already ate half on the way." He made a show of lowering his voice. "Don't tell anyone, but there was also this chocolate cake."

Josh's eyes widened. "Seriously?"

"Yeah," Lawton said. "And a side of beef, couple of hams." He shrugged. "A pie. A dozen donuts. After that, I lost track."

"Oh, you," Lauren Jane said with a playful pat on his arm. "Stop teasing that boy. He'll believe anything."

"No I won't," Josh said.

"Josh," Loretta said, "don't sass your sister. It's not polite."

Josh looked to his plate. "Sorry."

Lawton leaned over and said something in Josh's ear. Josh grinned.

Loretta cleared her throat. "Lawton? Care to share with the rest of us?"

"You mean salad?" Lawton glanced down at his empty plate. "Sorry, I didn't take any." He turned to Lauren Jane. "How about you? Got any spare salad for your mom?"

Frowning, Lauren Jane looked down at her salad plate. She gave it a worried look. "There's not that much here," she said.

Loretta pursed her lips. "That's not necessary. I wasn't referring to—" She made a little huffing sound. "Oh, never mind."

When the salad reached me, I took two small pieces of lettuce. Then I stood to return the bowl to the sideboard, located just behind Lawton. On the sideboard were silver platters covered with big, domed silver lids.

Loretta thought it looked upscale. Personally, I thought it looked like room service for twelve.

But I'd gotten almost used to it. Just like dressing for dinner, Loretta liked things a certain way. If things weren't always so tense, it might've actually been fun. But it was tense, and fun was a word I never associated with this house.

Walking back toward the table, I looked down and spotted Lauren Jane's bare knee rubbing against Lawton's leg. Either Lawton didn't notice, or he was choosing not to react.

I had a reaction, alright, but nothing I could act on. If sassing was rude, stabbing Lauren Jane in the leg with my fork was definitely off-limits.

So, with a stupid smile plastered to my face, I returned to my seat and glanced in Lawton's direction. With his muscles, tattoos, and T-shirt, he looked completely out of place, but somehow, it only made him look better, at least to me, anyway.

As I watched, Lauren Jane nudged her chair closer to his.

Okay, make that two of us.

As if feeling my gaze on him, Lawton looked up. Our eyes met. He gave me a smile filled with secrets and just the tiniest hint of amusement. He was laughing at them. Did they realize that? I looked around.

Apparently not.

"So I hear you're some kind of fighter," my dad boomed at Lawton.

Lawton turned to give my dad a deadpan look. "Yup."

My dad's smile faltered. "You're not gonna try any of those fancy punches on me now, are you?"

"Nope." Lawton smiled. "At least not 'til dessert."

My dad's eyebrows furrowed, and then he laughed, a big booming sound that rang hollow in the formal dining room. "Hah!" He pointed at Lawton with both his index fingers. "You got me there."

Lauren Jane giggled and leaned in close to Lawton's ear. "You're so funny," she said. She turned to my dad. "You'd better watch it, Daddy, or he's gonna get you."

Daddy?

Lauren Jane flipped her hair over her shoulder. "Speaking of funny things," she told Lawton, "did you notice that your name begins with an 'L' and my name begins with an 'L'?"

She gave me half a glance across the table. "Sorry, Chloe, I guess you're not in the club."

"Uh-oh," my dad said in mock concern, "My gal's name begins with an 'L', too." With a big chuckle, he shook his index finger in warning. "But you don't be stealing my Loretta."

I glanced at Loretta. She was giving Lawton a speculative look, like my dad's comment had gotten her thinking.

I jumped up. "Want me to get the turkey?"

Loretta's cool gaze slid in my direction. "Are you the hostess?" she asked.

Oh crap. There it was. That look again.

"No," I said. "But I'm happy to help." I paused. "Unless you'd rather do it?"

With a little sigh, Loretta pushed back her chair and stood. "So much for a relaxing dinner," she said. "Chloe, will you please sit? You're making everyone nervous."

So I sat. And with a solemn air, Loretta started delivering platters to the table, lifting the silver lids to murmurs of appreciation, mostly from my dad, as she announced what each dish was. There was baked turkey and stuffing and mashed potatoes, along with dinner rolls, whipped butter, and homemade cranberry sauce.

The mashed potatoes were making me nervous. I knew we'd probably have them. Almost everyone had mashed potatoes for Thanksgiving, especially with the turkey. So we'd be having turkey gravy, right? But as each dish was revealed, and no turkey gravy had been presented, I started to get that sick feeling in my stomach.

She wouldn't do it. Not again. Would she?

And then she brought over the final platter, a small one with a tall silver lid. With a great flourish, she lifted the lid. My hands grew clammy. There it was, a small silver gravy boat filled to the rim.

I couldn't afford to be obvious, but I was desperate to know what it was.

But soon, I didn't have to guess, because with a thin smile, Loretta announced, "and finally, my very own holiday specialty, oyster gravy."

Shit.☐

☐

CHAPTER 60

I glanced at Josh. His face was deathly white as he looked down at his plate. Next to him, Lawton looked completely oblivious as he listened to Lauren Jane chatter about her latest trip to Cancun.

I tried to catch his eye. Why, I had no idea. What could he do? What could I do? Should I spill it? Pretend to faint? Grab Josh and run for the car?

But Lawton never even looked in my direction.

Slowly, I let my gaze drift to Loretta, who'd resumed her seat and sat with her hands steepled in front of her. Our eyes met, almost like she'd been watching for my reaction.

I knew exactly what she wanted. She wanted me to freak out. I'd look like a total idiot, especially in front of a guest. This posed an even bigger question. Would she make Josh eat it in front of company?

This shouldn't be a big deal. I was blowing things out of proportion. It'd be fine. Maybe.

Slowly, the dishes starting making their way around the table. I took a little of everything, even the cranberry sauce, which I'd never liked.

So far, the gravy was just sitting there, uncirculated and unmentioned, except for Loretta's introductory remarks. But the longer it sat, the more tense the table became. I could feel it in the air – anticipation, dread, or in my dad's case, probably a mixture of both.

And then, someone reached for it.

Lawton.

He picked up the gravy boat and surveyed its contents. "You said oyster gravy, right?" He took a big, whiff of it and grinned. "My favorite. Did you know, my great-grandma, she was a fishwife on the Detroit river, this was her specialty too?"

I snuck a glance in Loretta's direction.

She bared her teeth in a pale imitation of a smile. "How nice."

Lawton shrugged. "Not really. She stunk like fish something awful. But man, she made the best gravy."

As I watched, he ladled a scoop onto his mashed potatoes, then kept going, one ladle after another. Loretta hadn't made a whole lot, probably because only two people were expected to eat it. Soon, the entire gravy bowl was empty.

Lawton's eyebrows furrowed. He looked toward Loretta. "This wasn't all of it, was it?"

Loretta sat, her back straight and her eyes narrowed. "I'm afraid it was."

Lawton looked down at his plate. "Oh jeez. I'm sorry." He held out his plate toward Loretta. "You want mine?"

"No," she said. "That won't be necessary. But thank you."

"Oh well. More for me." And Lawton started digging in.

I watched in absolute horror, and more than a little admiration, as he started to devour everything on his plate, gravy and all. In mid-bite, he looked up. "You guys are eating too, right?"

Suddenly, it occurred to me how incredibly rude we were all being, watching him eat like some kind of zoo animal. I grabbed my fork and started eating too. Soon, Lauren Jane and Josh followed suit. Finally, with a shrug, my dad joined in.

He looked at Lawton. "Boy, you sure have a good appetite," he said.

"Can't help it," Lawton said. "I never eat this good at home." He offered up a conspiratorial grin. "And if the tabloids are true, I have two French chefs."

According to the tabloids, he also had a pet leopard and a dick the size of Texas. Only half of that was true.

And it wasn't the leopard.

My dad dug into his plain mashed potatoes. "Two chefs, you say?" he boomed across the table. "Lucky me, all I need is Loretta."

I slid my gaze in Loretta's direction. Her fork still rested by her plate. Slowly, I realized I wasn't the only one looking. We all were.

"Gee Mom," Lauren Jane said, "aren't you gonna eat anything?" She rolled her eyes. "You're not on another diet, are you?"

"No," Loretta said through a clenched jaw. "I'm not on a diet."

"Then dig in, honey," my dad said. "This is some darn good eatin'."

I turned to stare at my dad. Was it Talk-Like-a-Cowboy Day or something? This wasn't the way he usually spoke, even in front of company. Usually, his grammar got better, not worse, even with his volume turned way up.

Unless – was this for Lawton's benefit? Was this my dad's way of trying to sound tough? It might've made sense, except for one thing. Lawton wasn't a cowboy.

Lawton grinned at me. He leaned back and rubbed his stomach. "It shore is, ma'am. Mighty thanks."

I glanced at his plate. It was empty. Oh my God. He'd

actually eaten all of it. The man deserved a medal. Or a stomach pump.

Loretta pursed her lips and made no response.

"Gee Mom," Lauren Jane said, "aren't you gonna say 'you're welcome?'" Lauren Jane leaned her head close to Lawton's and said in a loud whisper. "Parents can be so rude."

Loretta was looking daggers at her daughter. "So can daughters," she said.

Lauren Jane smirked. "Well at least I say you're welcome when someone thanks me."

Loretta cleared her throat. "Lawton, I apologize. Of course, you are quite welcome.'"

"See?" my dad said. "Now honey-bun, was that so hard?" He pounded his fist on the table. "Now what do you say we rustle up some dessert?"

I stood. "I'll get it."

And then, remembering what happened last time, I froze in mid-motion. I looked toward Loretta. "Unless you'd rather?"

She waved her hand loosely toward the sideboard. "Go ahead. Whatever." She reached up to rub her temples with both index fingers. "I give up."

I retrieved the dessert dishes and started to serve everyone a slice of cheesecake and a piece of apple cobbler.

Lawton waved the dessert away. "None for me, thanks."

"You sure?" I said. Didn't he want something to wash away the taste of fish barf?

He nodded and reached for his nearly full water glass. He downed it in one long, gulp. Concerned, I reached for the pitcher of ice water and refilled his glass. He looked up, meeting my gaze. "Thanks, dumplin'."

I snickered and then caught myself, turning it into a poor

imitation of throat-clearing.

"Oh you," Lauren Jane said, giving Lawton another playful swat to his arm. "How come you never call me dumpling?"

"Stop it!" Loretta said from her end of the table. "I don't know what's gotten in to all of you, but I've just about had it."

My dad's brow wrinkled. "What's wrong, Sugar Cube?"

Loretta glared at him. "I. Am. Not. Your. Sugar. Cube." And then, as if remembering herself, she gave him an stiff smile. "Alright?"

My dad held up his hands in mock surrender. "Woah. Hear ya loud and clear, chief. No more sugar cubes." He looked around the table. "Got that, everyone?"

"Oh for Heaven's sake," Loretta muttered, reaching for her wine glass.

"So," Lauren Jane said to Lawton, "you and my sister are just friends, right?"

Her sister? Just friends?

Although Lauren Jane and I had been stepsisters for years, I barely knew her. Funny too. The more I knew her, the less I liked her.

Across the table, Lawton grinned at me. "Chloe? You wanna answer that one?"

I smiled back. "Not particularly."

Lauren Jane's brow wrinkled. Again, she turned to Lawton. "So how'd you two meet? Was she your waitress or something?"

Lawton leaned back in his chair. "Nope."

My dad gave another slap to the table. "Don't be shy, son. Go on. Tell us how you two met."

Lawton looked at me. "Chloe, you wanna tell the story?"

My mouth opened, but no words came out. What story should I tell? The one where I saw Lawton kick two guys' asses in the parking lot where I worked? The time I showed up on his doorstep, soaked and looking for a dog that wasn't even my own? The time I fell half-naked over his fence?

"Never mind," Lawton said, leaning forward. "Lemme tell it." ☐

☐

CHAPTER 61

I reached for my own wine glass and downed what little remained. I glanced at Josh. He was grinning from ear to ear, with both eyes on Lawton.

Lawton looked around the table. "It was right after this underground fight in downtown Detroit. I'd just had the worst beating of my life. Total massacre. And I'm lying there in a pool of my own blood—"

"Oh for the love of God," Loretta muttered.

"Mom!" Lauren Jane said. "Don't interrupt." She gripped Lawton's arm. "It's just getting good." She leaned closer to Lawton. "Go on. We're all dying to hear the rest of it."

"And I look up," Lawton said, "and I saw this girl, and she was the most beautiful thing I'd ever seen."

Lauren Jane's brow wrinkled. "Who was she?"

Josh spoke up. "It was Chloe. Wasn't it?"

Lawton nodded. "Yup." He gave Josh a significant look. "And you know what?"

"What?" Josh asked.

"She probably saved my life."

"I knew it!" Josh said.

Loretta was frowning. "That's some story," she said.

I tried to keep from laughing. It sure was. I'd never even been to one of Lawton's fights, not the real ones, anyway.

Lawton held up a hand, palm out. "All true, I swear."

Lauren Jane looked at him with narrowed eyes. "But you've never lost a fight in your life." She straightened in her seat and announced, "I know everything about him, probably even more than Chloe."

I snorted. If she had to ask him about secret tattoos, she was way behind the curve on that one.

"What's so funny?" she said.

I blinked back at her. "Nothing." I gave a little pat to my throat. "Chicken bone."

Her jaw clenched. "We had turkey."

"Oh. Turkey bone then."

She pushed back from her seat. "I'm bored."

"Then maybe," Loretta said, "you can do the dishes."

"But I don't wanna do the dishes," Lauren Jane said. "I know. Make Chloe do it." Lauren Jane turned to me. "I mean, you're used to it, right?"

Lawton pushed back his chair too. "Sorry," he said, "but Chloe and I have to get going."

Loretta frowned. "Why?"

"Prior engagement," he said. "A thing at the hospital. You understand, right?"

"Oh," she said. "Of course."

My dad stood. "I guess we'll let you two cowpokes head on down the trail, then."

"Oh for Heaven's sake, Dick," Loretta said. "Enough already!"

My Dad's eyebrows furrowed. "What?"

Lawton looked at me. "Chloe? You ready?"

I glanced at Josh. He was still smiling. I glanced at Loretta. She was glaring at my dad. I glanced at my dad. He was reaching for another piece of cobbler. I glanced at Lauren

Jane. She was looking down at her lap. Texting?

"Lauren Jane!" Loretta said. "For the last time, no phones at the table."

Lauren Jane did a mimicking voice. "No phones at the table."

"Young lady," Loretta said. "Are you mocking me?"

I looked to Lawton. "Yup, I'm ready." I turned to Josh. "Wanna walk us out to the car?"

At the table, the argument between Loretta and Lauren Jane was heating up by the second. I heard words like "old bag," "ungrateful snot," and something about a cut in someone's allowance.

Walking toward the door, Lawton leaned in close to me. "She still gets an allowance?"

I shrugged. "Maybe not for long."

By the time we reached the front door, the argument had turned into a wrestling match, with Lauren Jane holding on tight to her phone while Loretta struggled to pry it out of her grip. Other than Josh, no one acknowledged our departure at all, which was just fine with me.

Standing in the driveway, I gave Josh a goodbye hug. Then Lawton shook Josh's hand, man-to-man.

"Best Thanksgiving, ever," Josh said.

Surprisingly enough, I had to agree.

When we pulled out of the driveway a minute later, I was surprised to find myself actually smiling. "You know what?" I said. "You're right. That was fun."

"Told ya," he said as hit the accelerator.

"Oh my God," I said. "That whole story about how we met—" I shook my head. "Where'd you come up with that?" I laughed. "I can't decide if I should kiss you or scold you for lying."

"Baby," he said, "I'm a lot of things, but a liar isn't one of them."

I rolled my eyes. "Yeah, right." I glanced out the window. We were practically flying. "Hey Lawton," I said. "We're not running late anymore. Wanna slow it down?"

"Sorry. Can't."

"Why not?"

"Because," he said, "I figure we got about fifteen minutes to make it to the hospital."

"You weren't kidding?" I said. "You really do have plans there? Oh jeez, I'm so sorry. Why didn't you say something when I first called?"

"Because when you called, I didn't know we'd be going."

"Huh?" I stared over at him and felt myself tense. "Lawton," I said, with a voice far steadier than I felt. "What's wrong with your face?"

He leaned over to glance in the rear-view mirror. "Huh. That's not good." Returning his gaze to the road ahead, he hit the brakes and skidded to a stop on the side of the road.

"What is it?" I asked.

Still gripping the wheel, he looked down and shook his head as if clearing the cobwebs.

"Are you alright?" I said.

When I reached out for him, his hands slipped off the steering wheel. I looked down. The hands were so swollen his fingers looked sausages about to pop. I glanced again at his face. Gone were the lean lines and sharp angles. In its place was a swollen mass of facial features I barely recognized.

"Oh my God," I said. "What's wrong?"

He leaned his head against the back of his seat. Slowly, he turned to face me. His words were so garbled, I had a hard time understanding him. But I'm pretty sure what he said was,

"Baby, can you drive a stick?"

And the answer, which I was terrified to give, was no. I couldn't.

CHAPTER 62

"Damn it," I said, squeezing Lawton's hand, "you are such an idiot."

"Please," the nurse said for like the tenth time, "no yelling at the patient."

"I wasn't yelling," I said. "Much."

With a look that told me she thought otherwise, she checked off something on his chart and returned the clipboard to the foot of the bed.

We were in a private hospital room, surrounded by machines, IV stands, and a whole bunch of other stuff that did who-knows-what.

Lawton was lying in the hospital bed, groggy, but more or less awake. How, I had no idea. They'd given him so many shots, and then there was the IV drip, and I'm pretty sure they pumped his stomach too, although for the sake of his dignity, I tried not to ask.

If I'd just had my stomach pumped, I sure as heck wouldn't want anyone asking about it.

The nurse adjusted his IV drip and left the room, but not before giving me a final look of warning. I guess I couldn't really blame her. Idiot was probably the nicest name I'd called him.

Seriously, who eats a whole crapload of oysters, knowing

damn well they're allergic to shellfish? Correction, deadly allergic to shellfish? Crazy people, that's who.

Blinking hard, I looked down at Lawton. "You're looking a lot better," I said.

He gave me a shaky grin. "Yeah?"

"Yeah," I said, "but you're still an idiot."

"Not this time," he said. "So, you know how to drive a stick, huh?"

"No. But I know how to call an ambulance." I bit my lip. "I think I forgot to lock your car."

"Eh, no biggie."

"And, uh, I might've left your keys in the ignition." I winced. "I'm sorry. Your car's probably long-gone by now."

"Don't worry," he said. "It'll turn up. Or not."

I scooted my chair closer and leaned down to press my face close to his. "You shouldn't have done that." My voice caught. "The doctor told me you could've died."

"They always say that. Hasn't happened yet."

"Seriously," I said. "Why on Earth would you do that? It was really stupid." I gave him a stern look. "And don't try to tell me you didn't know."

"I would," he said, "but like I told you, I'm not a liar."

"So why'd you do it?" I said.

"Because," he said with a faint smile, "I couldn't stand to see you hurt."

"You think I like seeing you hurt?" I said.

"This?" he said. "It's nothing."

"Okay," I said. "Now you're a liar."

Weakly, he shook his head. "Baby, I'm not lying. Seeing you cry? Hurts way more than this."

I reached up to wipe at my eyes. For his sake, I tried to laugh. "Oh so, now, you tell me." I closed my eyes to blink away the tears. When I opened them, he was asleep.

I sat there with him for the longest time. I kept expecting someone to make me leave. But by some strange twist of fate, or maybe a simple oversight, no one did.

Watching him, I thought of all the twists and turns our relationship had taken since that very first day I'd seen him, standing outside his gate. If I'd only been honest with him from the get-go, things would've been a whole lot different.

I reached out to stroke his hand, relieved to see his long, strong fingers returning to their normal shape. I moved my hand upward, tracing the lines and shapes of his tattoos. Feeling the ridges of his muscles steady beneath my fingers, it made me feel just a little better. Like he was solid and real, not just a figment, and not just wishful thinking.

Except for the faint humming of equipment and Lawton's steady breathing, the room was eerily quiet. Thankfully, I hadn't spent a lot of time in hospitals. There was that time my mom fell off our apartment balcony, and then a couple years later, that crazy accident with Erika's Porsche.

In mid-motion, I felt a stillness overtake me. This scene, right now, it was all too familiar – a different time, a different place, a different person.

Or – I swallowed – maybe it wasn't. Slowly, I let my gaze travel the length of his arm, trying to see beyond the lines and patterns of his tattoos. And then, just when I started calling myself crazy for even looking, I spotted them, faint, but unmistakable, even with the inky camouflage.

Cigarette burns.

Oh my God. It was him.

CHAPTER 63

I remembered it all too well. It was the night Erika crashed her Porsche. I'd been standing just outside a side entrance, trying desperately to reach her parents before they spotted her car at the end of their driveway and assumed the worst.

Erika was somewhere on the fifth floor, getting X-rays and a few stitches. I'd brought her to the hospital myself, in my piece-of-crap Fiesta, which, come to think of it, wasn't quite as crappy back then.

I'd just finished leaving another message on her dad's cell phone when I heard the steady beat of techno music, growing louder with every second. I glanced up just in time to see a huge white SUV squeal up to the curb. It had dark tinted windows and bright gold rims that kept turning even after the car stopped.

The rear passenger door flew open, and a body tumbled out. It rolled a couple of times, then stopped, face down on the sidewalk just a few feet away from where I stood.

I watched, in frozen shock as the SUV squealed off, leaving whoever – definitely a man – lying there on the concrete.

"Oh my God." Without thinking, I rushed over to crouch beside him. "Are you okay?"

He wore no shirt, no socks, no shoes, just some dark

running pants. I saw spiky dark hair and the body of someone I guessed to be in their twenties, at least based on his physique, which was embarrassingly magnificent.

Instantly, I took in the hard lines and sinewy muscle. And bruises. And blood. And – I swallowed – cigarette burns all up and down his arms.

I looked frantically for signs of life. "Somebody help!" I called.

It was stupid really, considering I was the only one out there. Tentatively, I reached out for his hand. Was he breathing? Did he have a pulse?

My own pulse was jumping so much, I couldn't be sure of anything. "Help!" I yelled again. "Somebody's hurt over here!"

And then he spoke in a groggy masculine voice with just the barest hint of humor. "No," he mumbled. "I'm good."

I heard myself gasp. At least he was alive. It was better than I feared, given the blood pooling around his head.

"Uh," I stammered. "I, uh, I don't think you're exactly alright."

Desperately, I looked around. Where the hell was everybody? But I knew exactly where. I'd been at the hospital for the last couple of hours. I'd seen plenty of people inside, or lingering by the front entrance, or even near the emergency room doors.

This door was next to the dumpsters. No one wanted to hang out here. But that's exactly why I'd picked this spot in the first place, for some privacy.

I pulled out my phone. "Hang on. I'll call for help." I started to dial 911, and was immediately struck by the sheer stupidity of it. They'd just send an ambulance, which would take him to a hospital.

He was at the hospital. "Wait here," I said. "I'll get help."

"No. Wait," he said in that same groggy voice.

"What?"

With a small groan, he lifted his head and turned it in my direction. "Don't go."

He couldn't be serious. He needed help. "Don't worry. I'll be right back. With help. I promise."

At this, he gave me such a piercing look that I felt my own gaze shift from his swollen eyes to the rest of his face. It was covered in so much blood that I felt the color drain from my own.

"No. Stay," he said. "Please."

Did he think he was going to die? Maybe he didn't want to die alone? I tried to keep my voice calm. For his sake. Still, when I spoke, it came out as a ragged croak. "What happened? Were you shot or something?"

At this, he laughed. Seriously laughed. "That bad, huh?" The laughter died abruptly when it was replaced by a choking fit.

At this, I went into full panic mode. "Help!" I yelled. "C'mon! Someone's hurt over here! Please? We need help!"

But nobody came. I was afraid to leave him. And more afraid of what might happen if I didn't.

His lips moved. "Stop."

"Stop what?"

His mouth moved, like he was trying to form a smile, but couldn't quite manage it. "Stop yelling."

In spite of everything, I felt vaguely insulted. I'd been yelling for his sake, after all. I was still holding his hand. "Then I'll be right back," I said, pulling away.

Somehow, he managed to grab my wrist. For someone in such rough shape, the grip was amazingly strong. "Don't tell," he said.

I stared at him. "Don't tell what?"

"Anything. Whatever you saw, it didn't happen."

Frantically, I looked around. Was he talking about the white SUV?

"Stairs. Fell down 'em. No big deal." He rolled onto his side and clutched his stomach. "Be fine in a minute." A spasm shook his body, and his eyes fluttered shut.

Shit.

I leapt to my feet. "You hang on, I mean it!" I told him. A waste of words, really. It was pretty obvious he couldn't hear much of anything. With a final glance at his scarily still body, I sprinted around the side of the hospital, heading full speed toward the emergency room entrance.

CHAPTER 64

Three hours later, I sat beside him in a not-so-private hospital room. He had a whole bunch of injuries – broken ribs, head trauma, and just enough internal damage to make them talk about operating.

But they didn't.

They'd checked him for identification. He had none. They'd asked his name. He couldn't answer.

For the dubious privilege of staying by his side, I told one little lie. That one lie led to another. And another after that.

Before I knew it, I was filling out forms, answering questions, talking to doctors, and holding his hand like a real sister might.

Except I didn't feel like a sister.

I felt like an interloper. A fraud. And something else. The something else was complicated – wrapped up in guilt for not getting help sooner and tinged with something I didn't want to think about. Curiosity? Concern?

I imagined his face, free of bruises, blood and bandages. I still had no idea what he actually looked like. I hadn't seen him. Not really. But I wanted to. And that's when I identified that mysterious something.

Longing.

Here was a guy who laughed – literally laughed – after

getting beat almost to death and dumped onto the sidewalk. Some days, I had a hard time laughing at all. But I needed to. If not for me, then definitely for my younger brother. He deserved that.

Sure, my mom wasn't around much, and my dad was dating someone who hated kids. Well, his kids anyway. But we were doing alright. At least compared to this guy.

When he woke up, all hell would break loose. The name I'd given wasn't real, and neither was the address. If I wasn't gone by the time he woke up, I'd be in some serious trouble.

Until that point, I watched him as he lay there, heavily bandaged, and even more heavily sedated. I talked to him in whispers, relaying every silly thing I could think of. Stories about my Polish grandmother, cartoons I'd read in the paper, ridiculous things my little brother liked to say.

If this guy were awake, he'd be bored out of his mind. But for now, he was John Livingston of Maple Drive, and he was utterly fascinated with everything I said.

And I kept my promise. Except for some made-up history, I told them nothing. Insurance? No idea. Medical history, didn't know. If nothing else, these things at least were the absolute truth.

Some sister I was.

I'd fallen asleep in the chair next to his bed when my cell phone buzzed. I answered with a hushed hello.

"You still at the hospital?" It was Erika.

"Yeah, why?"

"A heads-up," she said. "My parents are there looking for you."

"Really? Why?"

"My guess? They're heading on that cruise tomorrow. And they want to thank you before they leave."

"Thank me? For what?"

She laughed. "For saving their beloved daughter's life, of course."

"Oh shut up," I said. "I just gave you a ride." And I would have given her a ride home too, if her latest boyfriend hadn't shown up to reclaim that honor.

"Yeah. Just kidding," she said. "Actually, they want to give you a birthday present. You know, the big eighteen."

Neither one of us mentioned what my parents had gotten Erika. Nothing. But she couldn't feel too bad. They hadn't gotten me anything either. "Awww…they didn't have to do that," I said.

"Yeah, well you know how they are."

I did. They were amazing, slightly overprotective and maybe a little extravagant, but one-hundred percent wonderful. If I didn't love Erika like a sister, I might've been consumed by jealousy. When it came to parents, she won the jackpot. Me? I got the booby prize. Two of them, actually.

"Anyway," Erika said, "They're at the hospital now."

"Really? They're here?" I felt myself stiffen. "What'd you tell them?"

"About your mystery man?" she said. "Nothing. I just mentioned you were visiting a friend."

"Well, he might be a mystery man," I said, "but he's definitely not mine."

"Whatever. I'm just mad that your story's more interesting than mine is."

I rolled my eyes. "You don't think totaling a Porsche is interesting?"

"Not the way I did it," she said.

I saw her point. It's not like she was drag-racing. She'd left the car in neutral at the top of her parent's steep driveway.

She'd also forgotten about the parking brake. The car rolled down the drive, drifted onto the street, and got T-boned by a dump truck.

She wouldn't have been injured at all if she hadn't tripped on the driveway chasing after it.

"You know what?" I said. "Come to think of it, your story's way more interesting

"Stupid's more like it," she said. "Hey, I just got a text. They're in the cafeteria. They wanna know if you can meet them there."

I glanced at the guy in the bed. He hadn't moved. "Tell them I'm on the way." When I disconnected the call, I reached out for the mystery guy's hand and gave it a quick squeeze. "I'll be back in a few minutes." I made myself smile. "Don't go anywhere, alright?"

The joke was lame, but it wasn't any lamer than the story of Josh's imaginary friend. Humor heals, right? Even bad humor? Shaking my head, I left the room and headed three floors down to the cafeteria.

I returned with a ruby pendant, way too extravagant, but impossible to refuse – and not because I hadn't tried. But I couldn't help but smile as I felt the ruby resting against my skin.

But as I returned to that hospital room, I felt my smile fade.

He was gone.☐

☐

CHAPTER 65

As I sat in a totally different hospital, under a totally different scenario, I thought again of that mystery guy, trying to assemble the pieces in some way that made sense. That was how long ago? Five years?

That had to be just a month or two before Lawton had rocketed to fame and eventual fortune, all starting with some Internet video of a gritty back-alley fight. I'd seen that fight myself, with Lawton in all his tattooed glory, beating the living crap out of some guy who'd supposedly been unbeatable.

Unbeatable. The thought made me frown. Supposedly, Lawton had never lost a fight either. But on that very first night, something terrible had happened. The injuries, I might've chalked up to a fight gone wrong, but the cigarette burns made no sense at all.

So what had happened?

Thinking about it, I must've dozed off, because I jumped in my chair when I felt a touch on my shoulder. I whipped around to see Bishop, standing just behind me.

"Oh," I said. "It's you."

He glanced toward Lawton. "Is he alright?"

I nodded. "Mostly."

Bishop shook his head. "What a dumb-ass."

"Hey!" I said. "That's not very nice."

He gave me a look. "Just so you know, I talked with the nurse."

"Oh." I cleared my throat. "So, uh, she told on me, huh?"

"Pretty much."

"How'd you find out he was here?" I asked. "I would've called, but I didn't know how to reach you."

"Eh, heard it through the grapevine," he said.

"What grapevine?"

He shrugged. "So he gorged on seafood, huh?"

I nodded, feeling my eyes water just a little. "Here, I just thought he hated it," I said.

"Of course he hates it." Bishop flicked his gaze toward Lawton. "Look what it does to him."

"But why on Earth would he do something like that?" I said.

Bishop gave me a deadpan look. "My guess? He didn't want to see you hurt."

"But you don't even know what happened," I said.

"It's not hard to figure out. Here, lemme guess. And you can tell me how close I am."

I crossed my arms. "Alright. Go ahead."

"For whatever reason, it was either you or him. Or maybe it was either someone you care about, or him. Either way, he took the bullet so you didn't have to."

"It wasn't a bullet," I said. "It was oyster gravy."

Bishop made a face. "Is that real?"

"Unfortunately."

"How much did he eat?" Bishop said.

I glanced at Lawton. "A lot."

"Well, that's love for ya." Bishop shook his head. "Poor bastard."

"Hey!"

He shrugged. "I'm just saying."

I gave him a look. "So how about you? Haven't you ever been in love before?"

He glanced at Lawton, and then back at me. His voice was oddly quiet. "Yeah. Once."

"What happened?" I asked, suddenly curious.

Bishop was silent a few beats. And then, he reached into the back pocket of his jeans and pulled out his wallet. He opened it up and slid something out of an interior pocket. It looked like a playing card, all folded up in a neat little square.

"What's that?" I said.

Silently, he handed it over. The creases were worn and the pattern was scuffed. Taking it from his cool hands, I had the feeling it had been handled a lot, and folded often.

Careful not to mangle it worse than it already was, I unfolded the card and studied the image. Obviously, it hadn't come from a regular card deck.

"Is this a tarot card?" I said.

He nodded.

I studied the image. "The Fool? Is this supposed to be you?"

He gave a humorless laugh. "No. Not if I can help it."

And then, I heard a groggy voice from the direction of the hospital bed. "Damn it. For the last time, just go find her already, will ya?"

CHAPTER 66

A half hour later, Bishop stood to leave. The three of us had spent the last thirty minutes talking, a lot about what happened at dinner, and a little about the very first time Lawton and I had met.

"So you're Hospital Girl," Bishop said. He glanced at Lawton. "You could've mentioned that."

"Why?" Lawton said. "So you could spend another five years giving me a hard time? No thanks."

"Hospital Girl?" I said.

Lawton gave a sheepish grin. "I didn't know your real name."

"Well, you could've mentioned it to me," I said. "I never gave you a hard time."

Bishop made a noise that sounded suspiciously like a snort.

"Hey," I said. "I didn't. Much."

I turned back to Lawton. "So why didn't you tell me?"

"Maybe," he said, "I wanted you to love me, not that guy on the sidewalk."

I rolled my eyes. "Because the guy on the sidewalk lost a fight? Lawton, don't you get it? Win, lose, it doesn't matter. I don't love you because of what you do or what you have. I love you because of who you are."

Lawton grinned. "You wanna say that again?"

"That's it," Bishop said. "I'm gonna go get your car. See ya in a few days."

"Um, actually," I said, "I think I lost his keys."

"Not a problem," Bishop said.

"So you've got a spare?" I said.

"Something like that."

"Hey," Lawton called out to Bishop, when he was halfway to the door. "Have 'em drop a car in visitor's parking, will ya? Something low-key."

Nodding, Bishop walked out the door, silently, just like he'd come.

"He's kind of scary," I said.

"Baby," Lawton said, "you don't know the half of it."

"Speaking of which." I turned to face him. "Since you're incapacitated…"

He raised his eyebrows. "Incapacitated? That's what you think, huh?"

I gave it some thought. I'd seen him walk away from a different hospital looking far worse than this. "Hey, I'll take what I can get." I gave him a stern look. "Time to answer some questions, mister."

"Oh yeah? Like what?"

I glanced toward the door that Bishop had just walked out of. "Just what is it that you two are involved in?"

His smile faded. "What do you mean?"

"Oh c'mon," I said. "Don't play dumb. You know exactly what I mean. You've got this bullet-proof car and all kinds of weird skills—"

"Like what?"

"Well, like getting into locked houses, for starters."

"Oh that."

"Yeah. That."

344

"Sorry," he said. "I can't tell you."

Silently, I studied his face. He didn't look sorry.

"Why not?" I said.

"Because I've taken an oath."

I rolled my eyes. "Oh please. Do I look dumb to you?"

"No," he said. "What you look is so damn beautiful, it hurts just to look at you."

"Now you're just sucking up."

"Yeah. But that doesn't mean it's not true."

"Are you ever gonna tell me?" I said.

"Yup."

"So why won't you now?"

"Because we're not married." He grinned. "Yet."

My lips twitched. "Yet?"

"A guy can hope, right?"

"C'mon, be serious."

"You think I'm not?"

"Honestly?" I said. "I'm not sure."

He grinned. "Good. Because whatever happens, I'm gonna do it right. Because you deserve it, and a hell of a lot more."

My knees were trembling, and I was having a hard time focusing. Was he saying what I thought he was saying? And if so, how did I feel about that? I heard a giggle. Oh God, it was coming from me. My face blazing, I slapped both hands over my mouth and tried to look serious.

Lawton reached up, gently tugging my elbow until I tumbled down next to him, lying with him in the hospital bed, shoes and all.

I was laughing so hard, I couldn't stop. "You're gonna get me trouble," I said.

"From who?" he asked.

"The nurse."

"Eh, if she gives you a hard time, we'll just leave."

"You can't do that," I said.

"Why not? We'll just walk out and take care of the paperwork later."

I believed him, too. "So tell me," I said. "What happened that night we first met? Obviously, you lost a fight, but–"

He shook his head. "I didn't lose."

"But I saw you," I said. "No offense, but you were a mess. If you won, then the other guy must've ended up dead."

I froze. It would explain so much, the cigarette burns, him getting tossed out of a vehicle that barely slowed down, his warnings for me to stay quiet.

"Oh my God," I said. "Is that what happened? You killed someone?"

He laughed. "No. But you should see the look on your face. It makes me glad I didn't."

"Oh stop it," I said. "So what did happen?"

"You're right about one thing. It was a fight, except I was supposed to lose."

"Why?"

"Remember that businessman I told you about?"

"The one who loaned money to your Grandma?"

"Yeah. Well, you know that old saying. He made me an offer I couldn't refuse."

"To throw the fight?"

"Yup. And he'd forgive the loan. Refuse and, well, let's just say he'd be very unhappy."

"So you agreed?"

"Yeah. I was young and dumb. I knew I shouldn't. But I kept thinking of getting that loan off her back. It seemed a small price, wrong as it was."

"So what happened?" I said.

"One fucking punch."

"What do you mean?"

"So I'm supposed to make it look good, right? Hit him a few times. He hits me back. He was supposed to be some tough guy, won a lot of fights. So I hit the guy. Just once. And it's all over. He was on the ground. The crowd was going nuts. The guy never got up. And that businessman, the one who paid me to take a dive, he saw the whole thing."

"So then what?" I said.

"Well, as you can imagine, he wasn't too happy."

My voice was very quiet. "So he tried to kill you?"

Lawton laughed. "Nah. He liked me. Had 'em drop me at the hospital, right?"

"Drop you?" I said. "I was there, remember? They squealed up and kicked you out. You could've died."

"Nah, it'll take more than that to kill me."

I reached out to trace one of the old cigarette burns, faint, but unmistakable now that I knew what I was looking at. "They hurt you," he said.

"Baby," he said, "whatever they did, it didn't hurt half so bad as losing you."

I felt my eyes grow misty. "Really?"

"Yeah. Even then. First time we met. That's why I couldn't have you talking about it."

"Why not?"

"Because them hurting me, I can deal with. But them hurting you, I wasn't gonna let it happen. I still remember that night. You were so sweet." He laughed. "And funny."

"I was not funny," I said.

"You were too," he said. "And so fucking beautiful. And your voice. Man, I loved the sound of it."

"You couldn't have loved it that much," I teased. "You left

without saying goodbye."

"I had to," he said, "for your sake. Those weren't nice people."

"That's for sure."

"And then, a couple months ago, when I'd almost given up on finding you again, there you were, walking right past my house, looking just the same as I remembered."

"This is totally unfair, you know."

"How so?" he said.

"I had no idea what you looked like." I smiled. "But what I did see, and heard, I liked. I liked a lot." I looked around the hospital room. "Want to know what I wish?"

"What?"

"I wish we were somewhere else."

He smiled. "Yeah?" He sat up. "Let's go."

"Oh stop it," "You're supposed to stay at least twelve hours."

"For what?"

"Observation."

He leaned close to nuzzle my neck. "The only person I want observing me," he said, "is you."☐

☐

CHAPTER 67

An hour later, we were pulling into the Parkers' driveway. Lawton was behind the wheel of a slick black SUV that had miraculously shown up in visitor's parking.

"I still can't believe you just walked out of there," I said.

He pulled up just behind my car and shifted the vehicle into park. "Wanna know what I can't believe?" he said.

"What?"

"That we've got another chance." He turned sideways in the driver's seat to face me. "And I swear to you, this time I'm not gonna screw it up."

I shook my head. "It wasn't just you. It was me too."

I looked toward the Parkers' house, dark and stately in the quiet neighborhood. I'd wanted so badly to belong here that I'd made excuse after excuse for not being honest. But I was done making excuses, to me, and to Lawton.

"I should've told you," I said.

"You should've told me what?"

I gave a small laugh. "Where to begin?" I said. "About house-sitting, Grandma, Josh, my job." I heard a soft sigh escape my lips. "You know, Lawton. I never meant to lie to you." I looked down at my lap. "But I guess, if I'm being honest, it was nice to feel like I belonged somewhere for once."

"Hey," he said, his voice quiet in the darkened car. "I know exactly where you belong."

"Where?"

"Wherever you want to be." He grinned. "As long as it's with me."

I returned his smile. "While I'm apologizing," I said, "I guess I should apologize for flipping out on you."

He laughed. "Which time?"

"Hey!" I said, giving him a playful swat on the arm. "I meant about the whole hooker thing. But I've gotta tell you, I was pretty mad."

"Were you? I couldn't tell."

I laughed. "You are so not making this easy."

His voice grew serious. "Baby, whatever you said, I deserved it and then some. I should've known what you meant." He shook his head. "But thinking of you with other guys, it made me so crazy I wasn't thinking straight."

"So you're pleading insanity?"

"And stupidity. Because I should've known that's not you. So, if anyone's sorry, it's me."

"Speaking of sorry," I said, "why didn't you tell me that Shaggy was the guy behind that sex tape?"

"Who's Shaggy?"

"Oh crap. I mean that Chester guy."

"Who?"

"The guy with that camera phone? You know, the one whose girlfriend pelted him with shrimp?"

Lawton shook his head. "He didn't have anything to do with that tape."

"He didn't?"

"Nah. Was a totally different guy. Remember the guy they caught screwing a pumpkin?"

"At the Tiger's game?" I did remember. A few years earlier, the guy had been the punch-line of countless late-night jokes, especially after he claimed the whole thing was a setup.

"That's the one," Lawton said.

"Wow, talk about karma, huh?"

"How so?"

"I mean, look, he set things up to violate your privacy, and then his um, sex act was just as infamous. And talk about embarrassing. Funny how that works, isn't it?"

"Yup." He glanced toward the house. "Want me to come in with you?"

He'd never been inside the Parkers' house before. Well, not by invitation anyway. The Parkers definitely wouldn't like it. It would violate my agreement and cause all kinds of grief if they found out.

I smiled. "Yeah, come on in," I said.

When Chucky saw Lawton, he went berserk, diving for his legs so ferociously that it would've toppled a lesser man. Lawton crouched down to ruffle his fur, and Chucky bounded up on him so fast and so frantically that this time, Lawton did let himself get toppled over. And before I knew it, they were wrestling with each other across the hardwood floor.

I rolled my eyes. "Boys will be boys." I set my purse on the kitchen counter and called out to Lawton. "Could you take Chucky on a little yard walk while I grab some stuff?"

"How little?" he asked.

"Five minutes."

When he left, I dashed upstairs to grab a few essentials – my toothbrush and makeup, along with a small overnight bag with a change of clothes.

I looked around the guest room. If the situation with the Parkers continued to slide, I wouldn't be able to stay here much longer. But leaving Chucky wasn't an option. The plants, well, they were on their own.

I felt grubby after those hours in the hospital, or maybe it was from spending time at Loretta's. But either way, I needed a shower. When I heard the front door open and shut, I felt myself smile. I didn't plan on showering here, and I sure as heck didn't plan on doing it alone.

I tossed my keys into the overnight bag and practically flew downstairs, where I grabbed Chucky, and dragged Lawton out the front door, locking it behind me.

Lawton made a show of looking around. "So, uh, is the house on fire?"

"Nope," I said. "But I am."

CHAPTER 68

Five minutes later, we were wet and naked in his shower, surrounded by clear glass on three sides and smooth marble on the fourth.

We stood in a timeless embrace, our hot, wet bodies pressed against each other, while the steaming water cascaded over us. I wanted to be closer, to feel him inside me, and wrap my legs around his waist and beg him to pound into me like it was our last night on Earth.

And I wanted to step away, to watch the streams of water dance over his glorious body, to see his muscles and tattoos shift and glisten, to watch the thick soapy lather slide down his skin while my hands and fantasies ran wild.

I wanted it all.

I lifted my head and met his gaze. He lowered his head, and his lips met mine. I felt a strong hand caress the back of my neck as my wet hair slid over his long, strong fingers.

Desperate to be closer, I rubbed up against him, savoring the feel of his muscles and the rock-hard proof of his arousal.

Already my breaths were already coming short and fast. I was drowning in desire, and wet inside and out. Stifling a groan, I reached for the soap and moved backward, breaking the embrace while my eyes feasted on this fantasy guy come to life.

I rubbed the bar of luxury soap between my hands, watching a thick white lather grow between them. Then, I brought my hands, soap and all, to his chest, rubbing in slow, steady circles over those glorious pecs, feeling the muscles tighten and shift in time with my movements.

I lifted my eyes to gaze at him through my eyelashes, taking in his wet hair, his smoldering eyes, and his lips that parted as he stared down at me with an expression of such love and desire that I felt my heart soar and body tremble.

Breathing hard, I ran my palms across his chest, watching the lather gather between my fingers and slide downward, cascading in soapy waves over his washboard abs and lower still.

My hands drifted lower, sliding over those tightly defined stomach muscles as the sudsy water danced between my fingers. Desperate for more, I splayed my fingers, stretching them out as far as they could go, trying to touch every ridge and to catalog every sleek line of his amazing body. I ran my hands over his lean hips and reached around to caress his backside, relishing the hardness of his ass and the shift of his muscles.

He felt like a dream, a work of art come to life, and with every shift of his body and every movement of my hands, I marveled that I was actually here. With him. And that in spite of everything, this dream guy was actually mine.

I worked up some more lather and moved my hands back to his front. I wrapped one slippery hand around his rigid tool, sliding my closed palm up and down the length of him, the whole time marveling at his amazing size, his perfect shape, and the smooth hardness that felt so magnificent in my tight wet grasp.

His arousal pulsed in time with my touch, and when I

tightened my grip, he moaned my name. "Chloe."

I lifted my gaze to his face and felt myself smile. His eyes were shut, and his lips barely parted. But then, as if feeling the heat of my gaze, his eyes slowly drifted open, and slowly, he smiled that heart-stopping smile.

"Turn around," he said.

"Why?"

"Do I need a reason?"

I smiled. "But I'm not done yet."

"Me neither. And I don't want to be. Not yet." He reached out for my shoulders and gently turned me away from him. I felt a strong arm wrap around my stomach, and Lawton's front pressing against my back. His body was hot and hard, and slippery with soap suds and cascading water.

As for me, I was slippery with something else. Hot desire that coursed through me like a greedy life-force with a mind of its own. I wanted him now, and I wanted him always.

I heard his voice in my ear and felt his lips on my neck. "Baby, I love you so much it hurts."

A sigh escaped my lips, and my head fell back against his chest. "I love you, too. And God, I've missed you. I've missed this. I've missed everything."

He wrapped both arms me and squeezed me tight, gathering me against him and whispering. so low I could barely hear. "You're mine. And I'm never letting you go."

His words, sultry and sweet, turned my insides to butter and my heart to mush. I ground my hips back against him, urging him closer, and wanting him forever.

I reached up, arching my back as I placed my hands around the back of his neck, feeling his hard, corded neck muscles against my palms and his wet, soft hair brush the backs of my fingers.

I closed my eyes and felt his hands slide upward until they reached my breasts. He cupped their undersides, gently squeezing them together and then cupped them upward into the cascading streams of water as his lips pressed into my neck, and his hot erection pressed into my back.

When a moan escaped my lips, his hands moved higher, caressing my curves with sweet persistence until I trembled against him, panting for more.

When his fingers brushed my nipples, I arched into him, wanting more, and more again. Soon he was toying with my nipples, stroking them, rolling them between his hot, wet fingers, and gently tugging at them until they were hard knobs of taut desire.

When I ground my backside into him, I felt one of his hands drift lower, sliding down past my ribs, over my stomach, and drifting down toward my pelvis. When I felt his fingers slide back and forth on either side of my hot center, I moaned and ground my hips forward, my need so desperate that my body was begging.

When he rubbed his thumb along my clit and ran a long finger across my hot, wet opening, I couldn't stand it one second longer.

I twisted around and coiled my body against him, feeling my breasts flatten against his chest and my abs contract with desire. I reached between us and took his rigid length into my eager hands.

I wanted to climb up him, to cover him with kisses and sheath his hardness with my hot, slick opening until he filled me completely.

"Lawton," I said, more a moan than a word. "I need you so bad."

He lowered his head, silencing my words with a long,

drawn-out kiss. I reached up, wrapping my arms around his neck and savoring the feel of his wet lips on mine.

As his sighs mixed with my own, his hands drifted downward. He cupped my ass and lifted me up around him like I weighed next to nothing. I wrapped my legs around him, savoring the tightness of his hips and the muscles of his back.

And then, with a low groan, he was sliding into me. I moaned and wrapped my legs tighter, feeling his hot, hard length thrust deeper and deeper. Lost to everything except this, I ground into him, feeling my legs tremble and stomach clench.

He was so strong and so beautiful, it seemed like a dream. But it wasn't a dream. I knew this by the ragged sound of his voice as he said my name over and over again.

And then, I was convulsing. I felt my walls tighten around him, and his hardness pulsing with every thrust. Soon, the pressure was almost unbearable. I felt my insides convulse and my legs shake.

I called his name and hung on for dear life as waves of our united pleasure trampled all my doubts, all my inhibitions, and all my fears in a sea of sound and sensation that threatened to carry us away to who-knows-where.

Together, we sank down into a trembling heap, letting the steaming water wash over us as we stared into each other's eyes, oblivious of everything except each other.

Slowly he reached out, running the back of his index finger across my jaw. "If I wake up, and you're not here, if this is all a dream, I don't want to wake up at all."

I felt myself smile. "Me neither."

CHAPTER 69

Ten minutes later we collapsed, still naked, onto his bed with wet hair and damp skin. He was sprawled on his back, and I was cuddled up next to him, with my head on his shoulder, and my hand resting on his chest.

The air was cool, but my skin was warm. I sighed into his shoulder. "Best Thanksgiving, ever." I winced. "I mean aside from the thing at my dad's. Um, and the hospital. And losing your keys." I lifted my head. "You know what? I'll shut up now."

"No. Don't do that," he said in a sleepy voice. "I love to hear you talk." He pulled me closer. "It was the best. But you know what?"

"What?"

"Next year, it'll be even better."

"How do you know?" I said.

"Because we'll make sure of it."

I smiled into his shoulder. "Yeah," I murmured, feeling myself drift. "I can see that."

I woke in the darkened room to find myself wrapped in Lawton's arms and covered with a soft fleece blanket. I glanced at the clock. It wasn't quite nine.

The night was still young. I'd slept barely an hour, but felt wide awake – no surprise, given the fact that for someone like me, who worked nights, this was practically the middle of the day.

Gently, I slid out of Lawton's embrace and got out of bed. I spotted Chucky, curled up near the footboard, with a furry paw resting on Lawton's ankle.

Smiling, I made my way to the bathroom, and returned to the room a couple minutes later for my overnight bag. Determined not to wake either of my two favorite guys, I lugged my bag into one of the spare rooms. Quietly, I dug out some casual clothes, got dressed, and ran a brush through my still-damp hair.

It was a big house, so there wasn't any shortage of things to do, or places to do it in. But what I really needed to do was figure out what to do about the Parkers. It was beyond obvious that things weren't exactly what they seemed.

I had received no returned calls, no replacement checks, and no instructions from the financial guy or anyone else. Planning to check my phone, I went to retrieve my purse and stopped, confused, when it wasn't in its usual spot. And then I remembered, I'd left it on the Parkers' kitchen counter when I'd gone there earlier with Lawton.

"Oh crap," I muttered, suddenly feeling very naked – and not in a fun way – without my purse and everything it contained, my phone in particular. I glanced toward the quiet stairway and considered the timeframe.

It was still relatively early. If I knew Lawton, he'd be awake in an hour or two and ready to make up for lost time. Now was probably the perfect time to make a quick dash back to the house. I could grab my purse, maybe throw in some laundry, and be back before Lawton even noticed I was gone.

A minute later, I was lacing up my tennis shoes and shrugging into my jacket. I grabbed Lawton's spare house key, along with my own small ring of keys, and shoved them into the front pocket of my jeans.

I walked out Lawton's front door, feeling happier than I had in forever. My job stunk, and my career was going nowhere, not to mention my house sitting troubles. But somehow, I was having a hard time caring. All that stuff, I'd work it out somehow.

Walking down the quiet street, I thought of how much had changed, not just today, but over the past few months. No matter what, I vowed, I was going to be myself from now on. If people didn't like it, well, then that was their problem, not mine.

I was still smiling when I opened the front door and went inside the darkened house. I turned toward the side table and reached for the lamp.

From somewhere in the darkness, an unfamiliar male voice said, "Touch that light, and you're dead."

With a gasp, I whirled toward the sound and spotted what I should've seen earlier. The hulking figure of a man, standing near the far wall of the front room.

I couldn't make out his features, just his clothing. Black pants, black jacket, black shoes. Or maybe it all just seemed black in the shadows. As my eyes grew accustomed to the dark, I noticed what I should've noticed earlier. Upended plants and bare walls where the shadows of framed artwork should have been.

Slowly, I backed up until my backside hit the easy chair near the front window. I opened my mouth, but no words came out.

"Where's our money?" he said.

My heart raced, and my hands grew clammy. In a strangled voice, I said, "What money?"

"The money you owe us, bitch."

"I don't owe you any money."

The hulking figure moved closer. I looked wildly around. I needed a weapon. A baseball bat, a lamp, something.

And then I heard it, the click of a gun.

Shit.

CHAPTER 70

From somewhere near the kitchen, I heard a crash and a thud.

"Hey!" the man called over his shoulder. "You break anything good, and it's coming out of your ass!"

Oh God, how many people were in here, anyway?

"Whoever you are," I said in a far too shaky voice, "you've got the wrong house."

"Well, Louise," he said, "that's where you're wrong."

Louise? As in Louise Parker?

"Because," he continued, "we have exactly the right house. And you have exactly one minute to start talking, or we're gonna break more than some vase or whatever the fuck that was."

"But I'm not Louise," I said, "She's not here."

"Sure." He chuckled, a deep, ominous sound that echoed oddly in the quiet house. "I believe you."

"It's true," I stammered. "I can give her a message if—"

"Shut the fuck up," the guy said.

"But I'm not Louise. I don't even —"

"I said shut up!"

I clamped my lips shut and reached behind me. The Parkers kept a letter opener in the small drawer of the side table. If I could only reach it, maybe — shit, I didn't know.

363

But I'd feel a lot better if I had something, anything, in my hands.

Slowly, the man moved closer. His shoes made a faint, padded sound against the hardwood floors.

My heart racing, I tried to make out his features. I looked wildly to the left and then to the right. I wanted to run, but I didn't know where.

He had a gun. I had nothing.

Maybe I could dive across the floor, and take cover under the coffee table. Yeah, right. Like the coffee table was bulletproof. Suddenly, my breath hitched, and my eyes felt too big for my face. Behind the stranger, something was moving – a shadow shaped like a person.

Oh my God. I knew that shadow, because no one other than Lawton moved like that. As I watched, it crept silently toward the stranger with deadly purpose.

If the stranger saw him, we were both in deep trouble. A flash of consequences went through my brain, ending with Lawton dead on the floor. I couldn't let that happen.

I made my voice sound small and weak, not hard to do, given the circumstances. "Please," I said. "Don't hurt me."

His laugh, low and deep, turned my insides to mud, but I forced myself to speak again. "I'll do anything you want. And I mean—" I swallowed. "Anything."

"Oh yeah?" Slowly, his right arm lowered. "You bet your ass you will."

Suddenly, the shadow behind him moved, barreling into the stranger at lightning speed. The man flew forward, and I jumped out of the way. The darkened forms slammed, hard, into the end table.

The table tipped, sending the lamp crashing to the floor, and the stranger with it. I saw the shadows of fists, and the sound of their impact, along with grunts and curses.

Desperately, I looked around for the gun. It had gone flying, right? But I didn't see it. I rushed toward stairway and dove for the light switch. I flicked it on.

The shadows became people, and the destruction became obvious. Near the front window, the man on the floor was still, his face a bloody mess and his arms limp at his sides. The fingers on one of his hands looked twisty and mangled, like they'd been stepped on hard, or beaten with a sledgehammer.

At last, I spotted the gun, a dull black thing with a short barrel, lying where the stranger had last been standing. I stepped toward it.

"Wait," Lawton said in a low, urgent voice. "Don't touch it."

I stopped and looked over at him. He got to his feet and gave the guy a final vicious kick. The guy didn't budge.

He rushed toward me, and I fell into his arms, feeling his strong chest at my cheek and his hands clutch me close.

"There's someone else here," I told him in a low whisper. "Toward the kitchen."

When I tried to pull back, he gripped me tighter. "There was," he said, "but not anymore." He glanced toward the back of the house. "Now c'mon, we're leaving."

On the way toward the door, he pulled the sleeve of his hoodie over his right hand and stooped down to pick up the gun. He thrust it into the hoodie's front pocket and reached for my hand.

"Wait," I said. "My purse."

"Screw the purse," he said, hustling me out the back door and into the Parker's back yard. Silently, we made our way through the back yard until we reached the tall iron fence that marked the beginning of Lawton's estate.

He made a foothold with his hands. "Over the fence," he said. "And don't stop 'til you're inside the house."

I looked down at his hands. "But how will you get over?"

"I'll jump it," he said. "But not right now."

"Why not?" I said.

"Because I've got to take care of something."

"What?"

"Chloe," he said in a deadly serious voice, "I don't want to boss you around, but if you don't get your ass over that fence right now, I'll have to toss you over. And you could get hurt. I don't want that. So just listen to me, alright?" His eyes were pleading. "Please, baby. Just go. You need to do this, alright?"

"But I want you to come too," I said.

"I'll be there in a few minutes, a half hour tops. You know how to close the gate, right?"

I nodded.

"Good. Get in the house. Lock the doors, and hit the control for the gate. I'll see you in a little bit."

"Wait," I said. "I should call the police, right?"

"No."

"What?"

"Trust me." He flicked his head toward his hands. "Now c'mon. You've gotta go, alright?"

Gingerly, I stepped up into the foothold, and a moment later, I was launched over the fence, landing hard on my ass on the mulchy surface. I glanced back and saw Lawton, watching me, his eyes fierce and his grip tight on the two closest fence spires.

"Go," he said.

And so I did.

When I reached the patch of shrubbery that would hide me from his view, I turned back for one last look. He was still there, watching me in the shadows. Conscious that as long as he was watching me, he wouldn't be able to watch his own back, I turned and plunged toward the house.

Inside Lawton's house, I watched the minutes tick by – ten, then fifteen, then twenty. With every passing minute, I felt a fresh wave of guilt and uncertainty.

I should have never left him there by himself. What was I thinking?

But he'd been so insistent. And the way he talked, I had the distinct impression I'd be putting him in more danger if I stayed.

But why did anyone have to stay? He should've returned with me. I should've made him, even if I had to drag over the fence myself. And why couldn't I call the police?

My head swimming, I vowed to give it five more minutes. And then, I was going back there. Or I was calling the police. Or both.

Exactly forty-three minutes after I'd burst into the house, I heard the back door open. I flew toward it and met Lawton just as he entered. I plowed into him and threw my arms around him, hugging him close.

"I was so worried," I said into his chest. "What were you doing?"

"Well that," he said, "is complicated." He stepped back, holding both of my hands in his. "Do you trust me?" he said.

Foolish or not, I did trust him. I hadn't always. But if I wanted us to have any chance at all, those days were over. I felt myself nod.

"Say it," he said.

"I trust you."

"Good," he said, "because in about an hour, you're gonna have to lie like a rug."

He was gripping my hands tighter now. If he squeezed any tighter, I was sure the bones in my fingers would shatter.

"Why?" I said, giving a little tug at my hands. "I didn't do anything wrong."

He looked down, and his fingers loosened, but he didn't let go. "Was I hurting you? Shit, I'm sorry."

"Tell me why I have to lie," I said. "I didn't do anything."

"Baby, I know. But these people, they don't think like you and I do."

"What people?" I said. "Who are you talking about?"

"People I used to know. That's who." He pulled me close, wrapping his arms around me. "And I won't let 'em hurt you, but you've gotta help."

CHAPTER 71

From what we pieced together after the fact, the Parkers owed everybody and their brother, including a certain unsavory businessman who specialized in high-interest loans of the leg-breaking variety.

Apparently, the Parkers were fond of their legs, if not their pets, which over the last ten years had included a couple of Bengel cats in Baltimore, a parakeet in Tampa, and a Siberian Husky in upstate New York.

When they ran out of money, they did what they always did – hired some sucker to keep up appearances while they set up shop in a new town under a new name.

Their house was leased, their furniture was rented, and most of their portraits were totally fake, including every single one that included Mr. Parker, the so-called retired surgeon who had also posed as an architect, a hedge fund manager, and a personal injury lawyer.

Although I didn't realize it at the time, I'd met Mr. Parker after all. Turns out, he was the flashy financial guy who'd shown up on that doorstep with a wad of cash. Why they paid me anything at all, I didn't understand, until Lawton put it in perspective.

"They needed you to stick around," he said. "You were the fall girl, the one who'd pay the price when the bills came due."

"But I didn't have any money," I said.

"I'm not talking about money," he said. "Think about it. The Parkers give you this wad of cash, which they're probably planning to steal right back anyway. Then later, when someone comes looking for the big money, they're long gone. But you're not."

"But that night," I said, "I told that guy I wasn't Mrs. Parker."

"Yeah. Because nobody lies when they're about to get their legs broken."

"But they would've found out eventually," I said. "I mean, let's consider the worst-case scenario. Let's say they killed me—"

"No," he said. "We're not saying that, even as a what-if."

"But the point is," I said, "those guys would've found out pretty quick that I was just someone staying there."

"Yeah. But so what if it's the wrong person? You were living there, taking care of the dog, handling all their stuff. It would be easy for someone to get the idea the Parkers wouldn't want to see anything bad happen to you."

Over the course of the next few days, I talked to the police, the FBI, and even a couple of guys from Homeland Security. I told them all the same thing, that I'd mostly quit the job a few weeks earlier, when the checks started bouncing.

That's where the lie came in. If the neighbors were watching, they'd certainly know that I'd been in and out of the Parkers' house. But with my car dead in the driveway and a bunch of dead plants inside the house, thanks to whatever Lawton did that night, the lies made a weird sort of sense.

But all this misinformation wasn't for the police or anyone else in law enforcement. It was for the boss of the two leg-breakers left half-dead in the Parkers' house.

Officially, I wasn't there. And Lawton wasn't there. And Chucky, well, he'd supposedly run away the previous week. How sad.

As for the Parkers, well let's just say that a certain businessman in downtown Detroit isn't too happy with them right about now. Unsurprisingly, he doesn't take kindly to someone not just stiffing him for a whole bunch of money, but also jumping the guys who came to collect.

We were snuggling on our favorite sofa about a week after Thanksgiving when some other pieces started clicking into place. I turned to Lawton and said, "You know what? I know what your big secret is."

"You do, huh?"

"First," I said, "you've got to agree. If I guess right, will you tell me the truth?"

"Maybe."

I gave him a serious look. "No maybes. You won't lie to me, will you?"

"Never."

"Alright," I said. "You, and Bishop —" I narrowed my gaze "—is there anyone else?"

"That sounds like a question," he said, "not a guess."

"Hard-ass," I said. "Fine. Here's my guess. You fix things."

He raised his eyebrows. "Like cars?"

"Oh shut up. You know what I mean. You right wrongs."

"Interesting theory."

"It's more than a theory," I said. "Look what happened with me and those two guys in ski masks. You and Bishop, you did to them exactly what they were gonna do to me." I bit my lip. "Well, I guess not exactly, since you beat them up too, but I'm thinking that's mostly incidental."

SABRINA STARK

"Mostly incidental, huh? Where have I heard that before?"

"Stop distracting me," I said. "Am I close?"

"Keep going," he said.

"Alright," I said. "So then with the Parkers, they were trying to get me in trouble for the things they did. But the way you worked it out, they're not just on the hook for all that money, but also for beating up a couple of their enforcers."

"Since when," Lawton said with a grin, "do you talk about enforcers?"

"Since I started hanging out with the likes of you."

"So you're saying I'm a bad influence."

"Definitely." I edged up to lean my forehead against his. "Am I right?"

"Ask me in three months," he said.

"Why? What happens in three months?"

"You'll see."

CHAPTER 72

Until things settled down, Lawton insisted on driving me back and forth to work. Just as well, given the sorry state of my car, which now had its own place in Lawton's massive garage.

He offered to buy me a new car, and I'd be lying if I didn't admit that the offer was tempting. But I still didn't want to be that girl, bought and paid for, no matter how crazy in love I was, or him with me.

As for Chucky, he was my dog now, and no one was going to tell me differently. Somehow, Lawton had magically acquired papers to prove it, even if he wouldn't say exactly how he'd made that possible.

Chucky loved hanging out at Lawton's place, and Lawton seemed to love having him there. So that's where we were staying, except of course, for when I was visiting Grandma and Josh or waitressing.

Work was getting crazier every day. The flu had passed, and we were once again fully staffed. For me, this meant shorter shifts on the worst nights. Shaggy was there practically every night, standing there with his stupid cell phone as if waiting to catch me and Lawton getting naked in a corner booth.

When I confronted him about that story he told me –

about producing that infamous sex tape – he said, "I didn't lie. You just assumed."

"Yeah, I notice you didn't correct me," I said.

He shrugged. "You can't blame a guy for trying."

Oh yes I could. But still, he haunted my shifts like some kind of paparazzi poltergeist. After a while, I sort of got used to him, mostly because he irked the snot out of Keith, who hated to be filmed while pretending to work.

Exactly ten days after Thanksgiving, I was nearing the end of a six-hour shift when I saw Amber near the waitress stand. Looking around, she was busily tapping her foot like she'd been kept waiting a lot longer than necessary.

As usual, she looked like a million bucks. Her long blonde hair was loose and sleek over her shoulders, and she wore an expensive-looking silvery cocktail dress that fell in stylish folds just above her matching silver pumps. All in all, she looked way overdressed for dinner just about anywhere that didn't offer valet parking.

I kept my head down and rushed past her, eager to avoid whatever it was that brought her here.

"Chloe!" she called. "There you are!"

I stopped in my tracks. Slowly, I turned to face her. "Amber," I said. "There you are too. What a coincidence."

She smiled. "Yeah, I know, right?"

Well, at least she was being friendly. The least I could do was try to be the same, if for no other reason than to make this interaction as short as possible. "So," I said, "you're here to see Brittney?"

"No way," Amber said. "I'm here to see you."

"Why?" I asked.

"Because you're gonna need a bridesmaid, right?" She held up her arms. "Ta-da! Here I am! I'm thinking of this as my audition."

I stared at her. "What?"

"Yeah, I mean it's only a matter of time, right? With you and Lawton getting so serious, I'm totally hearing wedding bells, and I want to throw my name into the hat before all the slots are filled."

I couldn't help but laugh. "Actually, it's little premature, don't you think?"

"I am not," she said. "I'm totally mature. And besides, I throw a seriously wicked party. You've got to pick me. I mean, c'mon, you don't have any sisters, right?"

"No. but I do have a best friend."

"Fine. She can stand too. I don't care."

"Wow," I said in a deadpan voice, "that's really nice of you."

She flashed me a grin. "Thanks. And just so you know, when I marry Bishop, I'll let you be a bridesmaid too."

My jaw dropped. "You're dating Bishop?"

"Well no. Not yet. But c'mon. After you and Lawton get married, I figure it's only a matter of time, right? Especially with us being such good friends."

"Who?"

"You and me."

I decided to let that one pass. "But seriously," I said, "I'm not even engaged."

In spite of Lawton's innuendos in the hospital, it hadn't come up, which I told myself was just fine with me. Sure, he was my dream guy. And sure, I never wanted to let him go. But that was another girl I didn't want to be – the one who moved too fast when the guy wasn't quite ready.

"So what?" Amber said. "You totally will be." She looked around and lowered her voice. "My parents are friends with this jeweler, and I don't want to let the cat out of the bag, but somebody we know – meaning this totally hot guy, not that I'm supposed to notice now that he's off the market – anyway, he just paid gobs of money for the biggest rock this jeweler had ever seen."

I stared, speechless. What was I supposed to say to something like that?

Fortunately, I was spared the trouble of saying anything, because suddenly I heard a shrill female voice call out from the other side of the restaurant. "You!"

I turned around to see Brittney tottering toward us on those obscenely high heels of hers. Co-workers or not, we never spoke to each other, except when absolutely necessary. And the times we did speak, most of our words weren't exactly fit for public consumption, as Keith had warned me countless times.

Brittney elbowed her way between me and Amber. She gave Amber a long, scathing look and said, "What are you doing here?"

Amber tossed a long strand of blonde hair over her bare shoulder. "I'm here to see Chloe, not that it's any of your business."

Brittney's eyes narrowed to slits. She whirled to face me. "This is all your fault."

"My fault?" I said.

"Yes, your fault. First you steal my boyfriend, then you steal my best friend!"

I glanced at Amber. "Hey, I hardly know her!"

"You do too!" Amber said. "By the way, I look good in aquamarine in case you haven't picked your colors yet."

"See!" Brittney told me. "And I know you've been stealing my customers too. That Bolger guy, he won't even let me wait on him anymore."

"Yeah," I said. "Because you keep calling him fat."

Amber reached out and tapped Brittney on the shoulder.

Brittney whirled to face her. "What?"

"Do you know what the specials are?" Amber said.

Brittney glared at her. "What specials?"

"Duh," Amber said. "We're in a restaurant. You're the waitress. Seems like an easy question."

Brittney's jaw tightened and her nostrils flared. "How's this for special?" she said, reaching out to shove Amber with both hands.

Amber stumbled backward, and caught herself against the waitress stand. Her eyes narrowed, and she barreled into Brittney, knocking her back into the small crowd that had gathered to see what the commotion was.

The crowd shifted, and Brittney lost her balance, tumbling backward onto a table filled with dirty dishes. Her long blonde hair flopped into the remnants of what looked like blueberry pancakes topped with blueberry syrup.

With a string of profanity, Brittney toppled off the table and hit the floor. A split-second later, she dove, hard, for Amber's legs. Squealing, Amber toppled over, clutching at the necktie of the man standing nearest to her.

He lost his balance and toppled over too, landing halfway between Amber and Brittney, who dove for each other with the ferocity of rabid squirrels fighting over the last nut.

By now, the crowd was going nuts, with the woman watching in wide-eyed horror, and the guys cheering them on, except for the guy with the necktie, who took a heel to the gut, thanks to Brittney's flailing legs.

Frantically, I glanced around, looking for Keith, a phone, something. But what I found was Shaggy, standing there with his cell phone in his hand and a giant grin spread across his face.

"Sweeet!" he said.

"Oh for cripe's sake," I said, continuing to scan the restaurant.

I caught sight of Lawton, strolling in the front door. He stopped short at the sight of Brittney and Amber rolling around on the floor. I followed his gaze.

When a sticky blue stand of Brittney's hair whacked Amber in the face, Amber grabbed a fallen squirt-bottle of ketchup and aimed it at Brittney's face. Brittney shoved Amber aside just in time, and a geyser of ketchup streamed upward, raining down on both of them and pelting the nearest spectators with tiny red splatters.

By this time, both of the girls were covered in food-goo from the tops of their formerly blonde heads to the tips of their decidedly non-sensible shoes.

I heard a male voice off to my left say, "Somehow, I thought this would be sexier."

"Got that right," another male voice said.

And then, I heard a third male voice. It was Keith, who bellowed out, "What the hell is going on here?"

He waded in, separating the two girls amid a chorus of booing from the male spectators. I felt a hand on my elbow, and looked to see Lawton standing next to me, an amused smile playing across his face.

"So," he said in a low, amused voice. "How was your day, honey?"

I glanced at Brittney and Amber, who'd been hustled to opposite sides of a long booth for eight. "Eh, same ol', same ol'," I said.

Amber's eyes lit up. "Lawton!" she called. "Yoohoo! Over

here!"

Slowly, he turned to look.

"Have you heard?" she said. "I'm gonna be a bridesmaid!"

Lawton's face lost all its expression. He glanced at me. I didn't know what to say. He turned back to Amber, and his gaze narrowed.

"Oh c'mon," she said. "It's not like it's a big secret or anything."

Lawton looked down toward the floor. He gave a slow shake of his head. And then, he turned to face me. He reached out, taking both of my hands in his. Slowly, he sank to his knees.

I was having a hard time catching my breath. All around us, the restaurant had grown utterly silent.

"Chloe," he said, gazing up at me. "This isn't exactly the way I had it planned, but it doesn't change the way I feel. I love you more than life itself."

"Lawton, noooo!" Brittney yelled.

"Chloe," Lawton said. "Will you marry me?"

EPILOGUE
THREE MONTHS LATER

The day of the catfight was my last day waitressing – and not because I said yes a thousand times over. Lawton was my dream guy, and he was really mine. My heart said yes, and my mouth followed – no overthinking, no hesitation, and no more pretending.

As far as waitressing, I didn't quit. I was fired spectacularly amid ketchup splatters and pancake goo. Officially, it was for inciting a riot in the dining area. Unofficially, I'm pretty sure it was for calling Keith a pompous dipshit when he told me that I'd be the one paying for all catfight-related damages.

As for Grandma, she quit her fake mailing job the very next week. In her handwritten letter of resignation, she mentioned a new job, one that pays ten times better. She's still doing mailings, but instead of kittens and cooking supplies, these new flyers feature punching bags, sparring gloves, and other martial arts fitness gear.

Her favorite so far? Nun-chucks. She bought a pair the very next week and uses them for cleaning her rugs.

Coincidentally, a few weeks before Thanksgiving, Loretta had been fired from her job too, not that she'd told anyone. The rumor? Her colleagues found her impossible to work with. Go figure.

Fortunately for everyone, she found a new job to replace her old one, something that's enabled her to keep the house and Grandma's cottage, but also keeps her travelling all over the country. She's now the official food critic for an obscure publication dedicated to exotic cuisine.

The pay is good, but from what Josh says, it's not turning out quite the way Loretta hoped. Her editor, a mysterious recluse named John Livingston, chooses all the featured food. And his tastes are, well, let's just say, a bit on the eccentric side.

So far, Loretta has tasted fried rat, bat soup, maggot cheese, and my personal favorite, codfish sperm – not that I'd ever try such a thing. But hey, at least it's not oyster gravy, right?

I finally learned how Keith was able to tamper with my phone. According to Josie, a random building inspection turned up two hidden cameras – one in the restaurant's locker area and one in Keith's office.

The way it looked, it was the first camera that gave Keith a sneak peek at my locker combination, but it was the second camera that gave him a whole lot of grief. The first camera he knew about, but the second was a mystery to everyone, including the restaurant's owners. No one will say specifically what kind of footage it captured, but let's just say I wasn't the only person fired that month.

These days, Keith is working as the midnight manager at Sal's Shrimp Shack in the seedier part of town, where the only thing more fishy than the food are the late-night patrons. As for Brittney, she's gone to Hollywood, hoping to capitalize on her instant fame, resulting from a certain catfight video that went totally viral, just like Shaggy predicted.

And that wasn't the only video that went viral. Shaggy's footage of Lawton's proposal gave Shaggy over a million hits in the first month alone, and made him a small fortune when he sold the video stills to tabloids worldwide. He now has his own cell phone, his own internet channel, and his own locksmith – just in case Jen decides to change the locks again.

Just as Lawton predicted, Bishop is growing on me. But that didn't stop me from giving him just a little payback for all the hassle he'd given me in those hectic weeks leading up to the engagement.

Call me a sap, but I did agree to let Amber stand in the wedding after all. I simply couldn't resist, and not because she wouldn't take no for an answer. Mostly, it was because the idea of Amber chasing Bishop from one side of the reception to the other was just a little too hard to resist.

True, they didn't actually stand up together, with Bishop as Lawton's best man, and Erika as my maid of honor. Still, Amber gave Bishop one heck of a chase – not that it did any good. Turns out, he's a one-girl kind of guy, and his one girl couldn't be more different than Amber in every way.

As far as the Parkers, they're still missing in action. Maybe they'll show up. Maybe they won't. But one thing's for sure, they'd be smart to look over their shoulders.

The word on the street is that some very unhappy people are out looking for them, and not just to collect some money. Apparently, those certain people don't take too kindly to delinquent deadbeats beating up on their unique breed of collection personnel.

As for me, I've never been happier. I've got the man I love, who loves me right back. And as far as my career, it's on a definite upswing. These days, I'm using my accounting degree nonstop. As it turns out, managing a billion-dollar business is no small task, especially when you're never quite sure who you can trust.

But Lawton trusts me, and I trust him. And we have no more secrets, including the fact that my hunch was correct about his oath to give karma a helping hand. So together, we watch each other's backs, along with all those other more interesting parts. The way I see it – and a certain little dog would agree – a girl couldn't ask for more.

THE END

ABOUT THE AUTHOR

Sabrina Stark writes edgy romances featuring plucky girls and the bad boys who capture their hearts.

She's worked as a fortune-teller, barista, game-show contestant, and media writer in the aerospace industry. She has a journalism degree from Central Michigan University and is married with one son and two kittens. She currently makes her home in Northern Alabama.

ON THE WEB

Learn About New Releases & Exclusive Offers
www.SabrinaStark.com

Follow Sabrina Stark on Twitter at
http://twitter.com/StarkWrites